IFWG Dark Phases Titles

Peripheral Visions (Robert Hood, 2015)
The Grief Hole (Kaaron Warren, 2016)
Cthulhu Deep Down Under Vol 1 (2017)
Cthulhu Deep Down Under Vol 2 (2018)
Cthulhu: Land of the Long White Cloud (2018)
The Crying Forest (Venero Armano, 2020)
Cthulhu Deep Down Under Vol 3 (2021)
Spawn: Weird Horror Tales About Pregnancy,
        Birth And Babies (2021)
Caped Fear: Superhuman Horror Stories (2022)
Killer Creatures Down Under: Horror Stories
        With Bite (2023)

KILLER CREATURES DOWN UNDER

HORROR STORIES WITH BITE

EDITED BY

DEBORAH SHELDON

A DARK PHASES TITLE

Killer Creatures Down Under: Horror Stories With Bite

All Rights Reserved

ISBN-13: 978-1-922856-24-1

Anthology Copyright ©2023 IFWG Publishing International

V1.0

All stories are original to this anthology except for the following (first publishing instance): "Milk and Honey" by Jason Fischer, in *Ecopunk!: Speculative Tales of Radical Futures* (Ticonderoga Publications, 2017); "Species Endangered" by Deborah Sheldon, in *Perfect Little Stitches and Other Stories* (IFWG Publishing Australia, 2017).

Printed in Palatino Linotype and 28 Days Later Bold Italic.

IFWG Publishing International
Gold Coast

www.ifwgpublishing.com

For Allen and Harry

TABLE OF CONTENTS

Introduction (Deborah Sheldon)............................1
Corvus (Keith Williams)..5
Ixodes Holocyclus (Ben Matthews)..........................17
Bait (Anthony Ferguson)..27
Species Endangered (Deborah Sheldon)...........41
The Warrigals (Steven Paulsen)...............................53
Quoll Season (Helena O'Connor)..............................67
Every Part of Her (Antoinette Rydyr)...............83
The Best Omelette in Australia (Fox Claret Hill)...........99
Twisted (Renee De Visser)......................................109
A Pack Apart (Charles Spiteri)..............................115
The Seaside (Robert Mammone)............................131
Hell Gully (Pauline Yates).......................................141
Myiasis (J.M. Merryt)...149
No Frills Holiday (Geraldine Borella)...................159
Milk and Honey (Jason Fischer)..............................167
Nineteen Hours on Deep Creek Station (Tim Borella)...181
Boyfriend Material (H.K. Stubbs)..........................193
There are Things on Me (Matt Tighe) 207
Contributor Biographies 215

INTRODUCTION

I'm an Australian, born and bred, and I'm scared of animals.

Mostly wild animals, but domesticated types make me uncomfortable too. I was a toddler when I realised that cats were terrifying. Nothing has changed some fifty years later. *Please* don't put me in a room with your beloved moggy unless you want me to break into a cold sweat. Every cat I've encountered has wanted nothing more than to sit on *my* lap, even when other people in the room are making kissy-kissy noises and holding out their arms.

Cats gravitate towards me because animals know if you're scared.

When I was a teenager, I went horse riding with a company that apparently catered for the nervous beginner. While the rest of the group plodded along the nature trail on their placid, cow-like steeds, my horse got more jittery and excited in direct proportion to my rising anxiety. That damned beast kept trying to bolt. When it finally diverted from the trail to plunge headlong into a creek, the instructor repeatedly yelled at me, "Don't let him roll you!", which was unhelpful considering I had no idea what to do except scream. (The horse didn't roll — entirely the horse's decision — and this first ride also happened to be my last.)

But it wasn't until my early thirties, when our son was born, that I understood the full extent of my aversion to animals. On weekends, amongst other excursions, hubby and I would occasionally take our son to wildlife sanctuaries and reserves. These universally beautiful places, set in bushland, allow most of the animals to roam freely.

"Where are the fences?" I remember saying to my husband, as

a small mob of kangaroos and wallabies began lolloping towards us.

Our son (who's now a twenty-two-year-old man) sat in his stroller, happily transfixed by the sight and laughing joyfully, while I had visions of us getting disembowelled by slashing claws.

"It's okay," hubby said, "the 'roos are used to people."

And he was right, of course. Other tourists were handfeeding the marsupials with no sign of carnage. Hubby poured into our palms some of the kibble he'd bought from the ticket booth, and the animals pressed around us. I crouched beside our son's stroller, bracing myself to defend in case of attack. How silly! Our son had a wonderful experience. Meanwhile, I can still remember that first time a wallaby gripped my wrist to eat the kibble from my hand. Its paws were so hot, claws as smooth as polished jade, blunt teeth chafing harmlessly against my palm. I can remember the snort of its moist breath, and the thrumming of my heart as I tried not to panic.

Once I realised that I was unnerved by animals in general, I went to great lengths to avoid passing on my phobia to our son. That meant going to *lots* of sanctuaries and nature reserves. Feeding *lots* of wallabies. Patting *lots* of creatures like snakes and Tasmanian devils as they were held by keepers for limited "meet-and-greet" sessions. Exposure therapy didn't help me. At least our son—like his father—is not perturbed by animals.

However, I'm not averse to *all* animals. When I was young, I had a much-loved dog, but he was *family* and different from other dogs, which I assumed wanted nothing more than to bite off my face. Little furry animals have always appealed; put me in a petting zoo and I'll happily play with rabbits and baby goats. I was never afraid of my in-laws's chickens when they had a coop in their back yard. In fact, I love all sorts of birds, especially parrots. Ridiculous, isn't it? Of all the animal phobias, ornithophobia is common. (Our son has a friend who is not only scared of birds, but their feathers too—tough luck, I guess, that his father owns a cockatiel. Exposure therapy hasn't helped him, either.)

A flock of crimson rosellas daily eats blossoms in a tree out front of our house, and I like to watch them squabble, fossick and hang upside down. As I'm typing this, our six-year-old budgerigar, Zeus, is playing with his toys and chatting. He's happy to climb over me, and I'm happy to let him. He often sits on my finger while I kiss his beak.

But if he were bigger…?

Magpies are big birds. We've had a family of magpies living on our property for some quarter-century. Generation after generation, these birds have followed my husband as he's mown the grass, and gathered at his feet whenever he's dug through garden beds so they can snaffle up earthworms. This year, a particular magpie likes to perch on the wheelbarrow just to watch and ponder the mysteries of hubby's yard work. I *know* these magpies are friendly.

And yet… And yet…

Whenever I go to the letterbox, our magpies watch. Will they swoop and peck? Magpies tend to do that in nesting season. My superstitious precaution is to say, while pointing towards the letterbox, "Just checking the mail," as if I'm asking permission, as if the birds would understand.

Have I ever been swooped and pecked by a magpie? No.

Does my fear respond to rational thinking? Also, no.

Many people would understand my fear. Australia is known as the land where everything wants to kill you. That's actually a well-deserved reputation. Some of the deadliest animals in the world are native to Australia. For instance, we've got more venomous creatures than any other country, and eighty percent of the deadliest snakes are found here. However, it's also true that human deaths from animal attacks are relatively rare. Most Australians won't encounter any of these animals in their lifetimes.

Ah, whatever. People like me are scared anyway. Fear of animals is inbuilt into the human psyche. Without that fear, curiosity would have got the better of us, and we would have long ago expired as a species, right?

Right?

Animals are the perfect subject matter for a horror anthology because they have traits that we find inherently frightening. Wild creatures can be unpredictable, dangerous, and even downright repulsive to look at, let alone touch.

My idea for this anthology grew from my short story, "Species Endangered", which I've included here as a reprint. The story was first published in my multi-award-nominated and award-winning collection, *Perfect Little Stitches and Other Stories* (IFWG Publishing Australia, 2017). "Species Endangered' was well-received, and selected by Ellen Datlow for her honourable mentions list for best horror of the year. It also featured a real life Australian animal.

Since the publication of "Species Endangered", I've wanted to curate an anthology of horror tales about Australian critters of all persuasions. So, in 2021, I pitched the idea for *Killer Creatures Down Under: Horror Stories with Bite* to Gerry Huntman, managing director of IFWG Publishing Australia. The contract was quickly signed.

In April 2022, we put out an open call for submissions from Australian authors. (This is the first IFWG anthology that doesn't include work from commissioned authors.) The animals could be of any type—mammals, reptiles, amphibians, birds, invertebrates, fish, arthropods—as long as they were real creatures that are native to Australia. I put no restriction on subgenre. Over the three-month submission window, I received a wealth of stories. I've selected the ones that gripped me, unsettled me: stories that interpreted the theme in captivating, unexpected or shocking ways.

You're about to read an eclectic mix of disturbing tales that run the gamut from action to phantasmagorical to historical to futuristic to supernatural to psychological and more. My hope is that this anthology is the literary equivalent of a box of chocolates, assuming each chocolate is hazardous in its own delectable way.

And if, like me, you're scared of animals, please don't read this anthology at bedtime.

Deborah Sheldon
Melbourne, 2022

CORVUS

KEITH WILLIAMS

The ending of life comes to us in myriad forms. Any choice regarding time or method is rarely ours to make.

It is early morning. I sit at the kitchen table, a glass of Scotch in my hand and a loaded shotgun in my lap. Extra cartridges are lined up on the table like soldiers on parade. I am waiting. Death is coming. How did I come to this moment?

This is what transpired.

Growing up on a farm, one develops an affinity for most animals, but there are always exceptions. Foxes, rabbits, wild dogs, feral cats are genuine pests. For my father, mother and subsequently me, it was one specific pest that became much more than just that.

I remember Dad going out to tend the cattle each morning, always with a weapon strapped to the back of the quad bike. It had started out with the shotgun until the neighbours, although distant, apparently complained about the noise. He then downsized to the .22, but after one of his stray shots hit one of our prime beef steers, Mum would only let him go out with the slug gun, much to his chagrin and disgust. "May as well spit at them," he muttered that first time, but had reluctantly conceded to her wishes.

I still recall sitting on the back porch eating toast or cereal, watching Dad on the distant fenceline and hearing the *pop, pop,* of the slug gun as Dad fired into the small copse of trees. I asked Mum why he did that every day and what he was shooting at and why our cattle seemed to avoid that side of the paddock. She just shook her head and told me to never mind, I didn't need to know. Whatever it was, it was never mentioned in front of me, but I recall many heated yet whispered conversations behind closed doors. Growing up was mystery enough, but something much stranger was festering within my family.

Dad would always return from the morning chores in time to see me off to school, but even then, I could see his smile for me was somewhat forced. One day, when Dad came back from the morning run, I was waiting on the porch as usual, but this day I was steeling myself to address the family mystery. I watched as he climbed off the quad bike and glanced with disdain at the slug gun on the pack rack. He arranged his features into a semblance of a smile and climbed the steps. He was kicking off his boots when I summoned my courage and flat out asked him why he shot at the trees every day. He stared hard at me for what seemed an eternity, then closed his eyes for a moment as if deciding whether to travel down this road. He sighed, seemingly in resignation that this time had come.

He blinked, looked at me again. "Crows."

I frowned, knowing he was going to try and leave it at that. I pushed my luck. I felt I was old enough to know more. "Actually, they're ravens down here," I said, and his brow furrowed in anger. He did not like being contradicted. "And why shoot at them?"

Dad gritted his teeth. "Because they kill our young calves, that's why! They attack and mutilate our steers, that's why!" He made to move past me into the house.

"But ravens are just carrion eaters, Dad. They only eat dead things."

He turned on me and grabbed me by the arms, his big calloused hands shaking me hard, his watery blue eyes burrowing into mine. "You don't know anything, boy. Not a goddamn thing!"

He let go of me and stomped into the house, the screen door slapping shut behind him. I stared after him, open-mouthed and near to tears. My father had never yelled at me in such a way before. I had not only seen terrible anger in his expression, but deep-rooted fear. He was terrified of the birds and hated them in equal measure. I never brought up the subject again—until the day he never came home from his morning chores.

I had long since ceased my daily vigil on the porch, not wanting to spark his anger again, but could still hear the slug gun popping as he peppered the trees. Usually when the shooting stopped, we would hear the quad bike returning from the paddock as he dutifully came to see me off to school. Not this day. My mother was at the sink staring out the window, breathing hard and squeezing a dishcloth in her fists. I was a teenager by then and said I'd go check. I remember the tears in her eyes and fear on her face as I pulled on my boots and hustled out the door. Her reaction confused and frightened me. She seemed resigned to some fate I could not foresee.

I could see the quad bike down by the east fence, as usual, near the small grove of trees that bordered the paddock. I could not see my father. All our cattle had gathered by the west fence, seemingly as far away as they could get from the scene. I jumped into the farm ute and drove hard, not knowing what to expect but now dreading the worst. As I drew closer to the bike I could see a figure on the ground, motionless. The slug gun lay on the ground nearby. I skidded to a stop, piled out of the cab and ran to the prone body. It was Dad, of course. He was lying on his back, arms askew, face turned to a sky he could no longer perceive.

I moaned in horror at what was left of his features. His eyes were now nothing more than dark, bloodied holes, his ears mutilated, cheeks pocked with deep wounds like craters, lips ragged and bloody. I noticed his hands were torn, with some fingers missing altogether. In his gaping mouth were shattered teeth. Most of his tongue had been torn out.

I gasped for air, tears spilling from my eyes. The world had seemed to stop turning. My father dead? It made no sense. As I fell to my knees beside his lifeless body, I heard it. That unmistakable, deep-throated cry from high in the trees—*Ah-Ah-Ahaaah*—the last drawn-out note sounding like a cry of satisfaction. I swear I heard mocking laughter in that call. I picked up the slug gun. It had a thirty-pellet magazine which Dad fastidiously refilled every night. Rage and grief consumed me as I emptied what was left into the trees, firing blindly. I then threw the gun into the ute, covered Dad with a tarp and drove back to the house.

Therein began my own hatred and subsequent fear of the raven.

What followed was a cursory investigation and an autopsy. Official ruling? Heart attack and post-mortem predation by unknown animals. "Unknown" my arse. I watched the neighbours at the funeral. They knew. So did my mother, obviously. The secret they kept had exploded in our faces. I was an angry teen who had just lost his father and wanted an uncaring world to acknowledge that fact, but I was not stupid. Guilt and shame hung in the air like a pall.

I snarled at the neighbours as they filed away after the service, "You stopped him using the shotgun." They reeled back, eyes downcast, heads shaking, and hurried on. I could see the horror writ large on their faces. My mother pulled me aside. I turned on her. "You stopped him from using the .22 because a steer got a scratch." I pointed at the casket in the unfilled grave. "Remember what he looked like when the ravens had finished with him. I'll never forget."

I staggered away, grief and anger consuming me, and stood by another grave watching as everybody left. My breathing was ragged, a scream locked in my throat. If I let it out, I knew I would never stop. My heart felt like a brick in my chest. My mother waited by the car for me. I loved her. I hated her. I saw her pain.

As I tried to quell my anger, possibly directed at the wrong people, I felt eyes upon me. An eerie prickling at the back of my neck. My thighs and buttocks clenched as if I was standing on a high ledge with no support around me and only the inevitable plunge to my death awaiting. Vertigo had me swaying. I gripped the nearby gravestone as I turned and gazed into the Catholic section of the cemetery where huge Gothic monuments marked the interment of mostly unremarkable people. There, atop a stone angel, perched a large ebony bird, head cocked, eye staring at me malevolently.

I knew it was the one.

I cannot explain that knowledge, I just knew. I took several steps toward it, wanting nothing more than to choke the life out of the vile creature that had tormented and killed my father. The bird spread its obsidian wings and flapped lazily away, like black oil flowing into the sky. Its laconic cry, reverberating through the cemetery, mocked me yet again… *Ah-Ah-Ahaaah.*

I watched it diminish to a black speck in the distance as the inexplicable vertigo faded, then walked back to the car, got in and slammed the door. Vengeance was in my heart, but I needed to know more. There had to be more. My mother slid into the driver's side.

I turned to her. "We need to talk."

She stared out the windscreen, hands clenched tight on the steering wheel. She sighed shakily and nodded.

There was a wake for Dad at our house. I sat on the back porch staring down at the paddock where he had died, as relatives and guests came and left by the front door. No one stayed long. I wanted nothing to do with them and their hushed whispers and secrets.

When the last person had left, my mother came out to the porch. She carried two glasses of red wine and offered one to me as she sat. I guess we both needed fortification for what was to come. I could see ravens gathering in the trees by the distant east fence, but they were silent, as if in reverence or anticipation of the story to be told. My mother noticed them and her hands trembled as she sipped her drink.

Then she drew a breath and related the history of our farm.

Dad, apparently, was the third generation to live on this property, which had in turn been a sheep farm, a dairy farm and now us, running prime beef cattle. Or trying to, at least. As my mother understood it, the original owners, my ancestors, cleared the land of forest and animals in the most brutal and efficient ways they had available to them. She said there had been a lot of burning and no care for resident wildlife such as there is today. The land we sat upon had been a forest haven for the ravens, in particular. (She correctly called them ravens, not crows. I wondered if she had surrendered that argument to Dad. It hardly mattered.) The surviving birds had been driven away to the small copse next to our east fence, and from there they bred and watched their home overrun by farm animals and humans who cared nothing about the ravens or their fate.

The copse of trees was actually on a neighbour's property. They had fenced it off from the rest of their own farm as if in deference, or most probably fear, of what lived within. They also thwarted all attempts to rid the land of this last refuge for the birds.

The killings began immediately after the first season of lamb births. At first, the deaths were attributed to natural causes before the carrion eaters moved in. But then some lambs were left alive, their eyes, ears and tongues pecked away.

The message was clear. The war had begun.

Our ancestors tried baiting, trapping and shooting the ravens but could never rid the area of them. The more losses the ravens suffered, the stronger they bred. And always, there was one bird, the biggest and most powerful, that would make a true statement by killing the leader of the farm first and then the other family members.

I had finished the glass of wine, stunned and horrified by these revelations. Worse was to follow. Sixteen members of my family, past and present, had been killed in the same way. Eleven members of a neighbouring family had been killed also. It seemed a neighbouring farmer way back when had dared to help my ancestors in eradicating the birds. The ravens had turned on them. I knew of this family. A few years back, they had sold their farm and moved to the city. Both parents, my mother now told me, and their two young children, were found in their city home with eyes, ears and tongues missing.

"So, even moving away does not stop their quest for vengeance," she said. "You must understand, son, this is not a myth or legend or some fanciful fairy tale. It is all true." She stared into her empty glass. "When the time comes, the raven will approach at night and tap its beak on the window. The next day someone will die. Your father heard it the night before he…" She drew a shaky breath. "But he still went out."

I reached across and grasped her trembling hand.

She sighed, more a sob than an exhalation. "I was the one who pleaded with your father to stop using the shotgun and then the .22. I had hoped that if we stopped antagonising the birds, they would leave us in peace." She turned to me, tears flowing. "But it can never be, son. I'm so sorry, but this is our fate. When I first heard the story, I didn't believe it. But then I did." She looked away. "I refused to become pregnant. How could I bring a child into this madness?" She gazed at me, her expression one of utter sadness and regret. "You were an accident. A beautiful, terrifying accident. Love and fear have filled my heart since the day you were born."

I put my empty glass down and drew her into a hug as tears flowed down her cheeks and her body shook. She eventually pulled away, staring hard into the gloom at the distant trees. Her next softly spoken words shocked me to my core. "I wish with all my heart that I had never met your father." She got up and returned inside. I heard her sobs. In the descending dusk, I stared down towards that thick copse of cypress pines and a chorus of caws echoed up to me... *Ah-Ah-Ahaaah.*

I went inside and locked the doors. My mother was already in her bedroom. I could still hear her sobbing and a bottle clinking on glass. I opened my computer and got on the internet. I needed to know my enemy. Information was plentiful, except about what mattered to me.

The Australian raven—Corvus coronoides—is the largest member of the crow family in Australia. Okay, technically Dad had been right about the name and me pedantic. Huge beak. Mainly carrion eaters...mainly. There was some dispute about that depending on who you asked: a farmer or a so-called expert. They mated for life and were hugely territorial. I guess that explained a lot. Logically, it seemed their hatred of us for that original sin had filtered down, undiluted, from generation to generation.

I lay in bed wondering if there was anything I could do differently from all who had gone before. Or was our fate set in stone? I had no answers. My fitful sleep was punctuated by dreams— massive swarms of black birds, ebony wings closing over my head and raucous, mocking cries.

Time passed. I quit school and we ran the farm as best we could in difficult times. I despised them, but I did not declare my own personal war against the ravens. I avoided the copse when I could but carried the shotgun strapped to the back of the quad bike. We got by, my mother and I, and life was okay, yet the very real fear of what awaited still floated at the back of my mind, and I saw it in my mother's eyes every day. She grew greyer, gaunter, as if each passing day drew the inevitable.

Then, early one morning, I arose to find my mother sitting at the kitchen table. She had a glass of Scotch in her hands. I had never seen her drink at this time of the day. In fact, she never drank until the day's work was done.

"Mum?"

She looked at me with bloodshot, rheumy eyes. I realised this was far from her first drink. Her hands shook as she took a swig, swallowing hard. "It came last night, son."

"What…?"

"The raven. Tapping on my window. I heard it. It tapped and cawed."

I tried to hug her, but she could not, or would not, respond. My anger flared like a furnace. I remembered Dad shaking me that day and his words stinging me. I knew more now — and also what I must do.

The option of appeasement or doing nothing had been taken from our hands.

I left my mother sitting at the table, went outside, the screen door banging shut behind me, fired up the quad bike and sped down to the copse. I stood up on the bike and screamed into the trees. "Stay away from us! Stay away from my mother! I'll kill you all! I'll kill you all!" I screamed until I was hoarse. The trees swayed in the breeze, silent as the grave. I looked back at the house, sudden fear clenching my heart like a fist as I realised my stupid mistake. I raced back.

Too late.

My screams of horror, grief and anger tore apart the dawn.

Another cursory investigation and white-washed autopsy. I wondered what the local authorities knew of the history here. It mattered not. Another funeral, no wake this time. What would I say to these keepers of secrets? I guess they had to live with their own fears of being associated with my family. I heard whispers that I had left the back door open. An invitation to the birds.

Add guilt and shame to my anger.

I spent several weeks drinking and planning. I could not run the farm on my own and no one would work here. As a going concern, it was on its last legs. I eventually sold all the cattle for a decent sum. Enough to keep me going for quite a while. I would figure out my future when I could see that I had one. My current thoughts were somewhat short term in nature, and perhaps not even entirely rational, but I maintained and nurtured my hatred for the ravens in the copse. I also hated myself for my fatal error that day and conflicting emotions consumed my mind, yet I pressed ahead with my plans. I felt I had no choice now. I stayed out of the paddock and away from the trees, waiting patiently for their nesting season, hoping that no tapping on my window would come beforehand. It did not.

I drank Scotch and watched from the porch the activity of the killers. Their barking caws turned my stomach and fuelled my burning need to avenge my parents. I thought about the years of my father's mindless, pointless vendetta. I thought about my mother's heart, torn apart by love and fear, the choices she had made and the choices she had been unable to make. I understood.

At dusk one evening, four weeks into the ravens' nesting and mating season, I loaded the ute with what I needed and coasted down to the copse. It was time. I got out and looked into the trees. I could see the bulky shapes of the nests high in the branches. I grinned. I knew I had lost a part of my mind but was beyond caring. They should have left us in peace. This should not have been our war, but be damned if I'd let the brutal deaths of my parents pass without firing a shot. Literally.

I pulled the Remington out of the cab and the two boxes of shells

I had brought, and commenced to rain hell upon the creatures that had destroyed my life. Pine needles, branches, nests, and most satisfyingly, bloodied black bodies fell from the trees to the ground below as the gunfire echoed through the gloom. Birds that tried to flee were blown out of the sky. I think I was screaming with maniacal glee as I blew away everything I could see, and then exhausted the ammunition into all that I could not.

When I ran out of cartridges, I stepped over the fence and stomped on whatever was not dead and even that which was. My boots crushed eggs, nests and the broken bodies of adults and young. I was breathing hard and cackling like a loon as I hopped back over the fence and swapped the shotgun for a big container of fuel from the ute. I emptied it across the pine needles littered with the bodies of my current and future enemies. Standing clear, I pulled matches from my pocket and set fire to my war zone. I knew the pines would burn furiously.

The bonfire erupted with a huge *whoomph*. As the flames rocketed up the trunks, I shouted into the treetops, "Who's laughing now, you son of a bitch?"

I drove back to the house and sat on the porch with a bottle of Scotch, watching the enormous conflagration in the paddock. It lit up the night sky, illuminating the low clouds with an orange tinge. A vast column of oily smoke billowed away to the south. I heard distant sirens and knew I would likely be arrested. That was okay. The ravens could not reach me in prison even if any of them were left. I grinned at my handiwork and raised a toast to the pyre, "See you in hell, you black bastard."

The firefighters that arrived in the neighbour's paddock didn't try to extinguish the blazing trees; they didn't have enough water for that. They simply watched the copse burn as they protected surrounding farmland from catching fire. I didn't give a damn about this place anymore. I hadn't thought about any future beyond this night. The police didn't show up, which also explained a lot, so I went to bed with the last home for the ravens still burning furiously, the flames casting an eerie glow in the night.

Ah-Ah-Ahaaah.

I sat bolt upright. Had I just dreamed that mocking cry? It had haunted my sleep for so long I could not be certain. I rubbed my crusty eyes and listened for some time. The night was still, eerily silent after so many years of listening to grumbling cattle. I lay back down, waiting for my heart rate to slow.

Ah-Ah-Ahaaah.

No mistake this time. I tumbled out of bed and ripped the curtains aside, certain of what I would see. Backlit by the glow of the fire still smouldering in the copse, the big raven sat on my windowsill, orange light dancing across its oily feathers. Up close, it looked impossibly huge, as if bloated by rage. Its head was cocked to one side, a malevolent eye glaring at me through the glass. I saw a hundred years of hatred in that piercing gaze. I took a step back, swallowing bile. The raven turned its beak to the glass and nodded its head.

Tap, tap, tap.

And so, I wait, patient and grinning madly. I sip Scotch and stroke the Remington in my lap. Are fate and destiny sealed in stone? We shall see. Death is coming. I am ready.

IXODES HOLOCYCLUS

BEN MATTHEWS

"**O**w!" Alan leapt out of the bush, waving his arms, "Jesus, ow!"

"What's wrong?" Geoff said, garbage picker held out like a wand.

Alan had yanked up the sleeve of his forensic body suit and was examining the crook of his elbow. "I dunno, just, ow!" Alan struck at his arm.

Geoff stepped closer, trying to see what was happening. *Is it a spider?* If it was a spider bite, he needed to identify the spider before Alan destroyed it. That would mean the difference between calling an ambulance or telling him to harden up. Though he and Alan only dealt with the dead, they were still required to be fully trained in first aid.

"Hold still," Geoff said.

Alan hit his arm again. Now Geoff could see a dark black spot in the flesh of Alan's elbow. Despite how hard Alan was striking it, the speck didn't move.

Geoff breathed a sigh of relief. The only critter that could survive that kind of beating, that could remain fixed in place like that, was a tick. *Thank God it wasn't a spider.* "It's only a tick."

"A tick? It fucking hurts!"

Geoff tried not to smile. "Hold still."

"I've had ticks before. This really hurts."

"Relax, I've got it."

Geoff opened his bum-bag and retrieved a large pair of surgical tweezers. He'd never had to use them before, but they were standard issue for their job.

"Hold still." He wrapped his arm around Alan's elbow, slid the tip of the tweezers under the tick, as close to the thing's head as possible, and pulled.

"Shit!" Alan yanked his arm back. "Christ, that hurt!"

Geoff stuffed his forceps back in the pack, concealing his grin as he did so.

Alan rubbed his arm, "You reckon it's one of those ones that cause paralysis?"

"No idea." Geoff had heard of those, but he'd never met anyone paralysed by a tick. Was it even a real thing? He'd had plenty of ticks during his time as a farmer. "Maybe put some alcohol on it. Stop any chance of infection. If you're worried, go see the doc?"

"Mm." Alan took some square alcohol swabs from his bumbag and scrubbed the puncture in his arm. "I'm getting old. That hurt more than the time I nailed my thumb to a plank of wood." He held up the maimed digit to emphasise his point.

"You good? We've got a few more hours before sunrise." Geoff scanned the side of the road, taking in the enormous white gum, its bark shredded, the exposed trunk raw and yellow. He could still see the wreck in his mind's eye, a BMW wrapped tight around the tree like one of his granddaughters' hair-scrunchies. Even though the sky was lightening into a deep lilac, the ground was still inky and dark, with more shadows littering the ground than he'd expect for this time of the morning. He lifted his goggles and rubbed his glasses. Time for a break.

Alan and Geoff tossed their used polystyrene coffee cups into the back of their 4WD and pulled their hoods back over their heads. Then they put on goggles, and finally, their white face masks.

"This humidity is the worst," Alan said. "It never used to be this sticky in March."

"Reckon it's 'cos of global warming?"

"Whatever. It's making that 'roo stink even worse."

A large, dead kangaroo lay on the side of the road, its hide scratched raw. It wasn't involved in the accident, the cops had explained, and therefore was of no interest to their investigation. *They could have at least moved it away from the boy's remains.* It was offensive, both its stench and proximity to the crime scene. Geoff tried not to think that some of the smell might be that of the human remains they were collecting. Just in case, he'd taken the precaution of smearing camphor gel under his nose. It was worth having the menthol scent burning his eyes if it blocked out the meaty odour of rot.

"I'll go out wider," Alan said as he moved away, "and collect the last pieces of the kid. You wanna check over the ground we've already done?"

Geoff grunted in agreement. He disliked calling the deceased *kids*. Sure, most of them were actually kids, this one barely nineteen, but saying it aloud was too...*jovial*. The insincerity stung him. Besides, the word "kid" conjured too many positive associations for him and reminded him of his own children, and his grandchildren. Calling the scattered remains a *kid* drove home that the body parts splattered throughout the bush had belonged to a person. Child. Son. Brother. A body so perfectly obliterated that his family would never even get the chance to say farewell. All that was the stuff of nightmares.

That's why this job was only ever offered to old guys like him and Alan. When asked what he did for work, Geoff said he was retired. It wasn't a lie. He *was* retired. This job was a community service that made him a little pocket money. Geoff's job as a forensic cleaner meant he was responsible for cleaning up crime scenes after the paramedics had whisked away survivors and the police had finished their preliminary investigations. If a body was intact, the paramedics usually took it. When the body was in pieces—utterly obliterated in a car crash, industrial malfunction, or explosion—the forensic cleaners stepped up. It wasn't physical fitness that was demanded of them, but patience and experience. This was a job for men who had seen the world, lived through it, all its successes and failures, and witnessed both the best and worst of humanity. Men who were well and truly sailing away into the sunset of their twilight years.

Ironically, doing a job that was only offered to older workers made Geoff feel young and useful. Picking up the dead made him feel alive.

Alan trudged back in from the new area he'd covered, his biohazard bag already bulging. Snagged on the end of Alan's garbage picker was a long, blue length of gizzard, wet and slick like a fish. Geoff swallowed hard.

Alan flicked it into his bag with practised ease. "What were we talking about?"

"When?"

"Over coffee." Alan sealed the bag and dropped it beside their 4WD before retrieving another from the boot.

"I don't remember." Geoff lifted a blood-soaked rag from a tree branch overhead. "I asked how Marg was."

"Nah, not that. But she's fine."

"That's good."

Alan snapped his gloved fingers. "That's it! I was saying we should go see that new Batman movie. It's our turn to pick a movie. How many times have we seen an old-lady comedy?"

Geoff grinned. "Sonia hates it when you call them that."

"But they *are* old-lady comedies. And the last time I checked, our wives *are* old ladies. Just like we're a pair of old farts!"

A small breeze stirred up the abattoir stink in the bush.

Alan groaned, cursing the humidity again. "I don't think it's just the 'roo," he said, "more like a human-marsupial stroganoff made of offal." He giggled. "A *stroganoffal!*"

Alan, a lovely bloke, would be too loud and obnoxious at his own funeral. Geoff swallowed hard again. Even if the casualties were drunk, speeding, or not wearing a seatbelt, it wasn't Alan's place to ridicule them. Their families would live with shame enough. The deceased deserved respect.

Geoff located some shards of bone and swapped his garbage picker for the grabber that dangled from his belt. It wasn't much different to the mobility aids that the elderly use for retrieving things when seated in a lounge chair. A loathsome reminder of the fate that awaited him and Sonia as the years wore on. He placed the cigarette-butt-sized pieces of bone in his bag.

A sudden motion across the ground caught his eye, and he

stood, staring at the earth where he'd collected the bones. He blinked hard, not wanting to remove the goggles and rub his foggy glasses again. For a moment, it had appeared as though the shadows had retreated from the grabber. His eyes were playing tricks on him. *I need to get new glasses.*

"This is why young men shouldn't be allowed to drive sports cars," Alan said, a hunk of muscle on the end of his garbage picker.

Geoff didn't argue. The forensic scientists had ruled out alcohol or drugs as a cause of the boy's accident. The key sign, or lack thereof, was the absence of any skid marks on the road—he had crashed into the tree at full speed. "Likely lost control and was dead before he knew it," the forensic specialist had said.

Well, it didn't matter how the kid died. All Geoff and Alan had to do was make sure nothing remained by the time the sun came up. Before others began constructing vigils and placing photographs, flowers, and crosses at the scene. It never ceased to amaze Geoff how far body parts and organs spread from car accidents, like the deceased had leapt headlong into a tree mulcher.

Alan kept feeding meat into the mouth of his bag.

The less they talked, the less they breathed in the stench of rot, and the quicker they would have everything cleaned.

Alan's suggestion to ensure that nothing was missed was about as sensitive as he was: use pigs trained to eat human flesh. "Not like anyone is going to look at the bodies afterwards, anyway. Those pigs sniff out meat better than anything else on earth." At least he'd had sense enough not to repeat that to anyone but Geoff.

Geoff glanced at his watch. 3:15am. Three heavy bags of biohazard material in the 4WD, two more outside of it. Geoff estimated it would take one more to finish up the shift. Once the sun was up, they could do a last quick check of the area, radio it in, and he could head home to a warm cup of Milo and bed. Geoff took a rest, deciding against having another coffee. It would only make him groggy without taking the edge off his fatigue. He rubbed his left knee. It always began to ache when he stood up for too long. His eyes stung from the glare of the police spotlights, the reflective orange tape cordoning off the area, the naked tree trunk and the police markers. He was feeling the effects of being in the artificial light for too long.

"Whoa, check this out," Alan called from up ahead.

Geoff wandered over to where the fluorescent vest over his suit made Alan glow. He was hunched over a convex piece of muscle and bone on the ground.

Ribs, Geoff realised. Human ribs.

"Hey, don't get too close," Alan barked, prodding the ribs with his garbage picker. "Now look at this." He turned the ribs over.

The underside was covered in black scales. Except some scales were round, like berries.

"Ticks!" Alan said.

Disturbed, some of the larger parasites dropped from the ribs and crawled away. That's what they did, Geoff recalled. Fed until they were ten times their size, then dropped off, and disappeared into the bush.

"You ever seen as many as this?"

Geoff shook his head. "No. I've seen plenty in the ears of 'roos, but never this many."

"Do they swarm?" Alan asked.

"I don't think they are carrion feeders. There's no blood in dead tissue."

"Not much," Alan agreed. He very carefully plucked the ribs from the ground and dropped them in his bag. With uncharacteristic care, he stepped away from the ticks that were spreading out from their disrupted hiding place. "Christ, one of those little bastards hurt enough. Imagine what all of them could do."

"You okay?"

"Yeah. It's just...like being too close to a beehive. It makes my skin crawl."

Geoff stepped away from the ticks.

Alan said, "Do you think that's why there's no blood?"

Geoff frowned. "They can't drink spilled blood. Only suck it from a host."

"You sure?"

"Pretty sure."

"Okay."

The next few items they located were, thankfully, free of the tiny parasites. Alan had stopped talking and was taking more care than usual, trying to avoid the pests. Their body suits were no longer hot and constricting but a welcome protection against the arachnids.

After scooping pieces of liver out of some spinifex, Geoff headed back towards their 4WD. Strange how dry and grey the liver was. Was it the ticks? Had they drained the liver and disappeared? Were there so many ticks here that they could drain a nineteen-year-old's body in a matter of hours? It didn't make sense. Ticks only fed on living creatures.

Geoff's eyes found the kangaroo. Now it sat on the road, a smear of red dirt dragged behind as if in its wake. *Did Alan move it? No, I would have seen him.* Carrying his garbage picker like a spear, Geoff approached the kangaroo. Up close, he could see that the creature's exposed flesh was riddled with tiny pink puncture marks.

The kangaroo gasped.

Geoff jumped back, jarring his bad knee.

The kangaroo's dry eyes swivelled to stare at him. Then the creature again gasped for air, and vomited. A thick, black stream of ticks poured out of its body and rained across the ground like black rice.

What the hell!?

Alan's screams tore through the bushland. Geoff staggered backwards, his left leg giving way. He landed hard on his knees, heard a loud pop, felt pain explode from his left kneecap.

Move!

He forced himself upwards, the grinding sensation in his knee making him retch. He got his legs under him and lunged for the 4WD. The ground around him was disappearing beneath a black tide of parasites. The image in his mind was of a man trying to outrun a landslide. He felt itching all over his body, felt tiny sharp legs on his skin beneath the suit, but it was not real, just phantom sensations, because he was far enough away from them. Safe, yes, and far enough away. He pushed on, unable to quite believe that he was still free of the parasites.

Untouched, Geoff reached the 4WD and wrenched the driver's side door open. He flung himself into the driver's seat, slamming the car door shut. He stabbed the ignition button, and the engine roared to life.

A scream came from the side of the 4WD, and Alan, his outfit more black than blue, ran to the car, arms outstretched. Before Geoff could react, Alan had reached the vehicle. His hands were on the door handle.

Geoff screamed, "No, stop, no! Alan, no!"

Alan yanked the handle. The car shook with the force of his effort. The door remained closed.

"Oh, God," Geoff breathed. *The automatic doors locked when the ignition started.*

Alan tore his suit off. His skin was covered with glossy black ticks, as densely packed as fish scales. The parasites swelled before Geoff's eyes, expanding to the size of blueberries before dropping from Alan's naked flesh, then dozens more swarmed over the exposed skin. Alan screamed again. A fatal error, for the parasites swarmed up his chest and throat, forcing themselves into his open mouth. Clawing at his throat, choking, Alan sank out of sight.

Geoff wrenched the car into gear, and slammed his foot down on the accelerator.

Tyres spun, the car lurched, a thud reverberated through the vehicle as it rolled over Alan. Geoff ignored it. He would think about that later. When he'd survived. Right now, he couldn't afford to think about anything *but* surviving. Hands gripping the wheel so tight his bones creaked, he watched the speedometer's needle rocket up to seventy kilometres, eighty, ninety, and he tore along the road, out of the bush he had spent the night working in.

Now there was just him and the open road.

He clicked on the headlights, just as something brushed against the back of his hands. Geoff glanced down and screamed in terror. Ticks poured out of the air-conditioning vents, scattered over the dashboard, the steering wheel, onto his hands. More filled the footwell, tumbling into his boots. In seconds his lap was full of them. He could already feel them beneath the suit, their chainsaw-like mouths puncturing his skin. As pain erupted through his arms and legs, and the swarming creatures rose up inside the suit, up across his back, his neck, he tore at the suit.

Geoff's elbow hit the wheel, and the car was yanked right, momentum carrying it upwards, rolling the 4WD over. For a split second, he was weightless, the cabin filled with tiny floating orbs, their legs paddling in the air, tiny proboscises searching for him, probing the air. Even before the 4WD hit the tree, Geoff was flung through the windscreen, torn into hundreds of pieces of meat, bone and innards, and scattered across the night.

BAIT

ANTHONY FERGUSON

It was the sight of the hammerhead, breaching the spray, that did it for me. Couldn't believe the guy had hooked it for starters. Big, magnificent fish, with that strange tell-tale head. All part of the majesty and mystery of the sea. Which in turn is part of the opening spiel I give to all the guests who charter our little vessel. These guys were no exception.

Mind you, should have followed my instincts as I didn't like the look of them when they rocked up. Parked their massive SUV over the white line, like they didn't give a shit. Three of them: two regular-sized blokes, and one massive unit, looking like he was chiselled out of granite.

They were all buff, to be fair. The type of blokes who spend a lot of time in the gym, building massive upper bodies, shoulders, chest and forearms, but forget the bits below the waist, so they end up with huge torsos propped up on skinny little chicken legs. The big guy at least seemed to be in better proportion, and he was the one you didn't want to mess with. In fact, all of them had an air of menace, the kind where you didn't probe them too deeply on how they made a crust. They looked the type that would flick the switch over to psycho mode in a heartbeat. The sort of guys who get off on watching cage fighting.

Unfortunately, my gut instinct proved correct.

Terry, my offsider, gave me the look when we first clapped eyes on them.

"I know, mate, but what can I do? They made the booking by phone. Besides, we need the money."

We both cast our eyes over the *Liberty*. It was true, she had seen better days. With rent, taxes, and the overheads in keeping the boat afloat, we were barely making enough to feed ourselves. I knew Terry had a couple of under-the-radar side gigs, but for me, the boat represented my life-long dream of freedom, and I was buggered if I would let anything stop me making a go of it. Besides, it was all I had, since I cashed in my savings on it when I came out of the army. As far as I was concerned, looking over the ocean waves was the antithesis of staring across desert sand, waiting for a bullet with your name on it.

Terry had been my best mate since high school, and would often regale me with tales of his old man's and uncle's adventures in the fishing industry back home in Thailand. Terry was Aussie as, been here since he was in nappies, but you never lose your love of the place your family came from. I always told the prick he should've been a chef; he was that damn good in the galley. Some of the stuff he whipped up below deck was phenomenal. Then again, having a great sense of flavour is all part of their makeup across the water there. Give me Asian cuisine over the slop we grew up on here any day. No offence to my folks, but the old-world "meat and two veg" tucker just doesn't cut it.

However, I digress. We were contracted to take these three blokes out, give them a nice day's deep-sea fishing, and impart some knowledge about the waters off the Australian coast and the abundant life within. The trio seemed reserved, surly and untalkative, except among themselves. They pretty quickly revealed themselves as bigots, misogynists, homophobes and racists, by way of their group narrative and their attitude toward Terry.

I only had the name of the one who made the booking; I assumed it was the big bloke. They introduced themselves as Briggsy, Macca and Spud. They were all close-cropped and shaven-headed, so it was difficult to tell them apart. You could sense that Briggsy was the big fella in charge, while Macca was the follicly-challenged one, and Spud was as dumb as shit.

The first red flag happened when they tried to board with their own esky. I should've listened to my inner voice there and then.

"What ya got there?" I ask, pointing at the hold-all under Briggsy's burly arm.

"Just our liquid refreshments," he replies.

Terry and I exchange a glance.

"Nah, mate. No outside beverages on board. It's in the online contract. We got beers in the fridge here you can purchase at a good price."

A look of thunder rolls across Briggsy's face. "No, Skip. We like our own beer. Are we gonna have a problem?" Macca and Spud nod in agreement. "We already paid ya for the day."

The mention of money strikes a soothing chord, so we acquiesce, and cast off. All the while, I have this rising, nagging feeling in the back of my mind.

"So, what do you blokes do for a crust?" Terry asks, in his signature Ocker drawl.

Bloke is more Aussie than I am. Anyway, I can see it was a mistake, as I catch the look that crosses Briggsy's face, before he subsumes it under his regular human visage. It's a look that tells you he might snap and kill you in an instant. I've seen that look before, in the faces of guys who served in Afghanistan, and sometimes in blokes on the footy field.

"Aw, you know," says Briggsy, exchanging a grin with his colleagues. "We do a bit of importing and exporting, and we also do a bit of protecting."

Terry has sussed enough to stop probing, but I can't resist.

"Protecting what?" I can imagine what sort of stuff these guys probably import and export. I do a quick scan of their forearms for any bikie-related tatts, but nothing stands out.

"Oh, you know," Briggsy continues, "People, places, goods."

"Whatever people wanna pay us to protect," Macca joins in.

Spud just scratches his wispy beard thoughtfully, or with whatever passes for thought in his head.

I nod to Terry. I know he's thinking what I'm thinking. Something about standover tactics and the protection racket, and I'm running through several other wild thoughts, like how quickly can I get to the emergency flares below deck?

I decide to navigate the conversation into safer waters, by telling our clients about the sea, and the type of fish we are likely to hook up. That seems to engage them. Terry takes the wheel and steers us out into the strait. I point out on the sonar where some good schools lie. True to form, Briggsy and his boys are only interested in the bigger stuff. The bigger the better, much like their preference in motor vehicles and muscles.

"Yeah," I answer Briggsy, "these waters are teeming with big predators. Especially great white sharks. Good feeding ground for them around here. Plenty of tailor, bluefin, mackerel, and a seal colony on a nearby, otherwise-uninhabited rocky outcrop."

Macca's eyes glaze over at the thought. I can picture him interrogating a kneeling Afghan villager with an AK47. "How big do they get out here? The sharks?" He's almost salivating.

"Well, they can grow to about four-and-a-half to six-and-a-half metres, and weigh up to three-hundred-and-fifty kilos," I say.

"Jeez! How big is that?" Spud pipes up.

Briggsy punches his arm as if by reflex. "Big enough to swallow you whole, ya nong!" he says with a guttural laugh that sounds more like a growl.

"Except they don't swallow you whole," Terry interjects, unhelpfully as it turns out. "They get curious first. Circle you a bit. Size you up. Suss you out, and then they come in like an express train. Then you're stuffed. They'll take an arm, or a leg. Then the blood lust really kicks in as you bleed out. They slowly tear you apart. You just better hope you drown first."

"Jeez! Fuck that. I can't even swim," says Spud.

"Mate, all the better if a big Noah takes you quickly, eh? Save ya from drowning," Briggsy says with a grin that quickly segues into a nasty leer.

I manage to distract them from their *Jaws* obsession and get them hooked and baited up. They're happy enough sitting back in the chairs with their rods dangling, passing round cans of beer from the esky they insisted on bringing along.

Macca soon hooks up his first, a decent-sized mackerel. I give him a nod of approval, and toss it in the big tank for later.

Things go smoothly for a couple of hours. The spring weather stays balmy and the squall remains calm. The trio are distracted by the number of bites they are getting, only matched by the quantity of cans they consume.

"You got any grub on this rust bucket?" Briggsy arcs up as he detaches a tailor from his hook.

"Nah, not part of the deal. You read the flyer, I assume?" I take the fish and stick it in the ice tank. No need to measure this one either.

Briggsy gives me a stare. I look at Terry.

"I got a bit of fried rice left over from this morning," he says.

The boys turn their noses up.

"Good stuff," Terry looks hurt. "It's got shrimp, sesame oil, peanut oil."

"He's a great cook," I add.

"That's chogie food," says Macca.

"Yeah, we'll pass," says Briggsy.

"I need a dump," Spud announces.

Given that the trio had insisted on urinating over the side of the boat, against our wishes, I gather he wants to sit down for this one.

"Below deck," I say. "Can't miss it."

Macca hooks another bluefin and screws up his face when I insist on weighing and measuring. "No, mate. This one is too small. We gotta chuck it back."

"Bullshit!" He grabs at the fish protectively.

I exchange a look with Terry. "It's in the contract, buddy. Anything undersize we put back, to let it grow. You gotta replenish the ocean. The sea gives, and we give in return."

"Fuck off! It's my fish. I caught the bastard. I'm keeping it. Chuck it in the tank."

He goes to open the lid. I hold it down. "No, mate. It's illegal."

Briggsy interposes himself between us in a threatening manner and throws his two cents in.

"We're bloody payin' ya, Skip."

I swallow. "Yeah, and we're giving you a fun day's fishing."

At this point Spud returns from below deck. "Fuck me. They got a kitchen down there, a wok and all... What's the go?"

Macca turns to Spud. "These pricks are making us chuck me fish back... Are you alright, Spud? Ya gone very pale."

Spud rubs beads of sweat off his forehead. "Actually, no. I feel a bit crook."

Briggsy laughs. "Must be your delicate constitution, Spud. Macca and I are fine. Maybe we'll get this bloke to fry up some of our fish for tea."

Terry raises an eyebrow. "Your fish? Nah, mate. Those fish belong to us. All part of the deal. We might let you take a couple, out of pure goodwill, but technically, everything you catch on this boat belongs to us. Our rods, our bait."

Terry is correct, but what he leaves out is how the two of us cash in selling on the fish our clients catch to a small number of local restaurants with whom we have struck up a deal. All perfectly legit of course, and it helps us stay in business.

Unfortunately, this holds little sway with Briggsy. In fact, it's the proverbial straw that breaks the camel's back.

"Ah fuck this," he yells. "You two pricks are taking the piss! We're basically workin' for youse at this point. Breaking our backs to line your pockets."

"Too right!" says Macca

"I think I'm gonna chuck," says Spud, as he runs to the side of the boat and duly pukes.

By this point I'm a bit jacked off as well, with the attitude of these jerks.

"Look, mate. I keep telling you. It was all in the contract. Did you even read it?"

Briggsy reaches into the esky and pulls out a gun. "Yeah, bud? Was this in the contract?"

Terry takes a step back. "Shit!"

I flinch, but I know I need to calm the situation down. "Now hold on, mate."

Briggsy waves the pistol at me. "Nah, you've said enough, Skip. Me and the boys will take it from here."

"Too right," says Macca, opening the tank and throwing his undersize bluefin in.

"Aaaw Christ!" says Spud, as he spews over the side again, trails of yellow-green drool dangling from his lips.

It's at this point that I regret not mentioning to Terry the money I borrowed off a local loan shark to keep the boat afloat. I can guess what's coming, since I reneged on a few repayments.

Briggsy flexes his bulk and gesticulates with the gun. "Okay boys, let me give ya the bad news. Skip here owes our associate a lot of money, which he doesn't seem able to pay back. As a result, we've been commissioned to hijack this boat as payment and deliver it to our employer. Unfortunately, you two boys won't be completing the journey. You'll be going for a swim."

Terry gives me the death stare. All I can do is mouth a *sorry* back. Spud throws up over the side again.

"Macca, go help Spud. Lay him under that table on deck in the shade."

"We got a bunk downstairs," I say.

"Shut up, Skip," says Briggsy.

"We got seasickness pills downstairs too, and he needs water," I add.

"Alright." Briggsy nods. "You go get 'em, and don't try any funny stuff."

I go below and get the water and meds, and forgoing the flares, I grab the meat cleaver from the galley and stuff it down my pants.

Back on deck, I pass the meds over and Briggsy issues orders. "Righto, boys. You got a stay of execution as we need your help to deliver this bucket. In the meantime, you can entertain us. Forget the smaller fish, let's go shark fishing." He points at Terry, stationed near the wheel. "You, fucken Ho Chi Minh. Steer this boat to where the great whites hang out."

"You can't hook sharks on these lines. They're not made—"

Briggsy pistol whips me across the face and I go down like a sack of shit. The meat axe comes clattering out of my duds. Briggsy picks it up with his other hand.

"Jesus! Look what this prick was packing." He tosses the gun to Macca, who has finished depositing an ailing Spud under the table and forcing water and pills down his gullet. "Get this boat moving," he addresses Terry.

Macca points the gun in Terry's direction.

I get up, groggy, and wipe a hand along my stinging temple. It comes back slightly bloody.

Briggsy points the cleaver at me. "You got any burley on this hulk?"

"No." I shake my head.

"What are we gonna use as bait?" Macca asks.

"Maybe one of these two." Briggsy laughs. "Just grab some fish out of the tank there. That'll do for starters."

Terry pulls the boat up and anchors. A couple of seals frolic off the starboard side.

Briggsy and Macca bait a large mackerel each and throw the lines overboard, making sure to keep their weapons handy. The swell rises a little. The only sounds are the scream of gulls looking for scraps, and the occasional moan from the prostrate Spud beneath the table.

Half an hour passes, and the thugs grow impatient.

Macca scratches his arse. "This is boring. Shoulda brought some chicks with us."

"Why aren't they fucken biting?" Briggsy asks.

"We need burley," says Macca.

Briggsy throws me an accusatory glance. "You sure ya got nothing, Skip?"

I nod, still feeling the effects of the pistol blow. "We're not set up for shark fishing."

"I got an idea." Briggsy rises and moves ominously toward me. I back against the railings. Macca looks on with mounting interest. "Watch him," Briggsy barks, nodding toward Terry at the wheel.

Briggsy moves menacingly forward and grabs me by the arm.

"Stop it!" I try and yank my arm away but he's got a grip like steel.

He pulls my face in close enough I can smell his rancid breath. "Don't make this any harder than it has to be, Skip."

He stretches my arm out straight, and leans it against the starboard side. Looks over at Macca. "Whaddya reckon, Macca, the whole hand or just a couple of fingers?"

He laughs raucously and Macca joins in. Terry lunges, but Macca points the gun at him.

Briggsy pauses, then in one swift move he slides the sharp

blade up my forearm, dissecting the flesh. I scream and the claret starts to flow. Briggsy jerks my arm over the side of the boat, letting the blood stream into the water.

"This oughta get the Noahs excited," he says. "Hopefully bring a couple of big ones up."

The pain in my arm is sharp and excruciating, and in combination with the blow to my head, it feels like I'm going to pass out.

"You fucking wankers!" Terry yells.

"Shut up, choge, or you'll be next," Briggsy yells back. He yanks me upright again. "Harden up, ya pussy. I didn't go too deep. You'll be fine."

Despite the pain, I soon realise he's right. No major arteries are severed, and the flow soon slows to a steady trickle. Enough to make me woozy, though. I know I'm not much good to Terry like this.

Briggsy drags me across the deck and sits me in one of the chairs. He nods toward Terry. "You got a first aid kit on board I assume?" Terry nods in assent. "Go get it, and no funny buggers."

That's when Macca gets an almighty pull on his line, which starts flying out, the reel screaming.

In a few minutes it breaches the surface, silver skin glistening in the afternoon sun.

"Bugger me! It's a bloody hammerhead. Get stuck in, Macca," Briggsy screams.

They're both yelling with excitement and even I can't believe this clown hooked a hammerhead shark. Macca fights and strains, and slowly but surely, he starts to reel it in. It's a good two-metre fish.

Despite myself, the old instinct kicks in again. "Mate, you can't bring that one up. You gotta unhook it."

"Stuff that." Macca doesn't take his eyes off the fish.

"Yeah, piss off, Skip. We're in charge now," says Briggsy.

Using all his bulk, and with Briggsy's help, they haul the hammerhead on deck. Briggsy suddenly notices Terry's absence.

"Hey, where's the gook with the first aid? Go see what he's up to, Macca."

The poor shark is flipping and flopping on the deck, and

Briggsy yanks the hook out of its mouth.

"You can't torment this poor animal. Just let it go," I say.

"Get stuffed. This thing is a maneater. It's our trophy. The first of many."

"Hammerheads are not maneaters."

Briggsy's face turns and he raises the cleaver toward me. "Keep talking, Skip, and I'll cut that loose tongue of yours out for bait."

Briggsy's thought is interrupted by Macca returning from below deck. He's dragging Terry along by the scruff of the neck. "Caught this one trying to get into the flares. Bastard was gonna alert the authorities. Gave me a fucken slap too, the prick."

At that moment, the shark thrusts itself sideways and almost knocks Macca for a six.

"Jesus!" He gives the shark a kick.

"Don't torment it, mate!" Terry pleads.

"Yeah, alright," says Briggsy. "Gis a hand here."

He and Macca stand either end of the hammerhead and try and lift it, but the panicking shark is slippery. Briggsy loses his footing. Macca laughs at him. Terry and I try and help. Briggsy swears and barges us aside. He swings the cleaver into one of the shark's eye wings, almost severing it.

"Oops! I fucken slipped," says Briggsy, yanking the cleaver free.

"Hey, it's suddenly lighter," says Macca.

"Cool. Let's even it up then." Briggsy hacks into the shark's other eye wing.

"You mongrels!" Terry yells, but Macca pulls the gun and nudges him away.

"Might as well finish the job," Briggsy yells, and hacks into the wounded shark.

The deck is soon awash with blood. Macca pushes our protests aside with the gun. When he's done, Briggsy leans on the starboard rail, panting with exertion. He looks at Macca. They both look at Spud, who has now lapsed into unconsciousness.

Terry bandages me up to stem the flow of blood. Briggsy points Terry towards our destination, a suitably secluded inlet several kilometres up the coast, and he and Macca sit and ride out the early evening swell. Even the gulls cry off and call it a night. Spud talks in his fevered sleep intermittently, breaking the tension.

"Ya alright, mate?" Briggsy calls across.

There is no reply.

Briggsy casts his eye toward the darkening horizon and checks his gun. "Well, boys, looks like we're in for the long haul."

"Better strap y'selves in," Macca laughs.

Several minutes later, Briggsy stands, yawns and stretches. He looks over to Terry and me, standing by the remains of the shark.

"Stuff this. I'm fanging a feed. You hungry, Macca?"

His colleague nods in assent.

Briggsy nods toward me. "Get the chow to cook us some chow."

"Ask him yourself. He's right there."

"Don't get fucken smart, Skip. Just get downstairs and start cookin'. Ya got any decent tucker down there?"

Terry looks ready to explode, but then, a look of calm serenity crosses his face. He quickly disguises it, but not before I notice.

"Got some fresh seafood. How about some occy?"

"Occy?" Briggsy and Macca say in unison.

"Octopus, you know, calamari. You like squid rings I assume?"

"Aw yeah, decent tucker."

"Okay, I can whip up some occy. Chuck in some chilli, oyster sauce, onions, bit of garlic."

"Not too spicy," Briggsy says.

"I'll tone it down, western-style," says Terry.

We follow him into the hold. Terry fires up the cooker and layers the wok with oil.

"Hope this stuff is fresh," says Briggsy, laying the cleaver aside and seating himself beside Macca.

"Fresh as," says Terry, as he slips on a pair of gloves. "For hygiene," he explains, without being asked.

He reaches into a water-filled bucket next to the fridge, and I get an inkling of just what he's up to. The thugs blink as the chef lifts a pair of small, colourful octopuses out of the bucket. I bite my lip as I watch the cephalopods turn yellow, and Terry whips them into the oily wok before the tell-tale rings start to glow.

I watch our captors for any signs of suspicion, but they seem taken in by the sizzling of the wok, captivated by the smell of caramelising onion, chilli, capsicum, peanut oil and cooking flesh. I turn to Terry, who avoids my gaze and theirs. Beads of sweat are forming on his brow. Briggsy notices.

"Warm night, eh?" He fingers the blade, and as the thought hits him, he offers it up. "You need this thing?"

"Nah, all good," Terry replies, tossing the ingredients around in the wok like a master. "You can eat these whole."

Terry serves it up to them on tin plates. I am quietly grateful their innate selfishness stops them even considering sharing the meal. The pair of them wolf down the octopus and condiments in minutes.

I watch Terry watching them. I can sense his anticipation.

Briggsy leans back and wipes his mouth as Macca traces a greasy finger along his plate.

"Not bad... Terry! What sorta name is that for a slope?"

I watch the colour start to drain from Briggsy's face as he lets out a belch. It cracks right through the tension, and Terry visibly relaxes as he considers his reply.

"Actually, it's short and anglicised for my real name, Theera-phop, which translates as 'smart'."

Briggsy looks at Macca, who grins, then clutches at his gut and lets out a huge fart. "'Scuse I."

Briggsy belches again and a look of discomfort crosses his face. "Yeah, well you ain't so smart, are ya? Hooking up with this loser on his crummy boat."

Terry cracks a smile, and it's the most beautiful thing I've seen all day. "I was smart enough to cook the occy below two-hundred degrees Celsius."

"Huh?" Briggsy looks at Macca, whose facial muscles are starting to convulse. Briggsy's quickly follow suit.

"What...what the fuck did you feed us, mate?"

"Blue-ringed octopus, buddy. Highly toxic. Especially if you cook it at the wrong temperature."

Briggsy goes to rise, but he can't. He reaches for the gun, but his whole body is spasming now. His limbs start to stiffen. Terry yanks the meat cleaver out of his reach.

"Macca, what the...?" Briggsy starts to yell, but it's all he gets out before he begins to seize up.

Courage floods back into my veins with pumping adrenaline. I can barely feel the throbbing pain in my forearm as I jump to my feet to enjoy the spectacle. "Thanks for sharing your meal with us, fellas," I say.

"They didn't give us a single bite, mate," Terry says with a shake of his head.

"Not a mouthful," I say, as Macca's face turns into a rictus grin.

Within minutes both Briggsy and Macca are as stiff as a board. Just half-sat, half-stood in their seats, staring at us. Terry calmly rinses out his wok.

"Terry, what the hell just happened? Are they...?

"Dead?" He turns and examines them. "Not quite. Just about. You see, they're paralysed but still fully conscious." Terry points to parts of their bodies as he explains this like a demented university lecturer. "Their hearts have stopped beating and suffocation is starting, right about...here, by paralysis of the diaphragm. They can't breathe, Skip. It's like they're drowning internally."

It's awful to watch, but nonetheless fascinating. After a few minutes Terry closes their eyes, which is good, because I don't like the way they are looking at us.

We both sit down on the bench seat opposite them.

"How do you know all this stuff, Terry?"

"I read up on marine biology. I like to know what I'm cooking, and eating."

"Well, why the hell have you got a bucket full of blue-ringed occy on board?"

Terry grins. "I'm interested in toxicology as well. Besides, these things are actually a bit of a delicacy in certain parts of the world, as long as you cook them at the right temperature, or serve the right parts. You know, like blowfish."

"I'm just glad you're my mate, Terry." I look over at the two very dead crims. "So, what are we gonna do with them now?"

Terry shrugs. "This *is* shark territory, mate."

We lug them upstairs one at a time and line them up on deck. The sea is calm under a dazzling canopy of stars. I push my toe under Briggsy's corpse and hesitate.

"What if they don't…you know. What if one of them floats to shore?"

"Not much chance this far out, but just in case…" Terry pulls out his meat cleaver. "Turn around, mate."

I wince at the sound of steel hacking into flesh. I don't turn back again until I hear several loud splashes.

A whimper alerts us to the flensing table, where Spud stirs and shifts in his sleep.

"Shit! I forgot about him." Terry raises his blood-soaked cleaver. It glints in the moonlight. "Remember what he said earlier? He can't swim."

Half an hour later, Terry hauls in the anchor and I fire up the engine. I have made my full apology about the shit situation I got us in, and he shrugs it off as if it was all in a day's work.

"We can't go home though," I tell him. "When word gets back to the crim who hired those goons, he is not gonna be happy."

"Well, mate," Terry smiles, "we got nothing holding us back there. Maybe it's time we headed out to new pastures."

He takes the wheel, and I see that look cross his dial again.

"You got something in mind?"

Terry taps his nose and holds up his mobile. "Connections, mate. I got friends in low places."

I shake my head and smile. "You people, mate. You're…"

"Inscrutable?" he finishes my thought. "Yeah, I know."

Terry pushes the throttle down, and I see the lights of civilisation dim in our wake. I start to say something else, but I'm not sure if he hears me.

SPECIES ENDANGERED

DEBORAH SHELDON

The empty beach looked so sumptuous, so tantalising, that it actually made her mouth water. The colour of the sand reminded Helen of canned pineapple, while the Coral Sea shone with the kind of bright and luminous blue that she associated with travel brochures for infinity pools at five-star resorts. She slammed the car's passenger door.

"Last one in is a rotten egg!" she called, and broke into a run.

"Hoi, wait for me, you cheat!"

She had a good head start; Lou still had to get out and lock the car. Helen dodged through the palm trees and ferns that grew between the highway and the beach. The sand felt soft but hard-packed, easy to traverse. Hanging between the sea and sky sat a hump of land, presumably Dunk Island. Helen slowed, hopping on one leg to shuck a sandal. Lou flashed by, laughing, sprinting flat out. He kicked off his shoes and, bare-chested, ran into the sea.

"Rotten egg!" he shouted.

Cheeky bugger. Helen shucked her other sandal and waded in after him.

It was winter, July, but the dry season in tropical Queensland heated the seawater like a bath. The shelf went on and on at a gentle gradient. Helen caught up with Lou, who stood waist-height. They must be fifteen metres out or more. Fish darted. Sea grasses tickled her feet. She should have taken off her singlet and shorts. Now she would have to sit on a towel when they got back to the car.

"Come here, you," Lou said.

She moved in for his embrace. Instead, he gripped her waist, lifted her and dropped her. She came up, wet and giggling. He hugged her and kissed her crown.

"Babe," he said, "this has been the best holiday ever."

"Ditto."

Soon they would have to drive back to Sydney, to the cold wind and rain, to the noise, traffic, to their respective jobs; Lou at the building site, Helen at the start of third term with her rowdy grade five students.

Lou pulled away. "Did you hear that?" he said, facing the shore.

"Huh?"

"Listen."

There was the languorous whish and whoosh of the tide, the chatter of lorikeets, and something else: a low, almost subsonic growl from the lush vegetation.

"It sounds like a tiger," Lou said.

She laughed. "Or a truck's engine brake."

"Wait," Lou said, pointing. "What the fuck is that? You see it?"

Helen lifted a hand to shade her eyes.

Yes, now she could see it.

A shadow moved beneath the trees. She squinted. Whatever was slowly creeping nearer was tall, as tall as a man, yet impossibly slender and without shoulders. It resembled a head and spine with the arms torn off. Helen edged closer to Lou. They were alone on this stretch of coastline. The tyre iron Lou kept for protection while free-camping was in the car boot, their phones in the centre console. The growl sounded again.

"Can you see what it is?" she said.

"Not yet."

The figure stepped out onto the sand and into the light. It looked prehistoric.

Lou said, "Babe, is that an emu, a giant turkey, or what?"

For a second, Helen didn't know either. Then she recognised the scaly legs, huge and black-feathered body, the long throat which her imagination had suggested was an armless man. *The most dangerous bird in the world...* During first term, Helen had taken her students on an excursion to the zoo. Afterwards, each child had made a poster on an Australian animal. Most had chosen cuddly favourites—koala, sugar glider, wombat—but not Brianna. That quiet, intense little girl had formed her poster's heading with letters clipped from a newspaper like some kind of ransom note: *The most dangerous bird in the world.*

Helen said, "It's a cassowary."

"Yeah? Cool, I've never seen one."

"It's only found in north-eastern Queensland," Helen said, "and Papua New Guinea. I think it's endangered."

"How come it sounds like a tiger?"

"No idea."

Lou put his hands on his hips. "The fucker's looking at us."

The bird had stopped its advance a metre or so onto the beach. Now it stood completely still and silent, observing them. The high crest on its head (the *casque?* she wondered) looked made of bone. The face and neck were featherless. A wattle, two red and flabby tags of flesh resembling an empty scrotum, hung obscenely from the blue neck. Helen grimaced. Jesus, the bird was ugly. No, not ugly—*scary.* The bird must have come from the national park, drawn by Helen and Lou calling to each other. It must have crossed the highway, seen them, and decided to confront them. But why? They did not have any food. And cassowaries were not meat-eaters. Were they? No, the poster had featured pictures of fruits and berries. Yet the bird kept staring. The sneering beak and orange irises gave its face a grotesque, demonic cast.

The bird cocked its head, fast, and Helen jumped. The bird froze again.

"What's the matter, babe?" Lou said, and grinned. "Crapping yourself?"

"For sure. Cassowaries have killed people."

"Bullshit."

"Honest, I swear." If only she could recall every detail on the poster. "A boy got killed a long time ago. He and his friend had clubs or something and were trying to bash one. It turned on him, and cut open his neck."

"With what? Its beak?"

"No, its foot. Each toe has a long nail, sharp as a knife."

"Shit, hey." Lou rubbed his chin. "Well, it'll piss off into the bush when it gets bored. Let's just have our swim, okay?"

He floated onto his back and made leisurely strokes through the water. Helen paddled in his wake. The bird watched them. Lou swam parallel to the beach. Helen noticed that he kept the motionless cassowary in sight. Soon, the bird was a long way distant. Lou stood up and flicked water. Helen splashed him in return and tried to laugh.

"Stop fretting about the damn bird," Lou said.

"Me? You're as spooked as I am."

He looked past her shoulder, and his face tightened. She turned. The cassowary was treading across the sand in their direction, its gait slow and cautious, body and neck tense and rigid, eyes fixed. Helen's cat, Toby, moved in such a stealthy fashion whenever he hunted a pigeon. The bird's rasping growl started up again.

Lou said, "No wonder it's endangered. It's obviously thick as shit. Doesn't the bastard have sense enough to stay away from humans?"

"They're territorial," she said. "It must have a nest close by."

"Well, I've had enough. Let's head to the car."

Freestyle, he swam back the way they had come, parallel to the beach. His shoes stood out against the sand like a pair of black beacons. Helen followed but kept glancing behind at the cassowary. It watched them swim away.

Lou stood, shook the wet hair from his eyes, and strode toward the shoreline.

In her hurry to keep pace, Helen lost her footing in the slippery sea grasses and fell. Water closed over her head. She stood, coughing, blowing her nose.

Christ, she had to calm down. In a controlled manner, she began to wade using high and careful steps. Already, Lou was clear of the water. He picked up his shoes and clapped the soles together, knocking out sand. The cassowary, some fifty metres away, lowered its head and sprinted. It moved faster than Helen thought possible.

She screamed.

In the time it took Lou to turn and brace, the cassowary had closed the distance. It jumped. Both legs flew out in front of it, toes pointed, talons slashing. Lou lunged out of the way. The bird kicked again. Its rasping snarls sounded reptilian, primordial, like a dinosaur. Lou was a tall man, but the bird dwarfed him.

Helen cried, "Get back in the water."

Lou kept his arms outstretched, a shoe in each hand, trying to swat the bird away. Despite its massive size, the bird moved fast, bounding and springing, charging, thrusting its talons. One strike and Lou would be disembowelled. Helen rushed ashore. Waving her arms, she yelled as loudly as she could, stripping her throat raw. The cassowary baulked. Helen grabbed Lou's elbow. Together, they stumbled and floundered into the sea, scrambling backwards. The bird made a move to follow. Could the cassowary swim?

Yes. Oh, yes it could.

She remembered Brianna's penmanship, the cursive letters in hot pink pencil: *It swims like a champion in rivers and even the sea!* But the bird stayed onshore.

At waist-height in the water, Helen stopped and said, "Are you alright?"

"Nah," Lou said, panting. "The prick got me."

He had one palm held flat to his chest. Where were his shoes? He must have dropped them. God, was that blood oozing between his fingers? She dragged insistently on his wrist until he allowed her to look.

The gaping slash on his chest was about ten centimetres long. At its base, the flesh showed a glimpse of something white, something that must be, oh Jesus, must be bone...a rib bone. What if Lou had a punctured lung? Blood drizzled lazily from the wound. Surely, that was a good sign; if the talon had hit an artery, the blood would be spurting. *Don't freak out.* She tightened her grip on his wrist, felt his thready pulse beneath her fingertips.

"Can you breathe okay?" she said.

"Yeah, I'm alright."

The cassowary let out long, barking grunts, and stamped at the sand. Those legs belonged on a T. Rex. Helen wanted to cry but held on.

"So what do we do now?" Lou said.

Helen scanned the shoreline: deserted. Behind them, the Coral Sea was deserted too: no jet-skis, parasails or boats.

"We wait," she said. "Sooner or later, it'll leave for its nest."

He nodded. They held hands. The bird had again turned into a statue.

The black feathers were coarse and hair-like, falling on either side of its body as if from a central part. Where its wings should be were two stumps with blade-like quills. Perhaps these quills were secondary weapons. The bird kept hissing like a snake. Helen glanced at Lou. A flutter of panic started up in her stomach. He was pale beneath his olive skin, his green eyes glazed and sunken in their sockets.

"Pinch the edges of the wound together," she said. "That'll slow the bleeding."

He did as he was told. She squeezed his other hand.

Time passed.

The bird did not leave.

They began to speak quietly of many things: how much they had enjoyed their week in Cairns, snorkelling the Great Barrier Reef, trekking the Daintree Forest, river rafting at Barron Gorge; what they would do in Townsville, such as water-ski the Ross River Dam, hike Castle Hill; their work commitments; options to celebrate Lou's upcoming birthday, including a pub crawl, a party at the holiday house owned by Helen's parents on Phillip Island. Then the conversation petered out.

And still the bird had not left. And still it watched them.

The sun marched steadily toward the west. Its rays started to bite. Neither of them wore sunscreen lotion. This was supposed to have been a quick dip. During the drive south out of Cairns, the beach had kept peeking at Helen through the palm trees that grew alongside the highway. She had nagged Lou to stop.

"Are you in much pain?" she said.

"The salt water stings like fuck."

"At least you won't get an infection." She licked at her dry, cracking lips. "You realise the bird hasn't moved an inch."

"Yeah, I know."

"Maybe it's asleep," she said, and when Lou gave a snort, she added, "We don't know anything about this creature. It might sleep standing up, like a horse."

"With its eyes open?"

"Let's get low and walk sideways," she said. "We might sneak away."

They crabbed. The cassowary let out a shuddering bray and stalked the beach, following them. Helen felt the tears rise. At twenty-three years of age, she had not given death much thought, but she had never imagined dying from an animal attack.

"Oh, this is pointless," she said. "Let's stop."

The cassowary stopped too. It inflated its neck and made deep, booming sounds for a minute. Then it became silent and still. Its immobility chilled her.

She looked down at her bare shoulders. The skin glowed, a deep angry crimson. Lou's face and neck were reddening too. The blistering would soon start.

"How long do you reckon we've been out here?" she said.

"Couple of hours, maybe. We're gonna get heatstroke."

The reflection of sunshine on the water was giving her a headache. *Water, water, everywhere, nor any drop to drink…*what was that from, Coleridge? Something heavy bumped against her leg. A frisson of sudden terror made her shriek.

"What is it?" Lou said, clutching at her. "What's wrong?"

Shark.

Lou's blood must have attracted a predator, a fish with many teeth and an empty gullet. Her feet drew up involuntarily and her toes curled. But no, no, wait; it was a sea turtle. A bloody sea turtle… Relief made her sob.

"Hey," she said, and hiccupped. "Look."

The turtle swept its flippers and disappeared from sight.

Were there sharks off this coast? Saltwater crocodiles? Both? She had not seen any warning notices along the highway, but Australia's east coast was about a zillion kilometres. How could the authorities signpost it all? The expectation of teeth made her feel faint. She turned, scanned the vast expanse of the Coral Sea behind her, and saw the tip of a dorsal fin or the bump of eyes in every sparkling wave. The skin of her legs crawled in anticipation of the bite. *Don't freak out.*

"Find a stick or a rock," Lou said. "We'll have to smack the bird's head in."

"That's how the boy died, remember?"

"Yeah, but if we stay out here and do nothing, we'll die anyway."

Helen's heart pounded. "Don't say that."

"Babe, come on. Find a weapon."

Lou released her hand. Looking down, he searched the seabed. She did the same. There was sand and more sand, undulating grasses, fish, shells. The urge to scream began to build inside her chest. She clenched her jaw and swallowed hard.

"It's no use," she said at last, throat aching.

Movement from the cassowary drew her attention. Helen and Lou had drifted some distance apart. This must have confused the bird. It was pacing the beach, first one way and then the other.

"Check it out," she said. "It can't decide who to follow."

"There's our answer," Lou said. "We'll split up, put a hundred metres between us, and both make a run for it. The bird will have to choose which one to chase."

"What? Oh my God. Are you kidding me?"

"It's our best chance."

"No, that's a stupid idea." She swam over, grabbed him, and said, "We'll stay together and wait for help."

"There's no help coming, babe. Listen to me. The car's unlocked, keys in the centre console. Whoever gets to the car first drives over the beach and rescues the other one, okay?" He held her at arm's length. "Ready?"

"No. Shit, no. I mean, where's the car? All the palm trees look the same."

"Run in a straight line to the highway. You'll see the car once you're through the trees. Ready?"

"Please," she whispered. "I don't want to do this."

"Me neither." He kissed her crown and gave her a little shove. "Get going."

He loped through the water, heading north. The cassowary walked along the beach opposite him. Helen swam south. Her breathing sounded too loud. The pulse thudded in her ears. Every time the sea lapped at her mouth, she resisted the urge to drink. After a minute, she halted, stood, and looked around. The cassowary and Lou were a long way off. However, Lou must have been watching for her.

"Go," he yelled. "Hurry up."

Impatiently, he waved his arms. Helen stumbled towards shore. One step after another made the sea drop away, exposing her thighs, calves, ankles, until, oh God, her feet were on dry land. Had the cassowary noticed?

Yes. Even from this distance, she saw the bird turn to face her.

Lou—so brave, so gutsy—bounded from the surf. The bird sprinted at him.

Helen broke into a dash. The sand gave way beneath her heels, as if she were running in a dream, getting nowhere. The cool shadows of the trees and ferns seemed to mock her. Faster, she had to go *faster*. Her heart knocked chaotically.

Lou called, "Look out!"

She glanced. The cassowary was coming for her.

The bird powered over the beach, legs pumping. A fact from the poster: *It runs at fifty kilometres per hour!* Helen bolted into the vegetation. Branches whipped and lashed. Trampling sounded close behind. With a burst of speed, she emerged into the light. The car was some five metres to the north. She raced hard along the highway's shoulder. Gravel cut her feet. She focused on the driver's side door. Reaching out, she grabbed the handle, which stopped her momentum and spun her around.

The cassowary leapt.

Its huge, three-toed feet flew like a volley of arrows. Helen opened the door, creating an impromptu shield. The force of the kick pinned her against the car body. Pain flared in her collarbone. The bird dropped, preparing for the next kick. Helen slipped into the seat and slammed the door shut.

Relieved, panting, she pressed a hand to the stitch in her side.

The bird's head shot through the half-open window.

Its peck struck her scalp, ripping out a hank of hair. Dazed, Helen dropped across the front seats. Blade-like nails screeched against the door. Snarling, the bird lunged, its breath fruity and sour, beak snapping.

The window cracked.

Helen scrabbled through the centre console, found the keys, and started the engine. The bird squawked and withdrew. When she leaned on the horn, the bird shied, fled across the highway, and disappeared into the forest of the national park.

Gasping, Helen leaned her forehead against the steering wheel. Then she put the car into gear, swung the wheel and ploughed over the ferns, plants and grasses, crunching vegetation beneath the tyres. The car sank as it hit sand. Jesus, would the car bog? It was only a sedan, not a four-wheel drive. But no, it was okay, she was driving north and at a reasonable clip, but...

But where was Lou?

Fright gripped her by the throat. Had he fled to the water? She slowed the car. Nowhere, dear God, he was nowhere...and then she spotted him, about thirty metres away. Her relief quickly turned to panic. Why was he lying motionless on the beach?

Pulling up next to him, she left the engine running and got out.

His eyes were closed, his face grey beneath the sunburn.

"Lou?" she said, voice quavering. "Can you hear me?"

He opened his eyes. His gaze seemed blank, as if he could not recognise her. His shorts were covered in blood, and something else. What the hell was sitting on his hip? A steaming pile of greyish-purple, glistening loops...intestines...she was looking at Lou's intestines, extruded through a slash in his groin. Nausea washed over her.

"I think the bastard got me," Lou said. "Is it bad?"

Helen dropped to her knees and took his hand. "No," she lied. "Not too bad."

"So where's the bird?"

"Gone back into the bush."

Lou smiled. "Thank fuck for that. Help me up?"

"Hang on. Let me think."

If he tried to stand, the abdominal pressure would push more of his guts through the wound. First, she had to bandage him somehow. The car did not have a first aid kit. *Don't freak out.* Her mind raced. She took off her singlet and bra.

"What are you doing?" he said.

"Taking care of you. This might hurt a bit, okay?"

She wrapped her singlet around the top of his thigh, covering his guts, and secured the t-shirt with her bra. Lou did not react. Why not? He should be screaming in agony. She had to get him to hospital. They were midway between Cairns and Townsville, with nothing but sea, beach, and bush.

"Listen," he slurred, gazing blindly at the sky. "Can you hear that?"

A deep growl sounded nearby. Adrenaline shot through Helen's limbs.

"Sit up," she said. "Hurry. Roll towards me and lean on your elbow."

Complying, Lou grimaced. "Something doesn't feel right."

She draped his other arm over her shoulders and held his wrist. He smelled coppery, of blood and offal. Bile rose in her throat. Straining, she tried to lift him. He was too heavy. The growling came nearer. Helen did not have the breath to scream.

"Stand," she wheezed. "Put your feet underneath you and stand."

The car was only a metre away. Lou grunted. Short-winded, leaning his weight on her, he finally got up, swaying. A sharp pain twanged low in Helen's spine. She tottered beneath his arm, dragging him to the car. *Please don't let me drop him.* At last, she was close enough to open the back door.

"Get in and lie down," she ordered through her teeth.

As if unconscious, he collapsed across the back seat. The make-shift bandage at his groin bulged. The cassowary stepped from the vegetation. Helen grabbed Lou's ankles and hoisted his legs into the car. Pain lanced her lower back. Slamming the door, she limped to the front seat and fell behind the wheel. She locked eyes with the cassowary. A wild, crazy hatred flew through her body.

You're dead, fucker.

She aimed the car and floored the accelerator. The tyres spun in the sand. Hissing, the bird raised itself to its full height, glaring through the windscreen, its irises as orange as fire. Helen eased off the pedal. The tyres found purchase. Her fingers squeezed the steering wheel. The car lurched forward.

The cassowary turned and ran.

Helen bumped and smashed through vegetation in pursuit.

By the time she reached the highway, the bird was gone, lost in that vast, green forest across the bitumen. She braked. The bloodlust drained away. Now she could feel the pain in her back and collarbone, the cuts in her feet, the tight and hot scald of her sunburnt skin, the hammering of her heart. She grabbed a mobile. Perhaps an ambulance could meet them halfway. She thumbed the buttons. A bland, recorded voice said, "You have dialled emergency Triple Zero. Your call is being connected."

"Babe?" Lou murmured. "I don't feel so good."

"Don't worry. Everything will be alright."

Pressing the phone to her ear, Helen steered one-handed onto the highway and stamped the pedal. The bitumen felt smooth and flat. The speedometer needle climbed. Lou uttered a moan. Helen tried not to cry. The Coral Sea winked through the trees, and the beach shone bright, as yellow as pineapple straight from the can.

THE WARRIGALS

STEVEN PAULSEN

Archie Douglas awoke an hour or so before dawn. He rose fully clothed and pushed through the flap of his tent into the chill Ballaarat winter's morning. He stomped his booted feet and rubbed his hands together. His breath came out in puffs of misty cloud. He looked up. The sky was clear, the gibbous moon and myriad stars shedding light enough for him to work.

His Bakery Hill cookshop was comprised of a large firepit surrounded by a semicircle of logs and wood blocks—room enough for two dozen or more diggers to sit and smoke and warm their stiff limbs while they fortified themselves for their day's toil on the goldfields. He raked over the grey ash in the firepit, exposing a few dully glowing coals. He knelt to blow on them, coaxing them back to life with tinder-dry leaves and kindling, relishing the meagre warmth of the burgeoning flames on his face.

Normally, old Hugh McIntyre helped him with the fire, setting the kindling and tending it, splitting wood to feed it. When he wasn't drunk or hungover, that was. But he wouldn't be helping today because he was dead.

Murdered.

Word had gone around the Ballaarat goldfields last night that his body had been found in the gravel pits. Torn to bits. A bloody mess. *Poor bastard.* Some people might have considered him a tiresome drunkard, but Hugh McIntyre, a good bloke, didn't deserve that end. And he had been Archie's friend too.

Gossip said Jack No-Nose had done it. Archie doubted that because No-Nose and his dogs had not been sighted in the diggings since he had killed the butcher three days ago. Murdered him over a woman, and the irony was that he had shot the wrong man.

But Old Hugh hadn't been killed over a woman. He had been killed for gold.

Ballaarat was Australia's *El Dorado*, and men were flocking from around the world into the tent city every week, infected with gold fever, laden with tin pans, pick-axes, spades and shovels. Archie himself had caught the disease. He had been a merchant seaman aboard a three-masted sailing ship called *Brooksby*, but when the vessel berthed at Hobsons Bay in 1852, he had jumped ship without a backwards glance and made his way to the diggings. The work had been backbreaking and luckless. Some blokes struck it rich but like most poor blighters, he barely scrounged enough of the shiny yellow stuff to cover the cost of his food and grog.

Archie eventually realised he could make more money feeding the diggers than digging for gold, so he had set up his cookshop. Now, a year later, he reckoned he had more gold socked away in the Commissioner's Camp at Golden Point than three-quarters of the men working the diggings. And he didn't cheat them, either. On the contrary, he had a reputation for making sure his customers had tucker in their bellies even when they were down and out.

Old Hugh had been a *hatter*—a shaggy, unkempt lone digger scratching at a plot in the gravel pits. But he had become a regular at Archie's place and lent a hand with the cookshop chores, and Archie fed him in return. It helped that they were both Scots, and it wasn't long before they enjoyed sitting around the firepit together late at night, sharing a drink, laughing, telling stories, talking about the old country.

Drink was Hugh's downfall. Scotch whisky if he could afford it, but any rotgut the sly grog tents served up would suffice. He had started drinking early yesterday, and was already two sheets to the wind when he lurched into the cookshop shortly after lunch.

"Archibald!" he whooped. "I found a nugget."

The diggers sitting around the firepit stopped talking, ears pricked.

"Keep it down," said Archie. "How big? Where is it?"

"Big enough for me, my friend. And don't you worry, I cashed it in at the mining office this morning, and I've buried the spoils where they'll be safe." He laughed out loud, baring the stumps of his rotten teeth, his bushy grey beard bristling. "Now I'm going on a bender to celebrate, and I will see you on the other side. But first, let me draw you a map of where I put it so you can help me find it again if I forget."

Now he was dead, the silly old bastard, and would never bend the elbow again.

Archie wiped away a couple of unbidden tears, sniffed and steeled himself. He would have to bury Hugh's body—or what was left of it—later. He didn't relish the task, but somebody had to do it, and he was the closest thing Hugh had to family.

First, he had to make breakfast, because his hungry customers would start arriving soon. He hung a large, blackened cast-iron pot containing the remains of last night's stew over the firepit, and gave the contents a stir. He would need to add more water, some flour browned in dripping to thicken it, and spuds and onions to freshen it up. He would normally have added more mutton too, but since No-Nose had killed the butcher, meat was in short supply. However, there was plenty of flour and salt, so he would make damper to bake in the coals for the men to soak up the gravy. He took the big billycan over to the water barrel to fill it. When he tried to dip it in, it struck a sheet of ice, thick like a pane of glass, covering the surface of the water.

Someone laughed. Archie spun around in surprise. He hadn't expected any customers this early. The man who loomed out of the darkness was dressed in typical miner's garb: loose denim trousers from the Californian goldfields, a red flannel shirt that had faded to pink, and a bright blue-spotted handkerchief knotted about his throat. But he wore a broadbrimmed cabbage-tree leaf hat pulled low over his face—summer rather than winter headwear—and he was gripping a shovel over his shoulder in both hands.

Archie's eyes went wide.

Jack No-Nose!

And in that moment of recognition, the blade of the shovel swished through the air and *thwacked* Archie across the side of his head.

Archie groaned. He was shivering, teeth chattering. His head was splitting and he could taste blood. He tried to open his eyes, but one was swollen shut. He touched it and winced. It was puffy, sore, caked with dried blood. As far as he could make out in the faint flickering light, he was lying naked somewhere in a puddle of freezing, muddy water.

"Hello, Mr Douglas," a mocking voice said from somewhere above him.

Archie rolled over. The world shifted, his head spun and he vomited bitter bile.

He wiped his mouth and clambered shakily to his hands and knees. As he tried to stand, his left ankle gave way and he yelped in pain, dropping back to his knees.

He looked up.

A tallow candle, a wick burning in a tin of mutton fat, gave off a guttering, smoky glow. Enough for him to make out the silhouette of a man standing about ten feet above him. Archie realised he was lying at the bottom of a pit. Dogs prowled in the dark shadows behind the man. One of them gave an eerie howl, sounding more like a wolf than a dog.

The man lashed out with his boot. It connected with a *thud*, and the animal yelped and backed away. He kicked at one of the other dogs, but it ducked aside. The man struck a match and a kerosene lamp flared into life, its warm radiance illuminating him.

"No-Nose," Archie said. "You bastard!"

"I prefer 'Jack the Journeyman', if you don't mind." He smoothed his pencil-thin black moustache with a forefinger. "Or just 'Jack' will suffice."

He actually did have a nose, or the stump of one. The story was some bloke had bitten off the tip of it in a drunken brawl, but they say the perpetrator never lived to tell the tale. No-Nose had sliced him up bit by bit, and people claimed they could hear the poor cove screaming all the way to Yuille's Swamp.

Archie glanced nervously around the muddy bedrock floor of the pit. His torn and shredded clothes were strewn to one side on a small pile of rocks and rubble. "Where am I?"

No-Nose sighed. "If you must know, I've dropped you down an abandoned mine shaft out the back of Madman's Flat."

"The fall might have killed me!"

"I know a bloke who fell into a thirty-foot shaft, stood up at the bottom, brushed himself off and rolled himself a smoke," No-Nose said, laughing. "It's not that deep. And I dropped you feet first. Might have broken your legs at worst. Lucky there was a bit of mud at the bottom, I guess." He snickered. "It's not the fall that kills you, it's the sudden stop at the end of it."

"Let me out of here."

"Stop fuckin' about! I've got to leave town and I need Old Hugh's stash. It's not safe for me here since that butcher's unfortunate accident. Where's the map? I've searched you from head to toe. Well, everywhere I could without taking a blade to you."

Archie swallowed and shook his head. "I haven't got it."

"With his dying words, Old Hugh told me he drew you a map."

"That he did."

"Where is it?"

Archie snorted. "He drew it on the ground with a stick. It's been walked into the dirt by dozens of diggers since then. There's no trace of it left."

"Perhaps you need a little incentive to tell me what it said. How about I introduce you to my warrigals?" No-Nose pressed the tips of two fingers against his tongue and whistled. Three lean, snarling dogs leapt to the edge of the pit. One black, and two brindles. They stood tall on their toes, hackles raised, ears erect, their long, white-tipped bushy tails held stiffly high. They growled in unison, their long sharp teeth bared, eyes fixed on Archie.

"I'm not scared of you or your dogs," Archie said with bravado.

No-Nose scratched his head, a resigned expression on his face. "These aren't dogs, *mate*. Warrigals are dingoes, wild dingoes. Big bloody difference. Poor things are starvin' hungry. They haven't had anything to eat since they snacked on your old friend Hugh. Gave 'em a taste of human flesh."

"So, it *was* you!"

Archie leaped to his feet despite the searing pain in his ankle. He grabbed a lump of rock and hurled it at No-Nose, then launched himself up the wall of the pit, scaling it hand over hand. No-Nose waited until Archie reached the rim and booted him in the face, sending him sprawling back to the pit floor, blood spurting from his nose. Archie lunged for another rock, but before he could bring it to bear, No-Nose pulled a pistol from his belt, sighted along its barrel and pulled the trigger.

There was a flash and a loud *bang*.

Archie shrieked and clutched his left thigh, bright-red blood running between his fingers.

The sound of the shot and smell of blood sent the dingoes wild. They howled and snorted, snarling and thrashing their heads. No-Nose kicked the biggest one, the black dingo, and it gave a sharp, low-pitched *woof*. No-Nose raised a threatening fist and the dingo stepped back, the brindle pair slinking submissively away, low to the ground.

"I wouldn't try that again," No-Nose said, turning back to Archie. He hawked and spat. "This is one of Mr Colt's American-made revolving pistols, so I've still got five more balls left." He cocked the pistol and pointed it at Archie's other leg.

"Alright, alright," Archie said, raising his hands in surrender. "I'll tell you what you want to know." And he relayed a story that was pure cock and bull, but one that pointed at a location that would hopefully buy him enough time to escape.

No-Nose sighed again. "What am I going to do with you, Mr Douglas? I can't take you with me. I suppose I could just kill you. But what if you're lying? We might need to have another little chat."

"It's the truth!" Archie said, swallowing.

"Let's hope so." He tut-tutted. "Just to be sure, I'm going to leave you here with my warrigals while I go and check. I doubt you can get out of that hole with a twisted ankle and a bullet in your thigh, but let me tell you, if you were to somehow manage it, my warrigals will bring you down and eat you alive before you can hobble more than a few steps. I know, because I've seen 'em do it." He laughed. "More than once. And I'm taking the lamp, Archie. You won't need it and my warrigals certainly don't. They're night hunters."

No-Nose left. The yellowish light of the kerosene lamp gradually faded as he strode away. "I'm barring the way out, in case you were wondering," he called, his voice echoing. "And I'll give you a tip. Warrigals go for soft bits. So, I'd be careful. You with no clothes and all..."

His departure was followed by the sounds of construction, heavy thumps, the grating of timber and rock, and muted curses.

Finally, there was silence.

Archie licked his lips and crawled over to his shredded clothes. In the feeble light of the tallow candle, he ripped his flannel shirt into usable strips and bound his wounded thigh, gritting his teeth as he pulled the strips tight to stem the blood.

He dragged himself to his feet when it was done, choking down a sob as he put weight on his bad leg. At least No-Nose had shot him in the same one as his swollen ankle. Without one good leg, he would have been buggered. The dingoes above him growled, low rumbling sounds in the backs of their throats, as they circled the pit, triangulating him. Archie retreated against a rough wall, his gaze tracking them.

The diggings were always full of dogs, barking day and night. Strays knew to shy away from a well-aimed rock and he hoped No-Nose's warrigals were the same. He edged his way to the rubble pile and picked up a few decent lumps of quartz. He weighed one in his hand, took careful aim and flung it at the nearest brindle that was watching him from the lip of the pit.

From behind Archie, the big black warrigal sprang into the pit. It struck him hard between the shoulder blades with its large foot-pads, and drove him to ground, jaws snapping at his throat, searching for an artery. Archie lurched sideways and smacked the animal in the face with the other rock he was holding. The dingo yelped and shook its head.

The brindle pair circling above howled in agitation, tails held erect.

It was too damned dark. The light from the tallow candle barely shone into the pit. Archie could hardly make out what was happening. But the dingoes, he remembered, were nocturnal. *Shit!* They could see and he couldn't.

When it attacked, he sensed rather than saw it coming.

Archie twisted aside, but he was too slow, and the dingo's large, sharp canine teeth chomped into his shoulder, grating bone. He dropped the rock and grabbed the animal two-handed around the throat. He pressed his thumbs into its gullet and wrenched it away from him. Its vice-like bite ripped a chunk of flesh from his shoulder. He screamed in pain, but kept hold, trying to throttle it.

Teeth snapped at his face, spattering him with saliva. The animal might have been lean, but it was all muscle. He couldn't hold it... He slammed his right knee between the dingo's legs to little effect. It kicked and scrabbled, its claws raking bloody furrows on his chest. Any moment he expected the brindle pair to join the fight.

Oh God, he was done in.

He was going to die here.

Then he thought of poor Hugh, the unfairness of what No-Nose had done to him, and wanted revenge, wanted the brute to pay. Archie was not a church-going man, but he prayed. Not to God, but to Hugh. *Give me strength*, he asked.

Taking a deep breath, he heaved himself over and rolled on top of the dingo, slamming his knee into its soft belly. It yelped, jerked its head free, and slipped out from under him. Archie skittered backwards on his buttocks, gravel scraping skin, and chanced upon the rock he had dropped.

His last hope.

The light from the tallow lamp reflected in the dingo's eyes as it launched itself at him, head lowered, ears folded back. Archie swung the rock like a bludgeon. It smacked the animal squarely between the eyes with a sound like a hammer cracking open a walnut. The black dingo dropped and lay still.

Archie stared at it in disbelief.

Gingerly, he pushed it in the belly with his toe. Christ, it was done. It was dead. The poor bloody thing. Despite everything, he felt sorry for it. No-Nose had made it the way it was with his callous cruelty.

Archie stood. Breathing heavily, he leaned against the wall for support. He closed his eyes to try to make everything stop spinning. Then he took stock of himself. He was covered in mud and blood and sweat, and literally ached from head to foot.

Above, the brindle pair of warrigals were watching him.

He sighed. One down, two to go...

The climb out of the pit was agony. His shoulder was on fire and his left leg dangled most of the way, a useless impediment. He had almost reached the top when he froze, the hairs on the back of his neck standing up.

The black dingo in the pit below him had snarled.

Archie's heart missed a beat.

It leaped at him, its vicious teeth latching onto his foot, driving into the tender skin between his toes. His *left* foot! The damn thing had jumped almost two yards vertically up the wall. He shrieked and swore and kicked, and the dingo fell away, taking his little toe with it.

His vision clouded. The pulse pounded in his ears.

The black dingo howled, a long mournful cry.

Archie crawled over the lip, raised himself up, and roared as he staggered towards the brindle warrigals. But instead of attacking him, they dropped low to the ground, whimpering. He blinked and stared in disbelief.

Was his ordeal over?

The dingoes seemed cowed, ears flat and tails down. He approached, closer, closer. They lowered their heads, submissively avoiding eye contact. He touched one tentatively and it gave a small whine. Eventually, he picked them up, one at a time, and dropped them gently into the pit. They landed easily on their padded feet and joined the black one. Archie left them licking it and purring softly. He took up the tallow candle—the tin hot to the touch, the wick almost burnt out—and peered around.

There were two horizontal drive-tunnels leading away from the shaft at right angles to each other. One only went a few yards and came to a dead end, so he headed, half-limping and half-staggering, along the other.

The tunnel was about fifty yards long, but it felt like a mile. The walls were slabbed, the ceiling braced with timber. The glimmer of daylight at the end provided a beacon. It led him to an opening in a hillside, but the way out was blocked by heavy slabs of wood originally cut and split to shore up the walls of mine shafts and tunnels. Now they were stacked to block the opening. *No-Nose!*

In between the slabs, No-Nose had placed sawn-off tree branches, perpendicularly across, as bearers. The branches were about four inches in diameter and a yard long. Archie knew that, when used in such an arrangement, they reduced the amount of timber needed to block the entrance and provided air flow within the mine.

Archie's breaths came short and fast, his heart racing. Freedom! Despite his pain and exhaustion, his face split into a wide grin. He was getting out, naked and all. Damn the clothes! When he escaped, he was going straight to the Traps to tell them what had happened. He reckoned No-Nose wouldn't be back for at least an hour. And when they caught him, No-Nose would hang.

He grabbed the end of one of the bearers, pushing and pulling it until he worked it free. It was green timber, solid and strong. He then hefted it as a lever to pry the other slabs apart and move them aside. But before he had managed to dislodge the top one, he heard a horse approaching at a canter. He peered through a gap in the slabs made by the bearers.

His mouth fell open and his heart sank.

No-Nose!

Archie had not counted on him having a horse. He had no choice but to scurry back into the mine.

Archie concealed himself in the shadows at the entrance of the dead-end tunnel. He wasn't going back into the pit and there was no way he could climb the shaft above it. He was so weak and exhausted that he could hardly stand. He breathed heavily; nostrils full of the iron reek of blood. His own blood. Running down his leg from the throbbing bullet wound, dripping from the tip of his foot where his toe had been torn off.

"You sent me on a wild goose chase!" No-Nose yelled, roaring obscenities.

Light from the kerosene lamp he was carrying bounced and flickered as he charged along the tunnel. The warrigals howled and snorted at the sound of his voice. Archie sensed No-Nose pause his stride.

"What's going on here, Mr Douglas?" he yelled.

Archie swallowed, tightening his grip on the tree-branch. The light started to get brighter again as No-Nose crept forward, the Colt extended in his right hand, the kerosene lantern held high in the other.

Archie held his breath, his heart pounding.

When No-Nose's hand came level with the tunnel opening, Archie raised the length of wood and smashed it down on his wrist. It made a sound like a tree branch snapping. No-Nose howled and his pistol clattered to the rocky floor. He whirled around and swung the kerosene lantern. It caught Archie a glancing blow on the shoulder, before smashing against the timber-slabbed wall.

Burning kerosene splattered everywhere.

No-Nose rose up through the flames, like a demon from Hell, and launched himself at Archie, swinging his fist like a sledge-hammer.

Archie ducked under the blow and head-butted him in the gut. Flames singed his hair, burnt his throat. No-Nose kicked Archie's injured leg and Archie went down, crying out in agony. He still had hold of the tree branch and smashed it into No-Nose's knee.

The big man stumbled backwards. Archie thrust the branch like a battering ram, hitting him in the balls. No-Nose let out an *oomph* and bent double. Archie swung the branch again and hit him under the chin. No-Nose staggered and pitched back into the pit behind him.

Panting, Archie peered over the lip. No-Nose was already on his feet, lurching towards the wall.

"I'm gonna kill you!" he bellowed.

The kerosene flames were dying. The mine would be coal-black in moments.

Archie saw the Colt pistol on the ground near the edge of the pit and snatched it up. He cocked the trigger and aimed it at No-Nose's face. "How about I shoot you and leave you here in the pit with your warrigals?"

"You won't shoot me and they won't hurt me," No-Nose scoffed, regaining some of his mettle. "They do as they're told. They're scared of me. Just like you and everyone else. With good reason. Stop being a fool! Put that gun down and tell me where Old Hugh buried his stash. If you do that, I'll call it even, and let you go."

Archie shook his head. "Your warrigals don't like you, No-Nose. Nobody likes you, man or beast. But, in particular, I think your black one has just about had enough."

No-Nose laughed. "Tough words from a lifetime loser. You look a bit the worse for wear. Been playing with my pets, have you?"

Archie looked down at himself. The makeshift bandage from the bullet wound had come adrift and blood was running down his leg. A ripped flap of skin dangled from his shoulder, dripping blood down his chest. His swollen ankle had turned purple-black. His little toe was missing, his eye was swollen shut, and he was covered in blood, cuts, scratches and bruises.

"Think this is funny, do you?" Archie asked.

"Well," No-Nose said resignedly, "I did warn you."

"All this I might be able to overlook." Archie raised the Colt again, steel in his eyes. "But you murdered my friend, Hugh McIntyre."

No-Nose backed away, hands held up in appeasement. "I'll give you gold," he said. "Lots of gold."

Archie dropped the tree branch and planted his feet wide, levelling the pistol with both hands. "This is for Hugh," he said.

He fired. No-Nose yelped, an incredulous look on his face.

Blood spurted from his thigh and he crumpled to one knee. The dingoes howled, circling around him.

"And this one is from me." Archie cocked the hammer and fired again.

The bullet hit No-Nose in the gut and he doubled over, coughing blood. The warrigals were standing tall, snarling, their tails held stiff.

"Sorry, Jack. I meant to hit you in the leg. I'm not used to these newfangled American guns." He gave a wry grimace. "I guess I'd best go and get help. I'll leave you here with your warrigals to look after you."

The black dingo lowered its head, folded back its ears and leaped for No-Nose's throat. The brindles lunged from either side. Archie turned away, the blasts of the pistol still ringing in his ears, and limped out of the tunnel. Behind him, No-Nose began to scream.

It was five days before Archie felt able to search for Hugh's nest egg. The cookshop firepit was stone cold, the ashes muddy from days of intermittent drizzle. The only bums that had graced the logs and wood blocks in that time were the two Traps who came to question him, and the doctor.

The doctor pulled the lead ball out of his leg and stitched him up. It cost a small fortune: £2 for the visit, and another £3 to tend to his injuries. He was still sore, but healing well enough to get up and about. The butcher's widow, Mrs Blake, had tended to his dressings and made sure he had food and water. It was the least she could do, she said.

He hobbled through the diggings—past flapping tents, mullock heaps, and smoking woodfires—using a spade in one hand and shovel in the other as walking sticks. They weren't ideal for the purpose, but he figured he would need them when he got to Pennyweight Flat and found the spot that Hugh had described with his map.

Archie was exhausted by the time he got there, breathing heavily, with sweat on his brow despite the cold, even though it was less than a mile away. He eased himself down onto a small boulder and let out a slow groan.

The place where Hugh had dug his hole was right in front of him, a patch of quartz and clay rubble at the edge of a mullock heap. There was nobody working here anymore and he was alone. A chill wind ruffled his hair and brought colour to his cheeks. Even though nearly a week had passed since Hugh had been here, there were still signs the rubble had been turned; the colour and texture showed that someone had been digging here. Silly bugger. But it probably didn't matter, because most of Ballaarat had been dug over at some point.

Archie hefted himself to his feet with the aid of the shovel and limped across to the patch of worked rubble. He scooped the topping aside, the cutting edge of the shovel scraping tinnily in the gravel, and uncovered the lid of a wooden crate. He dug out one side of the tailings packed around it, then worked the blade of the spade beneath it and levered the box out of its resting place.

Archie examined the unlabelled crate and scratched his head. It was made of pine boards, the lid nailed shut. *Bloody hell, Hugh,* Archie thought. *What have you left for me?*

He worked the blade of the spade under the edge of the lid, and pried it open with a screech of nails being pulled. Archie brushed away the wood shavings covering the contents of the box and stared. He didn't know whether to laugh or cry.

In the end, he did both, the tears warm on his cheeks and salty on his lips.

He plonked down on his bum, pulled a bottle out of the crate and examined it. The thin wintery light shone through the amber liquid it contained, making it glow like spring honey.

The label on the bottle said: *Royal Brackla—Fine Highland Whisky.*

"Oh, Hugh," Archie whispered.

He uncorked the bottle and took a deep swig. The liquor was strong and rich. It burned a little as it went down, but left a pleasant malty aftertaste.

Archie sighed. "Rest easy, mate. See you on the other side."

QUOLL SEASON

HELENA O'CONNOR

The scent of eucalypt was cloying, even with the windows rolled up against the uncompromising red dust and summer heat. Rust-hued clouds surrounded the jeep as we bumped unsteadily over sheep grates, spattering rocks and pebbles in our wake. The jeep was a seasoned traveller and never faltered. That gum-tree smell was trapped in our air-con, having presumably entered when Dave cracked his window to barf. He was hungover—and baked as fuck, if the red eyes were anything to go by, though it was barely mid-morning.

"The cabin is beside a real authentic billabong," announced Stacey. He was driving. "Gus says there's some rare endangered species nesting there, too."

Gus's family owned the cabin where we'd be staying for our holiday. It was the '90s, and the nightmare of high school had finally ended for real. Stacey cranked up the radio—Silverchair was belting out "Tomorrow". We were doing our own version of schoolies since none of us were much into clubs and crowds. A secluded cabin was more our speed. Booze and card games, maybe a little *Magic the Gathering* if we were feeling nasty.

Stacey had to yell over the thump of grunge guitars and wailing vocals. "The place is called Red Moon Ridge. Cool, right?"

"Billa...*bong!*" yelled Dave, toking his hand like it was the best joke ever. He plucked a hand-rolled ciggie from his shirt pocket and fumbled with his lighter as the jeep hurled itself bodily down the road. He was more likely to light his face in his condition. Dave was a bloody moron. Seriously, in a horror movie, Dave would be the first to die.

Miranda, Stacey's girlfriend, caught my eye in the rear view, so I elbowed Dave in the ribs. "Shut up, Dave. And no smoking in the jeep."

"Geez, Steve-o, what's your problem?"

That's me, Steve. *Steve-o* if you're Aussie.

"Nothing, mate," I said. "Just a bit early in the morning. Besides, Jess doesn't like smoke and she's still sleeping."

I cocked my head to my left, where Jess was leaning against the window with her eyes shut, despite the noise. I was in awe of how that girl could sleep through anything. Jess was every bit as uncompromising as the staunch red Aussie dust. A final girl, if ever I saw one. I was wide awake, sandwiched as I was in the middle seat, between Jess's snoring and Dave's idiocy.

"Your girlfriend's a ballbuster, mate." He put the unlit cigarette away. "Cute as hell though."

"She's not my girlfriend."

Jess was a friend, who happened to be a girl. Dave maybe had designs on her, but Jess wasn't into stoners. As far as I knew, she wasn't into guys at all. I didn't want to be the one to break it to Dave. Like I said, it was the '90s, and back in those days, you never knew how people would react to that sort of info.

"A bunch of people died up at Red Moon Ridge. Hikers or some shit. Got mauled by wild animals." Dave cackled, like it was funny.

"Have a Fantale." I handed Dave a pack of lollies, hoping to shut him up for a while. I had no idea if he was right about the deaths, but that sort of talk felt like a jinx. Dave rolled his eyes, then sucked down every single one of my choc-caramels without offering them to anyone. Fucking stoners.

Our destination was out past Lake Wivenhoe, near the charmingly-named rural town of Crow's Nest. Stacey's "short-cut" across stretches of unsealed tracks saved us no time at all compared to the main road, especially with Dave hurling out the window at regular intervals. But it was apparently "scenic as hell" and Stacey had a girlfriend to impress, so I held my tongue.

We hung around the lake for a bit, skipping stones, then headed to the nearby town of Esk for pies and supplies. The cabin was a good four-hour drive from there, past Crow's Nest, on winding roads worse than Stacey's unsealed shortcuts. By the time we bounced up the rocky rabbit track to the cabin, we were all pretty queasy. Dusk was breaking over the horizon and there was a mountain chill in the air. We bundled everything inside with the last of the daylight, and hauled in some firewood from the pile near the front door.

Gus's holiday cabin was a rustic wooden affair, but thankfully still on the grid with running water and electricity. We flicked on the lights.

Miranda grabbed Stacey's arm and pointed. "What the hell is that?"

Her shriek made us all look. Perched on the mantel above the fireplace was one of those taxidermy creatures, a stuffed animal on all fours, fixed to a dark wooden plinth. A strange little thing. Like a bandicoot but smaller, with reddish fur and spots.

"A spotted rat?" Dave squinted.

"Some kind of possum?" Stacey wondered.

I walked up close enough to peer into the thing's beady little eyes. "It's a marsupial... Can't think of the name." As I pondered, the name came in a sharp flash, like a thought pressed into my mind from somewhere outside me. "Quoll."

"A quoll? Those are endangered, right?" Jess strode up and peered at the unfortunate critter. "Bit worse for wear, isn't he?"

I reached out a finger and stroked the sad, greying fur. "Been here a while, I guess."

"It's creepy." Miranda shivered and pulled Stacey's arms around her.

"Gus said his uncle was real woodsy and shit," said Stacey. "Hunting, fishing, whatever. He probably trapped and stuffed it himself. Sounds like he was pretty eccentric." A frown furrowed his brow. "He uh...came up here a lot towards the end."

"What happened to him?" Dave, unsubtle as ever, already had a beer in hand. He took a long chug. "He die up here, or what?"

"Dave..." I warned.

Stacey's jaw was clenching. "Yes, Dave, he did die here, actually.

Gus said this was his favourite place and he wanted to be somewhere he felt at peace. Don't talk about it when Gus gets here, or you'll bum him out, understand?"

"Geez, man, just trying to lighten the mood. Chill out—"

"What is your fucking problem!"

There was an uneasy silence. Stacey rarely raised his voice. It had been a tiring drive and he'd obviously had it with Dave's bullshit. But also, we were young and had little experience with death, or life—no one quite knew what to say.

Dave flopped on the sofa and drank his beer. "Whatever."

The rest of us stared at the taxidermy quoll. In my mind I saw Gus's uncle wandering the cabin, increasingly unsteady, talking to himself, talking to the quoll. I wondered if the quoll ever answered back. Our reverie was broken by the sound of tyres on gravel, the cut of an engine, and car doors slamming. The cabin door flew open, and Gus sauntered in with some of his football buddies.

"Gus. Maaaatttee!" Dave rolled off the sofa. "Heard your uncle died up here, man." He hauled some beers out of the cooler and tossed them across the room.

Stacey literally face-palmed, then went and got himself a beer.

Gus's football buddies were Baz and Tony, and Pete with his girlfriend, Anna. Miranda sorted out sleeping arrangements while we unloaded the other jeep. The cabin had one bedroom and an upstairs loft. The couples got the bedrooms, and the rest of us were sleeping in the lounge. Jess and I had discussed faking a relationship to snag a bedroom but decided against. Baz and Tony said they'd sleep on the porch in a pair of overstuffed sun chairs, even though we reckoned they'd freeze and it seemed pretty roomy in the lounge.

Someone plugged in a stereo and starting blasting Soundgarden. We stoked the fire in the hearth and got down to some serious drinking. I remember beer pong, "who would you rather", truth or dare, tequila shots, and not much else.

I woke briefly in the early hours. In the quiet of the wilderness, there were unfamiliar animal calls. Bats mostly, and something that might have been a dingo. Pete and Anna were having sex in the ground floor bedroom. Rookie mistake. The jock and the cheerleader. In a horror movie, they'd definitely have to die. In the silence after they quieted down, there came a scratching sound. An urgent scrabbling in the dark. It was close, perhaps inside the cabin. I pulled out my torch and shone a light around the room.

Dave was passed out on the floor, and Jess was curled tight in a sleeping bag stuffed into a wicker chair by the corner. As far as I could see, there was nothing inside but us. Yet the scrabbling, scratching sounds continued. As I listened, there was soft hissing and squeaking, and an occasional barking cough. Maybe field mice? Were they in the walls? Nesting under the cabin? We would have to check in the morning. It was too dark and cold to go exploring. Eventually the strange sounds subsided. Wrapped warm in my sleeping bag, with the soothing crackle of the fireplace, I fell into an uneasy sleep.

In my dream, I saw Gus's uncle pacing the wooden floors, talking. I realised he was talking to me. The perspective was all wrong, it was like he was a giant. The room was huge, and I was looking down at him from the wall. Eventually it dawned that I was sitting on the mantel over the hearth, in the same place as the taxidermy quoll.

"That's a lot of blood," Gus's uncle said, matter-of-fact.

My whiskers twitched in reply. Gus's uncle opened his mouth and screamed. His jaws cracked wide, dislocating in a mash of blood and gore. The scream went on and on.

I woke in a fright. Someone really *was* screaming.

"What's happening?" My brain was sluggish. I tried to get up but was still in my sleeping bag and rolled myself off the sofa with a thump. "Ow." When I opened my eyes, I was looking straight at Dave. Or what was left of him. I backed away fast, extracting myself from my sleeping cocoon as I went. "What the fuck?"

Miranda stopped screaming and started vomiting noisily into the kitchen sink. She must have come downstairs and found him. There was clattering and general noise as people converged on the lounge and saw what had happened. Stacey, bleary-eyed, went to help Miranda. Baz and Tony, who had come in from the porch to see what all the fuss was about, swore at each other. Anna sobbed while Pete held her. Jess was standing silent near the fireplace, hands over her mouth.

Dave had been *eaten*.

His face was chewed away, and parts of his jawbone shone in the morning light. One eye was gone. The other hung disconcertingly from its socket by a thin red thread. There was blood everywhere. I stared hard in disbelief. Who could do something like this? Who—or what? In the car on the way here, Dave had been talking about this sort of thing—about hikers mauled by animals. That was exactly what it looked like. But how would a wild animal get into the cabin, and why attack only Dave?

"Look." Jess was pointing to the taxidermy quoll.

I tore my attention from Dave, got up and crossed to the fireplace. The quoll had red streaks on the fur near its mouth. A shiver worked its way down my spine.

"Blood," said Jess, eyes wide.

"What are you saying? The stuffed quoll came alive in the night and ate Dave? Is that what you're saying?" I backed away, images from the dream still fresh in my mind. "Because that's..."

"I dunno." Jess put her face in her hands.

I felt like a bastard for yelling. I went back and put my arms around her. "Sorry. It's a lot to take in."

She buried her head in my shoulder and hugged me.

Stacey was swearing. "The cabin door was locked all night, right?"

Baz and Tony looked worried. "The key was outside, with us," Baz said, while Tony nodded. "We only unlocked the door when we heard screaming."

"What does that mean?" Pete wondered.

Stacey eyed us. "It means this wasn't an animal."

Gus hovered into view. "Phone's cut off. It happens out here. We'll need to go into town."

I made eye contact with Stacey, over Jess's back. "We should go together, find a police station."

"What if they think we killed him?" murmured Jess.

"They won't think that." I reassured her.

"I'm not staying here." Miranda marched past us, without looking at the remains of Dave, and disappeared out the front door.

"Guess we're all going into town," said Stacey.

We grabbed our wallets and keys and headed for the jeep. The sun was beating down—it was already close to midday. How the hell had we slept through what happened? The tequila shots must have really done a number.

"Are you okay to drive?" I asked.

Stacey's hands were shaking as he checked the mirrors. "Yeah." He inserted the key with some effort and turned it. Nothing happened. The jeep was dead. "The fuck?"

He tried it a few more times, but the engine made no sound. He hopped out to check under the bonnet. After a few seconds, he peered back through the window.

"Jeep ain't starting. The engine's been trashed."

We piled out of the jeep and went to look. The engine was like Dave, absolutely ripped apart. We ran to Gus's jeep, which was actually a black Range Rover, worth almost as much as my parents' house. Gus's father was some rich businessman. The fancy exterior hadn't protected the engine, though. Both our vehicles were finished. Someone, or something, really didn't want us leaving.

Stacey looked to Gus. "Took us four hours to drive up here. Not exactly walking distance. Is there a neighbour close by?"

"Yeah. Me, Baz and Tony, we'll go."

"Wait." I grabbed hold of Baz. "You guys slept outside, right. You see anything?"

"Nah, mate. Quiet as." Baz and Tony looked as rattled as I felt.

"How about...squeaking, like mice?

Baz gave me an odd look. "Nah."

Gus grabbed a bag of supplies, and the three set off to find a neighbour. I felt uneasy watching them go. Splitting up was worse than sending someone down into the cellar alone. At least they didn't say they'd "be right back".

"Did you hear something?" Jess grabbed my arm and leaned into me. "Last night."

"Did you?"

"I don't know."

We looked at each other. Christ. What the hell had happened to Dave?

Stacey hauled a tarp out of his jeep and headed back inside. There was nothing left for us to do except...have breakfast. No one felt like eating, but we had to keep busy. Pete and Anna volunteered to cook. That left us with Miranda, who was perched on the hood of the jeep, sobbing.

I looked pointedly at Jess.

"What?" she said.

"You're a girl, go...talk to her, or whatever."

She rolled her eyes at me but headed over.

I did a lap of the cabin. Mostly, I wanted to know if something could be nesting underneath. But there was no crawl space that I could see. The cabin was built right into the solid ground. When I went back inside, Dave was covered with the tarp. Breakfast was bacon and eggs. None of us ate much.

After an hour or two, Gus came back alone. Baz and Tony had apparently headed into town with the neighbour to alert the police. "Phones were down at their place too," Gus shrugged.

By this time, it was getting on for mid-afternoon. We were huddled together in the lounge, trying not to look at the lump under the tarp that was Dave. We couldn't move him until the police had been. We were trapped together, waiting.

"I don't want to stay here tonight," said Miranda, echoing what we all felt but weren't saying.

As twilight turned the sky red, Baz, Tony and the police were nowhere in sight.

"We'll take shifts," said Stacey, "keeping watch at all times." He nodded to Miranda, who shivered and rubbed her arms.

"It's a blood moon," said Jess, staring out the front door, above the tree line. "A blood moon at Red Moon Ridge."

I strode over and shut the door, since that view wasn't helping anything. As I slammed the bolts home, she nodded at the stuffed quoll.

"We should get rid of that thing."

I shrugged but left the quoll where it stood. It felt dangerous to give in to that idea, a supernatural fear that couldn't be controlled, to blame a taxidermy quoll for Dave.

At that point, I was still hoping for a rational explanation.

My shift was around midnight, not that I slept much beforehand. I sat on the sofa, rubbing my hands towards the fire, one eye fixed on the taxidermy quoll as if waiting for it to come alive and leap from its place. Gus arrived to sit next to me.

"Couldn't sleep," he said. "Feel like it's my fault, bringing you all up here."

"You couldn't have known. Besides we don't even know what happened." I scratched my chin. I hadn't gotten around to shaving, and it was itching. "Dave said some hikers died up here. Animal attacks or whatever. Could this be related?"

"Didn't Stacey say the door was locked?"

"Yeah."

"Probably not an animal then." He shrugged. "Look, I'm not sleeping so why don't you try. You look like hell, man."

My eyes felt full of sand. My body wanted sleep, despite the situation. "Wake me if anything happens."

"Obviously."

I nodded at Gus. He moved to an armchair, and I shuffled into my sleeping bag on the sofa. Jess was upstairs with Stacey and Miranda. It was just me and Gus in the lounge. I didn't know him much; he was Stacey's friend. I wasn't cool enough to hang with the football crowd. My high school years were pretty rough, looking back. But Stacey always stood up for me. As I drifted to sleep, I noticed an odd smell circulating above the woodsmoke from the fire. *Dave was starting to rot.* Not a pleasant thought to have, as I drifted to sleep.

I dreamed I was crawling across the floor. The room was huge, and I was small enough to squeeze through a crack in the door to the bedroom. Pete and Anna were lying together, clenched in an awkward embrace. Both appeared to be asleep. The sheets dangled to the ground, and I was able to claw myself up onto the bed. Anna's exposed ankle lay within reach, creamy and enticing. I bared my teeth and bit hard, breaking skin and bone. Blood spurted across the bed. Anna screamed and kicked, sending me flying.

I hit the floor and woke in the lounge, disoriented. The scream echoed in my ears. Was I dreaming? Above the fireplace, the eyes of the taxidermy quoll glowed bright as rubies.

"Steve-o! Wake up!" Gus hauled me to my feet.

The scratching, scrabbling sound was back, loud in the night. There was a rushing, like a flock of birds, coming from all around the cabin. Anna and Pete started screaming. We hurried to the bedroom, but the door was locked.

"Pete, let us in!" I yelled.

"Anna?" called Gus.

"Open the door!" I thumped my fists against the timber.

Stacey, Miranda and Jess clattered down the stairs from the loft.

"What's going on?" called Stacey.

"Something's in there with them," I said over my shoulder. "And they're not answering."

"Move!" yelled Stacey, and I got out of the way fast.

Stacey barrelled across the lounge and slammed into the door with his footballer shoulder. The wood exploded in a shower of splinters, falling inwards to the bedroom.

Pete and Anna huddled against the bedhead, shapes moving all around them. Stacey hit the light and we leaped backwards in horror.

The floor of the bedroom was a mass of squirming red fur. Quolls covered the bed, squeaking and scratching. Pete had his arms around Anna, shielding her. They were both covered in deep claw marks. One of his legs was twitching, and she wasn't moving. Blood ran in rivulets. The whole scene was carnage.

"Run!" came a gurgled whisper from the bed.

Wheezing, Pete swivelled his head towards us. Half his face was eaten away. As he moved, I caught a glimpse of Anna's throat, the slashed windpipe clearly visible through her torn flesh. A large quoll struggled over Pete's head and sank its fangs into his neck. His head rolled sideways and as the flesh tore, his head dropped to the ground with a soft wet *thunk*. The quolls on the floor turned with glee and began to feed. The quolls on the bed swarmed over Pete and Anna until they were buried beneath the pile of furry bodies.

We backed away and tried to shut the door. Thanks to Stacey's efforts, it was half broken and wouldn't close.

Miranda was already at the front door. "It won't open, it's stuck!"

The squealing of the quolls was growing louder. When they ran out of food, we were next.

"The loft," whispered Jess.

We ran up the stairs and bolted the loft door. Me, Miranda, Stacey, and Jess.

"Wait, where's Gus?" Jess looked around.

"Should we go back?" Stacey's voice was dubious.

The screaming of the quolls drowned out all rational thought. The rushing sound, like the wings of a million crows, was closing on us. Then the quolls were outside the door, scrabbling and scratching. A mass of teeth and claws, seeking our flesh.

Stacey leaned against the wood. "We can't go out there."

"We can't stay here either," I said. One way or another, those quolls were determined to get in. Who knew how long we had until they found a way?

"Check outside," said Stacey.

Under any other circumstances, I would have admired the loft. It was nice. A huge princess-style bed and rustic wooden furniture. I crossed the room and stared out the small window. The blood moon hung in the sky, bathing the trees in red. Otherwise, the night seemed quiet. No movement. "I don't see any quolls."

Miranda and Jess came up beside me to look. I noticed everyone had slept in their clothes, like we were waiting for this. Jess handed a jacket to Miranda, pulled one on herself, and shouldered her small backpack. I wanted to ask what supplies Jess had gathered, on such a wild dash through the house at midnight, but there was no time.

Stacey's face was strained. "Out the window!"

A splintering sound came from the door, and he leaped back.

A nose full of whiskers pushed through the gap.

Stacey grabbed up Miranda's curling iron. "Get out now! I'm gonna play some whack-a-mole." He thwacked the curling iron against the door, bashing anything that threatened to enter.

Jess cracked the window and crawled onto the overhang. "Come on."

Miranda followed. "Stacey?"

"I'll be right behind you!"

The door was disintegrating fast. There were more noses than Stacey could punch, and myriad rows of gleaming, murderous teeth. He didn't have long.

"Hurry!" I clambered out the window, creeping along the overhang with the others.

There were no quolls in sight as we jumped from the roof into the grass at the side of the cabin.

"Where's Stacey?" Miranda said, and took a lungful of air to yell for him.

Jess clamped a hand over her mouth. "Quiet!" she whispered. "We can't let them know where we are."

She dragged Miranda towards the trees. I looked but couldn't see any sign of Stacey. As we hit the tree line, there was an almighty howl from the loft. Miranda threw her hands over her face but kept moving. Jess and I grabbed her, one on each side, as we moved through the forest.

"Which way?" Jess panted.

"Towards the neighbour's place." I pointed to the path Baz and Tony had taken earlier in the day. Houses were acres apart in the country. At least we knew there was someone in that direction.

The smell of eucalypt was strong in the forest. The blood moon gave the trees an eerie crimson light, but at least we could see. As Jess pushed beyond a straggling clump of bushes, she tripped and gasped. She had stumbled over Baz's half-eaten leg. Baz and Tony lay there on the ground, chewed up like Dave, and every bit as dead. We stared in horror. This was too much. Jess sagged against a tree, breathing heavily.

"Fuck this!" Miranda lunged away, back into the forest.

"Wait!" By the time I pulled Jess to her feet, Miranda was gone. Jess looked at me. "What now?"

"Guess the police aren't coming." With no idea what to do next, we trudged in the direction Miranda had vanished.

"What about Gus, wasn't he with those guys?"

"And it was his watch tonight," I said, thinking hard. "And his cabin."

"Does that mean…" Jess's voice shook. "*He* did this?"

"Congrats, my dudes." Gus emerged from the trees, holding Miranda with a knife pressed to her neck. "You figured it out. Spare keys and sleeping tablets." He gestured back through the forest, and we all started walking.

"Is Stacey dead?" Miranda whimpered as we reached the cabin.

"Why don't you go and check?" said Gus.

He pulled open the cabin door, pushed her inside, then closed the door, leaning against it. There was silence for a moment. Then a rushing, scrabbling, squeaking. Miranda gave a blood-curdling scream, and all was quiet.

Gus smiled affably. "Gotta feed the quolls."

I reached out to hold Jess's hand. This was not looking good for us. "Did you kill those hikers?"

"Not me. But the cabin's been in the family a good while. This is my first blood moon, actually. I was nervous, not gonna lie, but things are going great so far." Gus grinned.

Jess squeezed my fingers. Then she stepped away from me.

"What are you doing?" I hissed.

"I'm guessing this is important." Jess rummaged in her backpack and pulled out a quoll.

My heart stopped, but the furry creature wasn't moving. Was it dead? I saw the wooden plinth. The taxidermy quoll from the fireplace. Its eyes shone ruby red under the blood moon. Why on earth had she grabbed that monstrosity?

Gus shifted nervously. "What are you doing with that?"

"Taking out the trash." She moved as if to smash the quoll on the ground.

"Give it to me!" Gus lunged at Jess, but she dodged out of the way.

Jess had been into martial arts for as long as I'd known her. She really was cool.

I charged at Gus and grabbed him around the shoulders. "The billabong, Jess—that way!" I yelled, jerking my head, and Jess took off.

She was fast, too.

Gus elbowed me in the stomach and gave chase. The door to the cabin exploded and a mass of quolls poured out, heading for the billabong. I followed, feeling sick to my stomach.

When I reached the billabong, Jess was holding the taxidermy quoll above her head. The quolls were circling but seemed unwilling to attack.

"I think it's their leader," she said.

I turned to Gus, who was standing at the fringes of the quoll circle, looking murderous. "Gus," I said, "how exactly did your uncle die?"

"He killed the wrong quoll, so they drove him mad. The voices, always talking, talking... Can't you hear?" Gus stared, transfixed, at the taxidermy quoll. "Can't you hear them?"

"We don't hear anything," said Jess.

"Feed them on the blood moon, or they'll come for us! That's the deal." Gus wrung his hands. "You get the picture?"

"Not really," I said.

"It starts with the dreams. Then the voices... They never shut up." Gus clutched at his head. "I have an important family; I can't just let them die. Anyway, who's gonna miss a few football jocks and two losers like you? I have to obey." He moaned, holding his head. He was writhing, twisting in pain. "I have to!"

"I don't think so," said Jess.

"Wait!" Gus tried to get to Jess, but a mass of quolls was in his way. More were piling up behind him, circling furiously, whiskers twitching.

Jess hurled the taxidermy quoll towards the billabong.

"No!" screamed Gus, desperate.

With superhuman speed he dove over the mass of quolls. I dove too, reflexively, hurling myself towards him. Gus caught the quoll as I slammed into him, the momentum carrying us both into the billabong. Gus gave a surprised yell as he hit the surface. The water slapped like ice. The quolls screamed, hurling themselves into the water, chasing their leader. The mass of bodies took Gus under, covered him in squirming red fur, drawing him inexorably down. The wake caught me too, pulling me underwater. I saw the taxidermy quoll, sinking like a stone, fading into the fog as water filled my lungs. Was this how it was going to end? Quolls were drowning all around me, the water thick with bodies. Gus was already gone. I surrendered to the dark.

A strong hand closed on my wrist. Jess hauled me out of the water. I lay coughing and gasping, as quolls streamed like lemmings, faster and faster into the water, until none remained. An eerie quiet descended over the billabong.

"Let's get out of here." Jess grabbed my soaked shirt and pulled me to my feet. "We'll walk until we get to town."

"And never come back," I agreed.

"They're endangered you know, quolls," said Jess as we walked. "I read a book in the loft."

I squeezed her fingers. "If I never see another quoll, I'll be okay with that."

We trekked through the forest as the blood moon faded. Dawn broke soft above the horizon. The sound of birds rang happy in the air. And all the way through the forest there was an underlying sound, a scratching, scrabbling, hissing, squeaking. Maybe it was just my imagination. The sun broke through the clouds, and I couldn't feel its warmth. Gus had said it began with dreams.

EVERY PART OF HER

ANTOINETTE RYDYR

Musca domestica, the common house fly and universal pest, has a life cycle of two to four weeks and is found throughout Australia.

When *musca domestica* flew into the cavernous maw of John Smith, she didn't realise that he was about to croak. John's mouth slammed shut and *musca* was trapped inside, but she made the best of it. She laid her eggs in the soft warm tissue of John's mouth, then buzzed about in search of an escape route. She emerged covered in mucus from John's nose. Wriggling her body and shaking her wings, she flicked off as much snot as possible and flew off.

When the police entered John's house, the first thing they noticed was the stench. Second, the abundance of small black flies that buzzed about the room. They vainly tried to shoo the flies away. The flies glued themselves to the officers' faces and hair.

The officers circled the morbidly obese man slumped dead on the couch. Small black flies were crawling over his face, in and out of his nostrils, his ears, his eyes.

"Been here a while. On the nose."

Suddenly, the corpse yawned, releasing noxious gas. A black cloud of newborn blowflies zoomed out of the man's open mouth and filled the room. The police furiously swatted at the malignant swarm before retreating outside.

Gymnorhina tibicen, the Australian magpie, is a territorial bird and during nesting periods may swoop and attack anybody in the area where it is nesting.

Alana ran screaming down the footpath, her hands frantically waving about her head as the magpie terrorised her from above. In her haste, she tripped on the uneven concrete and fell to the ground. The magpie didn't ease up. Talons extended, it fluttered about Alana's face as she tried to get up, and skewered an eye with a steely beak. With blood streaming down Alana's face, she continued to scream and shake her head. But the enraged bird dived in and popped her other eye.

Alana lay in a hospital bed with her eyes bandaged. Sitting in a chair by the bed was her sister, Marisa.

"It was him," Alana said.

"What were you doing there alone?"

"Cleaning his house, preparing meals, running errands. I spent a year there. Knew I'd found him."

Marisa raised an eyebrow. "And you didn't think to tell me?"

"Had too many false leads. Wanted to be sure this time."

"You could have called."

"I'd already spent a lot of time searching for John Smith." Alana paused, turned her head towards the window, allowing the sun to bathe her tortured face. "Do you know how many John Smiths there are?"

"A lot."

"A lot. And I sought out each and every one."

"We'd all been searching, Alana," Marisa said, a little terser than she'd intended.

"The others are gone and it was me who found him. And I needed to find my bracelet."

"*Our* bracelet."

"It was around *my* wrist."

Marisa bit her lip, didn't want an argument. "Didn't he recognise you?"

"I looked different, especially since dyeing my hair blonde. Don't think he likes blondes." Her voice trailed off in contemplation. "I guess I wasn't to his taste anymore. *Not young enough.*"

"But if he'd recognised you, he might have left, moved away. You would have lost him again."

"He wasn't going anywhere."

"You know he's dangerous. He could have hurt you. Hurt others."

"No." Alana smiled. "He couldn't do anything. Not anymore."

Bufo marinus, the cane toad, was a native of Central and South America and was introduced into Australia in the 1930s to control beetles decimating the sugarcane industry. It failed to control the beetles. Due to a toxic substance secreted from glands on its skin, the toad has been deemed a pest and its numbers are swelling across the country.

Holding two large bags full of groceries, Alana extended her fingertips to flip down the handle of a tattered screen door. She entered the ramshackle old weatherboard house through the back door which led directly to the kitchen, and called out.

"Hey, John, are you home?"

Of course you are, she muttered under her breath.

"In here." A low rumble echoed down the hallway.

Alana placed the grocery bags on the kitchen table, then wandered the rickety hallway to the living room. There was John slouched on the couch watching the TV. Not really watching, staring. *Reminiscing?*

"I brought your favourite for dinner tonight."

Everything was John's favourite.

John just grunted.

When Alana had prepared the dinner, she carried a large plate to the living room where John remained all afternoon. He always ate while seated on the couch in front of the television. He gulped it down, barely chewing.

"My, you have a healthy appetite, John."

"Is there more?"

"Certainly. I'll get you more." Alana scurried out.

"No," Alana reiterated. "He couldn't do anything. I made sure of that. John was a big man to start with, but in the time I cared for that slob, he doubled his weight. Thanks to my *special* diet."

Marisa's eyes widened. "You trapped him in his house."

A broad grin stretched across Alana's face. "I trapped him in his own *fat*."

John had readily accepted Alana's offer for home help and cleaning services. She did a thorough job and didn't charge much. What he didn't know was that Alana only had one client: John Smith.

He always paid cash. It was hidden all over the house in various concealments but that's not what had interested her.

"I knew my bracelet had to be in the house somewhere. John never went out. Too fat to move too far. And although I spent my days there, cooking, cleaning, washing, scouring every inch of that house, I never found it or anything linking him to what he'd done.

"But there was one place I *hadn't* searched. All day long he vegetated on that couch. The padding was flattened and spilling out of burst seams. I couldn't get near it so when I brought him his meal, I added a little something extra."

"What was in the pie?" John bellowed.
    "The same as usual, the way you like it: chicken, leek, celery —"
    "Feel sick!"
    "Can I get you something?"
    "Get outta my way!"
    John barrelled passed the woman, bumping his massive girth against her and knocking her to the floor. He lumbered down the hallway, crashing into the walls. Each seismic step shuddered the floor. The modest timber house trembled and groaned. John slammed the door of the bathroom. Sounds of thunderous flatulence and retching emanated from the toilet.
    He would be there all night.
    Alana got up off the floor and went to the couch to start searching. She immediately recoiled. The fabric reeked of a foul odour that had seeped into the material from John's loathsome body. Alana found him repulsive. How did she put up with him for so long?
    Holding her breath, she pressed on, and beneath the cushions

of the sofa was a storage compartment. It was full of mementos and trinkets, and *trophies*.

The bracelet.

"He sat on each and every conquest. It was definitely him."

Canis lupus dingo is an Australian wild dog that hunts alone or in cooperative packs when hunting large game. It is an opportunistic carnivore preying on native species, domestic animals and livestock.

Lying on his side on the ground, John coiled his body into a tight ball. A circle of older boys kicked and punched him from all directions.

Finally, they stopped and one of the assailants spat a gob of saliva as a parting gesture of contempt for the overweight boy cowering in the dirt.

"Eat this, fatso!"

John endured the beating and the pain for several minutes. But the humiliation etched into his psyche would last an eternity.

Covered in dirt and bruises, he made the long walk of shame home. Not for the first time. The beatings had become a regular entertainment for the gang of louts.

At home, the indifference of his stepfather added to the sting of abasement. He had never cared for his wife's child. The child of another man. And when she died, he had been stuck with the boy. The *fat* boy, who sought solace in food.

The only advice he cared to offer: *What's the matter with you? Stand up for yourself.*

That night, John blubbered in bed. His fists clenched and unclenched in an impotent rage. As tears stained his pillow, he gritted his teeth until his head throbbed.

In the morning, John awoke to blood caking his chin. During the night, he had bit his lip and blood had flowed from his mouth. At the grimy bathroom mirror, as he inspected and prodded the open wound, a tooth popped out and spun around the porcelain basin of the vanity. He ran his tongue along the rest of his teeth and they felt loose. More teeth fell out.

He tentatively touched his bloody gums and felt something

pointy. Leaning in closer to the glass, he could see his teeth were being replaced with sharp, serrated teeth.

That's when John discovered that he was becoming a monster.

Carcharodon carcharias, the great white shark, is an apex predator. With huge jaws filled with multiple rows of razor-sharp teeth, carcharodon carcharias has fatally wounded swimmers in waters off the coast of Australia, and strikes fear into the hearts of ocean goers all over the world.

A week later, John's tormenters were looking for another confrontation. But John had retrieved a small sledgehammer from his stepfather's shed and had been carrying it in his schoolbag ever since.

He whipped the hammer out and managed to get in a lucky blow across the face of the closest boy, pulverising his jaw and sending teeth, blood and bits of bone flying.

Time froze as all the boys were suddenly stunned by John's retaliation. Just as suddenly, they snapped out of it and turned tail to run off. But in that split-second pause, John brought the heavy hammer crashing down on the gang's ringleader. The boy crumpled to the ground. As the rest of the boys bolted, John crouched and caved in the boy's skull.

That night, John cowered in his bedroom as police spoke to his stepfather.

Head bowed, John was escorted out, while his stepfather gave him a look of disdain but, truth be told, he was glad to see the back of the lad.

John spent the rest of his teenage years in boys' homes where the cycle of violence continued until he was released, at age eighteen, onto an unwary world.

Trichoglossus moluccanus, the rainbow lorikeet, is distinguished by its colourful plumage of red, blue, green, orange and yellow feathers. It gathers in large communal flocks, frequently screeching and chattering, and is especially partial to fruit and nectar from flowering trees and shrubs.

John noticed a flash of light sparkling from the girl's bracelet as she rode her bicycle up and down the long driveway of the farm. It was like a colourful beacon calling him.

He parked his car on the gravel verge near the fence line of the property and when she reached the gate, he called to her. Asked for directions.

Laying her bicycle down, she stood at the wire-mesh gate and tried to help. But he struggled with a map and couldn't follow her instructions, so she squeezed out between the gate and the post and approached the car.

John had developed a taste for sweet things. The girl was thirteen, slender and petite. Good enough to eat.

And easy to grab.

He dragged her into a thicket of trees between the fence and the road.

Her struggles were ineffectual. Her fists sank into his stinking flesh as if she were punching butter. He slobbered over her frail frame. Ripped off her clothes with his meaty paws.

After plundering the girl's innocence, he took delight in breaking both her legs. Using brute strength, he tried to snap them off. When they stubbornly held, he lumbered off and retrieved a machete and spade from the boot of his car.

Upon his return he found the girl crawling through leaves, twigs and clumps of mushrooms. Grabbing her by her ponytail, he flipped her over like a rag doll and with two mighty whacks hacked off her legs.

Her protests and howls of pain urged him on.

She thrashed her arms and vainly clawed at his coveralls. Her fingernail snagged on a loose thread on the man's shirt. A yellow thread.

Vespula vulgaris, the European wasp introduced to Tasmania in the 1950s, has spread throughout Australia and become a notorious pest. Its striking yellow-and-black markings are an indicator of its dangerous and aggressive nature.

He swatted her pesky hands away, then took great delight in dislocating her arms before hacking them off too. It was easy for him, just like pulling the wings off a fly when he was a kid.

Her vision closed in on the embroidered name on her attacker's chest before being swallowed by darkness.

Scraping a shallow grave in the dirt, he placed the girl's torso within the depression, then carefully laid the arms and a leg across her body. Picking up the other severed leg, he stroked the smooth skin and brought it up to his nose, smelt the delicate aroma.

He removed his denture veneers and slipped them into his pocket. The dentures disguised two evil rows of shark teeth. Salivating as he grinned, he took a large bite out of the girl's tender thigh. Closing his eyes, he savoured her sweet flesh.

When he was done, he placed the remnants of the leg with the rest of the limbs.

He unclasped the bracelet glittering around her left wrist and held it to the light. The sun struck its many facets, tantalising his senses. He slipped it into his grubby pocket beside his dentures.

A perfunctory covering of dirt and branches finished the job. The dense grove of trees had shielded his obscene acts from prying eyes.

She was so small, so lithe, so desirable. Yeah, it had been easy to grab the girl. So easy.

Aquila audax, the wedge-tailed eagle, is the largest flying raptor in Australia. Its keen vision allows it to spot prey up to two kilometres away and its visual perception even extends into the ultraviolent bands.

The distant farmhouse was perched on a hump in the vast acreage. A long driveway stretched past paddocks to the gate. Beyond, flanking the driveway, was a large copse of trees, then the main road.

From the farmhouse, Evelyn Miller noticed the stranger emerge from the thicket of trees and get into his car. Not so unusual on a farm. The house was quite a distance from the road and sometimes people stopped to answer the call of nature amongst the screen of the trees or to search for magic mushrooms.

She saw the car skid off, its spinning wheels spitting up gravel. But something else caught her eagle eye. Something at the end of the driveway. A frame of some sort. A bicycle. Her daughter's bicycle!

"LAURA!"

She ran screaming down the driveway to the bottom of the property. Her shrieks alerted her husband. He halted his chores and ran after her.

When the girl was finally found, it was too late.

Megascolides australis is a giant earthworm found in South Gippsland in Victoria. It can grow to over two metres in length. With similar capabilities to ordinary earthworms, if cut into pieces, each segment can grow into a new earthworm.

Every part of her was starting to regenerate.

The family was aware of their strange genetic uniqueness. Secret knowledge of it had been passed down the generations.

They gathered the severed parts of their daughter and laid them on a blanket on the living room floor beside the open fireplace.

While the adults debated what to do, in the warm glow of the fire, an identical girl grew from each part.

Soon, five identical girls had sprung from the severed pieces and stood naked before their parents. With identical memories, they wanted revenge.

Every part of her.

"We have to call the police," Evelyn shrieked.

"And tell them what? That a psycho killed our daughter and hacked her into pieces? Oh wait, she's still alive. And there's five of her now."

Then one of the "sisters" collapsed.

Fifteen years ago, Stan Miller's wife left in the family car to visit her parents for a week, and he drove a tractor to a back paddock.

As the tractor ran over the uneven ground, it hit a rut and overturned, pinning his arm to a rock on the ground. He was trapped for a few days, slipping in and out of consciousness, becoming delirious. He couldn't determine how many days but knew he had to get out or die. If he could withstand the pain, he knew he could survive. He slipped his belt out through the loops and tied it around his arm as a tourniquet to stem the flow of blood. Using a multipurpose knife, he carved into his flesh.

After cutting off his arm, Miller staggered to the house.

By the time he got there, his arm was already growing back.

When his wife returned, they drove to the overturned tractor with winches, shovels and jacks. They found a fully grown, but gaunt, version of Miller lying naked on the ground, pinned under the tractor.

"Help me," he moaned.

"Oh my god!" Evelyn said. "I didn't realise the arm would regenerate a whole new you!"

"Now the chores can get done in half the time!" her husband quipped.

Evelyn flicked him an eyeful of daggers. "This is not the time for flippancy."

"Who's being flippant?"

"Be serious. How are we going to explain this?"

"Easy. He's my twin brother."

"But—"

"C'mon, let's get him out. We can discuss it later."

The ability of regeneration was not a superpower for the family. There was always a compromise.

Once regeneration occurred their immune system was impaired. A mild infection could have catastrophic consequences. A scratch, the common cold, could be fatal.

Or a bite.

When John bit a chunk of Laura's leg, the wound festered and infection rapidly spread during regeneration, killing her within an hour.

Similarly with her father's duplicate. Weakened from the ordeal of the tractor accident, her "uncle" only managed to survive for six months after regenerating from the severed arm.

Marisa stood before Alana's grave. The wounds to her eyes had not healed but had become inflamed. No amount of antibiotics could stop the infection from spreading.

The bracelet that Alana had retrieved now circled Marisa's wrist. She rubbed the cool metal as she spun it around.

As she was no longer whole, all the parts of Laura had adopted new names. Marisa walked along the row of graves of her "sisters", momentarily pausing at each one. Feeling their loss, losing a part of herself. They had all succumbed to circumstances that ordinarily should not have been fatal.

All her "sisters" had passed away. The part of Laura that was Marisa now was alone.

"I had a bad dream last night." Alana told Marisa as she lay in the hospital bed. "I was alone and imprisoned in a cage. The only thing I could do was to cut off pieces of myself and slip them through the bars so that they could regenerate and escape. I started chewing at a finger…" Alana trailed off.

Marisa squeezed Alana's hand. "I'm here for you," she said softly.

Marisa slipped on the disposable gloves before preparing the dye solution. Originally, Alana had dyed her hair blonde to look different from the other parts of her. Now Marisa prepared to dye her hair blonde to look like Alana, to become another part of her.

Marisa found the back door unlocked just as Alana had said it would be. John had never given her a key, always kept it on his person.

"Hey John, are you home?"

"In here." The expected answer.

Marisa placed some bags of groceries on the kitchen table, then walked down the dingy hallway. Alana had been thorough in her descriptions.

When she entered the living room, she had to stop herself from gasping. She had never quite imagined how immense John had become.

Sarcophilus harrisii, the Tasmanian devil, is a carnivorous marsupial with a voracious appetite that hunts prey but also dines on carrion. *Sarcophilus* has a loud screeching growl, and with its powerful jaws and sharp teeth can devour an entire creature, including the bones.

As a boy, John Smith was large. As a man he was a behemoth. And his personality had turned to poison.

"Where have you been?" John growled as he mindlessly scratched his arm. Flakes of skin were shedding and fluttering to the floor. "You've been gone a week! Couldn't contact you, went to voice mail."

"I'm sorry, John, my sister died and—"

"HUNGRY!"

Marisa jumped.

Although startled by the sudden ferocity of the demand, what chilled her more was the vision of John's mouth. It was filled with rows of shark teeth. White and pointy and razor-sharp. This was something Alana had failed to mention.

"Y-yes, of course, I'll fix you something, right away." Marisa hurried out to the kitchen.

As John impatiently waited for his food he flexed his jaw, opened and closed his mouth, grimaced and gritted his teeth. In the beginning, John pulled out his jagged shark teeth with pliers. Then had denture veneers made to cover them from public scrutiny whenever he was out. But now he didn't care and his mind started wandering and wondering about how delicious it would be to take a bite of living flesh again.

While John devoured the meal that Marisa prepared, along with multiple helpings, she did the dishes and continued the household chores, cleaning, washing. In the laundry, mountains of John's stale and soiled clothes were piled up.

In the living room she vacuumed the flakes of skin that had accumulated on the threadbare carpet around his feet. As she worked, she noticed that John's skin looked strange, scaly in texture, *not human*.

"I'm sorry, John, I couldn't get everything done today. And I'm too exhausted to drive home. If I stay the night, I can get an early start tomorrow."

John glared at her with cold, black eyes, mouth clenched, cheeks puffed. For a long moment, she thought he was going to erupt.

"I'm not paying you any extra!"

"That's perfectly fine, I don't expect you to. It's my fault, I let the chores pile up. I should have called you. Made arrangements."

"Yes, you should have!"

Another pregnant pause. Marisa held her breath.

Was it a trick of the light or did she see a membrane sweep across his eyes and his pupils contract to slits? Marisa blinked, trying to adjust her vision. *What have I got myself into?* she thought.

"You can stay in the back room." John's voice suddenly boomed. "There's plenty of bedding in the cupboards there."

Marisa expelled the air built up in her lungs. "Thank you, John."

The back room was a tacked-on extension to the house and was used for storage. There was no key in the door but there was a small sliding bolt and Marisa slid it closed. It looked too weak so she wedged a chair up against the doorknob to prevent it from opening, just to be on the safe side. Didn't want any unwanted visitors during the night.

A solitary low-wattage bulb hung from the ceiling, so dim it cast all furnishings into obscurity. Misshapen mattresses were leaning against the wall and Marisa flipped one down onto the floor. She retrieved a pile of blankets and sheets from one of the cupboards to make up a temporary bed.

The bedding had not been used for quite some time and smelled musty, but she was so tired…

Badumna insignis, the black house spider, is commonly found on window frames, under eaves and in various nooks and crannies. While the female remains in her web, the male will wander in search of a mate.

Marisa pulled up a woollen blanket around her neck. Engulfed in warmth, she fell into a deep slumber. Caught in the folds of the blanket was a silent assassin. A black house spider shrugged free and softly padded over the smooth skin of the sleeping woman. The woman stirred. *Badumna* reacted by biting her neck once, twice. Then thrice just below her jawline, before turning and crawling away.

During the night, Marisa heard John call her. She threw off the bedcovers, quickly dressed and raced to him.

John was in the bathroom groaning.

Marisa rapped lightly on the door. "John, are you alright?"

"Feel sick. Something's wrong," John groaned.

"I'll call an ambulance," she said through the door.

As Marisa headed for the phone, she heard a loud crash. She turned to see the bathroom door obliterated with splintered wood jutting out at all angles. In the middle of the chaos stood John. His shirt and trouser legs were shredded to ragged ribbons, revealing his massive and monstrous body. His flesh had turned a blotchy crimson and appeared to pour like slow-moving lava over his belt and boots.

His mouth opened impossibly wide, displaying jagged teeth. The monster heaved, and drool dripped from his mouth, sliding down his grotesque torso to a horizontal ridge running across his belly. The ridge opened up to reveal another mouth, a huge maw studded with multiple rows of evil, triangular teeth.

Marisa turned to run but suddenly her feet flipped backwards and her face slammed into the hardwood floor.

John had pulled the hall runner rug out from under her. He lurched forward. Tendrils sprouted from nubs running along the sides of his chest. They unravelled and whipped about, stretched and extended towards her.

Marisa quickly got up and skidded to the front door. A tentacle wrapped around her ankle and brought her down again. She pulled at the console table, knocking it down and sending the mirror atop it smashing to pieces. Picking up a shard, she stabbed at the tentacle until it released her.

Just as Marisa reached the door, a pudgy appendage slammed against it, preventing it from opening. More tentacles wrapped around her waist, gripped her arms, her legs, and lifted her off the floor.

John laughed at her ineffectual struggles as he brought her towards his gaping mouth. His foul breath stung Marisa's eyes and made her gag.

The mouth in John's belly was so huge she thought he was going to swallow her whole. But John had other plans.

In the living room, the monster that was John sat on the couch. His wide girth spread across the entire seat.

On the floor was a metal cage with Marisa trapped inside.

John stretched his tendrils through the cage and grappled with the woman. He pulled her leg through the widely spaced bars. Another tentacle gripped a machete and hacked off her leg. Then he waited for Marisa and her leg to regenerate.

When the leg had grown a whole new person, John grabbed her and tucked her into the diabolical maw in his stomach. He savoured her flesh and crunched down on her bones.

"*Sweet!*"

In this way, he would devour her again and again and again—

Marisa awoke from a feverish dream to the sound of John calling her. She threw off the bedcovers, quickly dressed and raced to him.

John was in the bathroom groaning.

"John, are you alright? What's wrong?"

"Stomach cramps. Can't stop spewing," he groaned.

"I'll call an ambulance."

As Marisa headed for the phone, she felt an itch on her neck. When she scratched it, she felt a raised lump. She peered at her reflection in the hallway mirror that sat atop a console table, and on her neck three angry welts stared back at her.

She knew that she didn't have much time left. John had finally killed her, along with all the other parts of Laura.

John was sick all night with diarrhoea and vomiting but eventually emerged from the bathroom and collapsed on the couch. Vomit had spilled down his multiple chins, down his shirtfront, and dried on his jowls. He looked pale and exhausted.

"Where's the ambulance?"

Marisa shrugged. "I didn't call them."

John clutched his massive stomach as a sharp wave of cramps washed across it. The flesh quivered like jelly. When the wave subsided, he stared at her slack-jawed.

"What was in that pie?"

Defiantly, she stood before him. "The usual, John. Chicken, leek, celery, *mushroom*."

She lifted her sleeve and a flash of light caught on the multi-faceted bracelet.

His eyes widened.

A wry smile crossed her lips.

Grimacing, he lunged at her, but was stricken with sudden pain and fell back in his seat.

"Don't try to get up. I've killed you, John Smith, just like you killed us. Although, I must say, we were much more merciful."

His face crumpled in confusion. "*We?*" he managed to utter before another wave of pain gripped him.

And a fly shot straight into his mouth.

As Marisa left the house, she noticed a cage amongst other junk in the back yard. *Had it always been there?*

After John's body was discovered, police found Marisa and questioned her.

She knew they were not finished with her and would return with more questions. Questions she couldn't, wouldn't answer.

But it didn't matter.

She flipped down her collar to inspect the spider bites on her neck. They had become enlarged and inflamed. The spider toxins were invading her body, ravaging her system. It was only a matter of time before she would succumb.

Every other part of Laura had already died. Now the last part of her sat waiting to finally join the rest of her.

THE BEST OMELETTE IN AUSTRALIA

FOX CLARET HILL

The rental car churns dust as Laurie drives along a winding dirt road in the middle of rural nowhere. Focused on not mowing down any suicidal grey kangaroos, Laurie doesn't spot the sign, but her girlfriend Lindsey does. It's in the shape of an arrow, and Lindsey squints at the faded, painted lettering to figure out the sign's message.

"The best omelette in Australia."

"Huh?" Laurie asks, her eyes still on the road.

Lindsey points. "That's what the sign says."

Laurie slows the car, cranes her neck, and lifts her oversized sunglasses to get a better look at the bush-concealed indicator. "Bold claim. Fancy giving it a go?"

Lindsey's stomach grumbles, desperate for something greasy after their particularly drunken venture to a pub the night before. The girls' good looks and foreign accents mean that the flow of drinks is often free of charge, but there's always a different price to pay when morning comes.

"I don't know. I was thinking more along the lines of fried chicken and chips," Lindsey whines.

"Come on, babe, we've only got one week left. You can have mediocre nuggets anytime you want back in Bristol, but this is our one chance to try Australia's best omelette."

Lindsey opens her mouth to protest, but big brown eyes render her mute, and she shrugs and leans back into her seat. Laurie beams, her thick curls bobbing in excitement, and she gives Lindsey a cheek-kiss of gratitude.

Lindsey's mouth curls up at the corner. "I don't really like eggs, though."

Laurie isn't listening. Keen to have a break from driving, she's already reversing and pulling into the driveway. The small parking lot is nearly full despite its location, and fanny-pack-toting tourists and suntanned locals occupy every outside table. Head pounding, Lindsey eyes the ramshackle building with uncertainty, examining its corrugated tin roof and tourist-trap decor.

"Don't judge a book by its cover," Laurie says, elbowing Lindsey affectionately.

Lindsey hums disapprovingly at the prod, her eyes still fixed on the café.

"Tell you what," Laurie continues, "if it's shit, I'll buy you a boneless bucket, and we can have a junk food picnic."

"Deal."

Lindsey hops out of the car, keen to get their visit over and done with, and get one step closer to popcorn chicken. Dressed in denim booty shorts and a crocheted crop top, she totters towards the entrance in high-heeled sandals and waits for the lecherous gazes and wolf whistles. None come, and as she looks around, she sees that her usually impactful arrival has been unable to part a single soul from the focused consumption of their enormous omelettes.

Or so she thinks.

Repetitive drumming attracts her attention to a chocolate-coloured cocker spaniel sitting and wagging its tail on the porch, eagerly watching the young woman approach. Lindsey jogs over, ankles rolling, and is greeted by enthusiastic licks and dirty paws. The well-worn tag on a muddy collar indicates that the animal's name is "Madi", and Lindsey turns to Laurie with a protruding lower lip.

"Aw, she has a people name. Can we get a dog when we get back?"

Laurie sighs as she locks the car and walks over, kicking up plumes of dust as she stomps in her combat boots. "Thanks, mutt," she says under her breath. "Now we have to have *this* conversation again." When she reaches Lindsey's side, she says,

"We live in a shoebox. We can't get a dog."

"What about something tiny? One of those teacup chihuahuas?"

"So, we can spend thousands on vet bills for something so inbred its eyes pop out? No thanks." The two of them love animals, but in different ways; Lindsey leans toward cute things and away from creepy crawlies, and Laurie would throw red paint at fur wearers if the resulting viral video wouldn't get you fired.

Lindsey's shoulders slump as she pets Madi.

Feeling guilty, Laurie kisses the top of her head and says, "Once we buy a house, we can get a dog."

"Which is never," Lindsey laughs.

"Never say never." She offers a hand, and Lindsey takes it, reluctantly parting from the dog. "Let's try this omelette."

Inside, the queue. Sunburnt sightseers amble lazily, and once they reach the counter, a surly woman greets them with a muttered, "What do you want?" The handwritten chalkboard menu indicates plenty on offer, but like everyone else, they order omelettes: one plain for Lindsey, and one with a variety of vegetables for Laurie.

The woman behind the counter is what Laurie calls a "granola-type"—covered in tie-dye, adorned with swinging crystal pendants, and sporting greying dreadlocks. Her pink skin has the texture of a sun-baked tomato, and when she forces a smile, she becomes a roadmap advertisement for sunblock. There's something about her that Laurie doesn't like, but Lindsey makes small talk while they order and pay.

"So, what makes your omelettes so great? What's the secret?" Lindsey says.

The woman shrugs. "Just eggs, butter and cheese. We make the butter and cheese right here, and all the ingredients are organic and locally sourced."

"Wow," Laurie says, interest piqued, shooting Lindsey—who couldn't care less about this sort of thing—an approving nod. "What breed are the cows?"

The woman stares blankly, and a long interlude of silence ensues as her brain seems to buffer. "Holsteins," she says suddenly. "The black and white ones."

"So, free-range too?" Laurie asks.

Lindsey glowers at her, mouth pulled into a straight line. "I'm sure they're free-range if they're local and organic, Laurie." Her tone is exasperated, and she picks up their table number before the woman can answer. She drags Laurie by the wrist to the booth by the large windows and places the number "14" on the table between them. The seats squeak as they scooch and adjust.

"I was only asking," Laurie protests.

Lindsey rolls her eyes. "I love you, but you can be really rude without meaning to be. Like asking those surfers last night if they had real jobs. It's your tone; it's accusatory."

Laurie throws her hands up in defeat. "Alright, I'm sorry. When you're right, you're right." She leans forwards, glancing around to ensure no staff overhears and lowers her voice. "Is it just me, or is this place a bit weird?"

"You were the one who wanted to come here!" Lindsey furiously whispers.

"I did. I do! It's just—" Feeling an argument brewing and noticing the owner's eyes on her, she stops midsentence and leans back. "You know what? Never mind."

Lindsey grins at the defeat, an expression that amplifies as steaming omelettes are dropped in front of them by a despondent server.

"This smells amazing," they say in sync.

Lindsey gets in the first jinx.

Laurie rolls her eyes and silently tucks into the meal. "Holy shit," she moans, immediately breaking the jinx. She looks at her girlfriend.

Lindsay's eyes widen, and she nods in agreement. "Holy fucking shit," she replies.

"This is the best omelette I've ever had. It's salty and sweet and tangy in all the right ways. It's...indescribable."

"It also barely tastes like an omelette," Lindsey says, cocking her head and pulling the yellow mound apart with her fork. "Am

I going crazy, or does it taste completely different to every other omelette you've ever had?"

Laurie stops and thinks, savouring the aftertaste of her last greedy mouthful. "You're right. It must be how they cook it, or maybe it's the cheese? Either way, it's amazing."

"You're right about that. Fuck a boneless bucket. I want to eat this every day for the rest of my life."

A sad silence forms.

"We're never going to be able to eat this again," Laurie says at last.

"Unless we stay another couple of nights, put off heading up to Sydney for a little longer. That way, we can come here twice more before saying goodbye."

It is an insane suggestion: completely dismantling multiple plans for *omelettes*?

And yet, Laurie agrees wholeheartedly, adding, "And if this motel can't take us, we can always camp out here. Maybe they'd let us stay in the parking lot if we asked. That way, we can have this for breakfast, lunch and dinner."

Lindsey's eyes are wide and manic. "Oh my God, yes, you're a genius."

Laurie pauses, examining the dilated pupils ringed by green. She feels her heart rattle against her ribs, more forceful than usual. "Do you feel a bit stoned?" she asks.

Pausing mid-chew, sunny-coloured slab of egg slipping from her lips, Lindsey examines her own vital signs. "Yeah, it's weird. Like a runner's high or getting the shit scared out of you. I'm all shaky." She raises her quivering hands to demonstrate.

The women pause, looking at the remnants of their meals, the alluring scent rising up and filling their nostrils like the way it does in cartoons. There's something *unnatural* about these omelettes. They both know it, and they know each other knows it—and yet, they both pick up their forks and continue to wolf down the delicacy. Once no morsel remains, not a crumb nor garnish, they excuse themselves from the café and make their way back to the car.

As they walk, they notice many customers sitting in front of stacked plates. People are returning for second and third helpings, unbuttoning their trousers and gorging themselves like it's Christmas Day. It's hard not to stare at the spectacle. One man appears to be on his fifth. The omelettes aren't small, nor are they cheap.

"Imagine spending $150 on breakfast," Lindsey says, except she *can* imagine doing so.

They both can. They're both desperate to turn around and buy another, and then another. Halfway across the lot, they begin to um and ah. They lie and say they could fit another one in even though they're already overfull and bloated...

Laurie stops in her tracks, and Lindsey comes to a halt. Together, they almost turn back towards the café, but at the last second, Lindsey spots Madi sitting in the shade by their car. Dogs are one of the few things that Lindsey likes better than eating, and so she drags Laurie by the hand away from the café and hurries towards her newfound friend.

As they pat the dog's soft brown fur, they feel their cravings fade, and they thank the dog via enthusiastic scratches for saving their stomachs. The dog patiently puts up with the abundance of affection, but when the smothering becomes too much, she ditches their hands with a shake of her shaggy coat. Dirt spackles the girls, and they recoil. In disappointment, they watch Madi as she trots towards the café.

Brushing grit from their clothes, they stand up, and when Madi stops and looks back at them over her shoulder, Lindsey squeals.

"She wants us to follow her!"

Laurie scoffs and looks sceptical, but when Madi barks impatiently, still staring at the girls, Laurie furrows her brow. "Okay, that is strange."

"Maybe she's a service dog. Her owner might be hurt!"

Before Laurie can stop her, her girlfriend sprints toward the dog and edges ever closer to the dangerously-tasty omelettes, leaving Laurie with no other option but to follow the pair.

To their surprise, the dog doesn't lead them to the café. Instead, she turns right, down a skinny path surrounded by clawing trees and coarse bush. Lindsey slips through easily, her waifish figure avoiding snags and cuts, but Laurie is less lucky. Sharp twigs prod and scrape every inch of exposed skin.

"Where the fuck are we going?" she hisses as a branch smacks her in the face.

"I don't know! I don't speak dog."

The path gets progressively darker as they proceed, the trees knitting together to form a tunnel, and though the path is well-trodden, it's clearly traversed by someone much shorter than Lindsey and thinner than Laurie. Despite the spiders hanging overhead and the creeping claustrophobia, they keep following the dog, neither wanting to reveal that they're too scared to hypothetically save a life.

Eventually, they see the light at the end of the tunnel and squeeze out into a clearing. In the centre of a field of dead grass sits a building. It's similar to the café—tumbledown and tin—but it's surrounded by barbed wire and lacks any windows. It appears like an omen of doom. Both girls' churning guts beg them to turn back. They don't, eager to win their game of chicken, and follow the dog to the back of the building, where a small section of the flimsy fencing has fallen over.

Putting her combat boots to good use, Laurie stomps the section flat, picks her girlfriend up, and swoops her over the spiky barrier to safety.

The dog sails over the obstacle with an elegant jump and guides the girls to the back door of the building. Laurie tries to open it, but it's locked, and she's ready to admit easy defeat until Madi whines and paws at the door. Sighing, Laurie gives it another go, and with a crunch, the door swings open, and Laurie falls into the dark mouth of the building. The remnants of the rusted latch lay scattered across filthy linoleum tiles, and Laurie quickly jumps up from the floor.

Lindsey runs to her side and is met by a wall of sauna-like heat. Next is the smell, emphasised by the suffocating temperature. It smells like a pet shop, all sawdust and acrid piss. Lindsey retches, nearly losing her breakfast, and Laurie nervously searches the rough, corrugated walls for the light switch. A single bulb flicks on, and their jaws drop in horror.

Two dozen furry platypuses are strapped into machinery and suspended in layers, one above the another. With the heat turned up, the animals sweat, and metal appendages squeeze the milk that oozes from their tender flesh. Multiple funnels beneath their bellies greedily swallow the liquid. Plastic tubes positioned at their rear ends catch and consume eggs from the moment they're plopped out. The platypuses' little webbed feet lazily paddle the air, their eyes are rolled back in their heads, and their beaks suckle feeding tubes. At four times their usual mass, the tortured monstrosities have clearly been overbred and hormone-pumped into being perfect battery-farm platypuses.

Stacked steel cages—fronted by bars and reeking of urine— rattle with life at the far end of the room. Something larger than those being drained growls from within—the males. The breeding bulls begin to thrash, unsedated and agitated by the human presence, and all the girls can do is stare.

"The best omelette in Australia," Lindsey whispers with horror as the realisation hits her.

"No cows or chickens required," Laurie sniffles. "They've got everything they need right here."

Madi begins to whine and lick at the most accessible of the imprisoned creatures, offering them some comfort in their pitiful state. Not needing to discuss it, the women get to work, gently freeing platypuses from drips, tubes, and restraints. The females come quietly, but the males writhe at first, aggressively wielding the barbs above their webbed feet. Laurie and Lindsey offer gentle touches and soft coos, until the males eventually calm in the girls' careful grasp. They set the creatures down on the ground, one by one, until about 240 kilograms-worth of platypus wriggles around sluggishly at their feet.

"Are they going to be okay?" Lindsey asks.

"I don't know."

"You're the vet nurse!"

"Yeah, but I've never worked with platypuses before," Laurie snaps.

She crouches to inspect the animals. Slowly, they seem to

wake from synthetic slumber, freed from their IVs and systems pumping full of adrenaline. They clamber over each other, rocky waves of umber writhing impatiently.

"I think they'll be okay," Laurie says. "They seem healthy. I think they just need to go find some water to live by."

As if listening to the conversation, Madi scratches at the back door. Once it's opened, the shaggy dog leads the group like the pied piper out of the building and back into their natural habitat. The girls are left behind, wide-eyed and dumbfounded, and by the time they shake out the shock enough to leave the building, Madi's troupe is already gone. So, there's nothing left to do except navigate back through the forest, get in their car, and drive to the hotel. They do so in silence, undetected by the owners or their patrons.

Back at the hotel, neither of them speaks as they pick at their boneless bucket. After seeing what they've seen, they can barely stomach it, and sick of picturing hormone-inflated chickens in tiny cages, they end up putting the bucket aside and turning on the TV.

Lindsey flicks through reality show after reality show, but finally stops when she reaches a pretty reporter standing in front of a familiar backdrop. She turns up the volume.

"Tragedy has struck at the Hidden Haven Café, a local foodie hotspot and popular tourist attraction due to its award-winning omelettes. The owner, Lisa Walsh, has been found dead along with nineteen customers and workers who have yet to be identified. Two police officers had stopped by for a late lunch when they discovered the harrowing scene. While the causes of death are not yet confirmed, the causation suggests poison, though it seems the food is not to blame. As far as we know, most, if not all, of the individuals involved are covered in puncture wounds, having been seemingly stabbed by some sort of unknown, poison-coated implement."

Lindsey turns the volume back down and turns to Laurie, her face shock white. "Do you remember what the keeper told us when we went to the zoo?"

Still staring at the screen with wide, watery eyes, Laurie nods. "That male platypuses have venomous spurs on their hind legs. It's agonising, but the dose is too small to be fatal to humans."

"Four times larger means four times the venom payload. Did we—?"

"No, it's not our fault," Laurie says firmly. "We did the right thing. We couldn't have left them like that."

All those people dying in torturous agony, red faces contorted into silent screams as they froth at the mouth and fade away.

"No. You're right." Lindsey repeats it in her head like a mantra until it starts to sound less hollow, and when Madi appears on the screen, she turns the volume back up and lets the reporter's words drown out her thoughts.

"The sole survivor is a dog that belonged to Marsh. She is heading to the vet for an examination and then will be looking for a new home. If that's you, call the number below."

The girls look at each other and then at the doe-eyed dog, who, for the first time, is no longer wagging her tail.

Laurie sighs. "I'll call the shelter."

Lindsey squeals, delighted, but turns sombre when the TV camera moves away from the dog and focuses on the banner hanging above the Hidden Haven's front door.

"Their omelettes weren't *that* good, were they?" she asks.

"No, they weren't," Laurie responds, and it almost sounds like the truth.

TWISTED

RENEE DE VISSER

The cold water, lapping gently at the soles of his feet, woke him out of his stupor and, for a moment, he forgot why he was lying there. Then he attempted to move, and it came to him in a rush.

From his position lying supine, he could see his backpack and camping gear up on the embankment above him. Beside him, to his left, his fishing rod and bait bucket lay where he'd dropped them after he had lost his footing on the slippery rocks at the edge of the river bank. As he had stumbled to gain traction, his right ankle had wedged between two rocks and twisted abruptly as he fell.

Twisted? That was probably wishful thinking.

With a groan, he pushed himself onto his elbows and looked down at his ankle. He had since pulled it free from the rocks—hence the passing out—and now he could easily see the bone sticking out of his skin to the right of the break. It was hard to tell how much blood he had lost into the water, but he guessed it was a fair bit. He was aware of a few other cuts and bruises on his left side from the fall, but it was his ankle that screamed at him, that kept him rigid and taking shallow breaths in an effort to reduce movement and pain.

He slowly lay down, eyes again drawn to his backpack. All his first-aid gear was far away in that pack. This was not good. This was not good at all.

And the afternoon tide was coming in. He probably had less than an hour to move to higher ground. There were bull sharks in these waters, and they were probably already aware there was a badly injured creature in their midst.

Cautiously, he lifted his left buttock and slid his hand into the back pocket of his shorts. He could feel that the glass was broken from the fall, and, yes, could immediately see that his mobile phone was dead. He was going to have to get out of this on his own.

With a grimace, he sat up and surveyed his options.

The bait bucket had tipped towards the water and the incoming tide was now lapping most of the bait out of it, floating it down-river. His rod was still beside him and he grabbed it now before he lost that too. He wasn't sure if the bucket could've been of any use, but maybe he could use the rod as a crutch.

Or...*a splint!*

Carefully, he started to pull the line out from the reel, leaving the hook safely secured against the rod. Then, when he surmised that he had enough slack to loop it around his leg a few times, he stopped and considered how the splinting was actually going to work. There was no denying it—this was going to fucking hurt. A *lot*.

Gingerly, he placed the rod, handle end down, against the out-side of his right leg, and looped the line loosely several times over his foot and around the rod. Then the moment of truth—he had to lift his foot to bring a couple of the loops under his heel and up his leg. He braced himself, holding his right calf muscle with his right hand and his right heel with his left. And lifted them both together.

HOLYSHITHOLYSHITHOLYSHITHOLYSHIT!!!

Trembling, sweating, maybe even, yes, weeping, he took a moment to gather himself once more. Then, with a shuddering breath, he moved the three fishing-line loops so that they were evenly spaced—one around the arch of his foot, and the other two up his leg. Then he pulled the line just tight enough to bring the rod firmly against his limb, before falling back in a quivering, weepy heap.

He must've briefly passed out again because, suddenly, the water was fully covering his lower legs and lapping at his knees. The sun was hidden by clouds that swirled above his camp and the wind was picking up, the day turning dim and gloomy. It would rain again soon, which would make the water murkier. He needed to get his injured ankle out of it *now*.

He glanced once more to his left at the lost bucket and caught his breath. Something was meandering down the beach.

What the fuck is that?

Propping himself on his elbows, he squinted up the beach and realised he was looking at a large goanna. It was moving across the rocks, and seemed to be following some sort of scent towards him. No, not a scent, it was following the bait, the dead prawns that had been washed further up the river bank like a trail of bread crumbs.

I just made myself a new friend, he thought. As an avid adventurer, he was used to seeing the big lizards scavenging around tent sites, looking for scraps. It was generally known amongst campers to secure food inside tents and to keep sites clean from rubbish and scraps. Other than that, goannas tended to avoid humans and were generally seen as harmless unless they were cornered.

Still, it was probably time to start moving up the embankment and out of its path. He had used his rod as a splint, so he didn't really have anything else on hand to ward it away if it got curious. Plus, the ever-present threat of sharks and other opportunistic river life in the rising water remained.

Moving, however, was not going to be easy. Hopping on one leg was out of the question—the rocks were slippery, and sharp in some places. He would have to kind of shuffle backwards on his butt, keeping his ankle raised so it didn't drag against the ground. That was where the rod would help. It was a pretty shitty splint, as far as splints went, but it would help with that.

"Enjoy your feed, buddy," he said. His voice was hoarse. And then, swallowing hard, he lifted his right leg and the rod at the same time, so that his foot lifted too. There was a white flash of incredible pain that made him feel nauseous, but he managed to stay conscious.

Determined and concentrating hard to keep the rod as still as possible, he used the left side of his body to scoot up, back and down, up, back and down, up, back and down. It was slow going and, once he had made it past the worst of the rocks and out of the water, he had to lay on the sand to rest for a few minutes. He was sweating and his heart was racing with the exertion, but it was a start and it would get easier over the smoother sand. He was going to get out of here.

The tiny nip on his little toe was quick and sharp.

"Ouch! Motherfucker!" And he sat up to find the two-metre lizard squatting in front of his mangled foot. Lazily, it backed away towards the water.

Why the little... "Get! Get out of here! That's not a damn prawn!"

He found a pebble to throw at it and, as expected, it hissed and scurried away. He watched the lizard warily as it wandered back out to the water to investigate the floating bait bucket.

"Motherfucker," he grunted, moving off again. "Going to need a damn tetanus shot or something now."

Yes, the sand was less treacherous to navigate, but it was also softer and gave way beneath him, which made it more difficult to gain ground than he'd first hoped. Also, as the terrain started to climb towards the embankment where he'd initially made camp *(what, an hour ago? Two?)*, he found himself slowing with the exertion of lifting his whole body up a hill whilst leaning towards his left side. He was also thirsty. He was needing to rest more frequently.

At least I'm out of the water. No shark bait here, folks.

The flies, mosquitoes and midges, however, were relentless, and they naturally targeted the inflamed, hot and bloody skin around his wound. Without the water to shield it, he was literally being eaten alive, one tiny bite at a time.

And then there was the goanna, his ever-watching silent companion.

It had followed slowly behind him, like a game of "Statues" — whenever he moved, it moved; whenever he stopped to rest, it also stopped. At first, it stayed just out of reach of any missiles he could throw, but now it grew bolder, seeming to recognise that he was running out of projectiles as the sandy ground covered in shells and pebbles gave way to dirt and grasses.

And it can smell my blood, he realised.

He estimated he was about three-quarters of the way up the embankment when the goanna first took a run at him. He screeched as it approached, a sound borne more from fear and surprise than any feeling of might or power. The screech made it hesitate for a second, but then it darted again, and this time it delivered a solid bite to his big toe. With a yelp of pain, he kicked out with his other foot, hitting it squarely in the nose. It hissed and retreated, but not before its tongue flicked over the bite it had left. And then, as the rain began to come down, the goanna began to slowly pace back and forth at his feet.

"Motherfucker! Oh, motherFUCKER!" he screamed, and, lifting his leg and rod again, began moving backwards up the hill as fast as he could.

This is not happening, this is not happening, this stuff just doesn't HAPPEN!

He dared not stop to look, but he could sense that he was now close to his camping spot. Both of his arms were trembling with the exertion of moving one half of his body whilst simultaneously trying to keep the other half as still as possible. His ankle, now swollen to twice its normal size, was throbbing and made worse with every thud of his backside as he shuffled backwards up the hill as quickly as he dared. He was panting, spurred on by the primal fear of being stalked by a wild animal, and his tongue felt dry and thick. Everything felt like it was on fire, and yet all of that faded into the background when the goanna came into view again through the sheets of rain, heavy tail swaying from side to side like an angry cat.

As he watched, it rose up on its hind legs and made a run at his shattered ankle.

In one movement, it grabbed hold of his shin with its left claw, his foot with its right, and closed its jaws around the bone that jutted from his leg. There, it began to shake its head from side to side like a dog playing tug o' war. Screeching with pain, he lashed out at it with his other foot and attempted to punch it with both fists, but it held firm, repositioning and digging its claws in further in order to keep its grip.

Sobbing now, he fell back, reaching around him for something, *anything*, to defend himself with. Auspiciously, his hand fell on a large branch and, with a roar, he lifted it and waved it blindly. The lizard dodged his blow in a final yank that also splintered part of his shin bone from his leg. Its prize won, it backed away slowly *(Was it actually growling?)*, then turned and scurried off without looking back.

Everything went black.

He gained semi-consciousness a few times, just enough to register that the rain continued all night and into the next day. No campers or hikers went past him and his twisted leg and, if they had, they probably wouldn't have noticed him, assuming that any person stupid enough to be camping in such weather was taking shelter in the tent.

And so, weak with blood loss and barely conscious, he was still there two days later when the sun finally made an appearance. His right leg was covered in deep lacerations below the knee that were already showing signs of infection. His ankle was a mangled mess of angry, inflamed tissue and shattered bone, and it continued to bleed without clotting. His tongue was swollen, and he was shivering violently from being cold and wet for days.

So, when he did hear the sound of someone approaching, it was all he could do to lift his head and open one crusty eye.

"Oh," he croaked. "Hello."

The goanna, settling in beside him, didn't offer a reply.

A PACK APART

CHARLES SPITERI

"Do you know how to play football, wog?" Janson grinned.

Eight kids circled Joe in the playground, watching him, a rat in their trap.

"Yes, I can play football very well."

Back in Malta, he would sit with his father during the World Cup to watch England play Italy. Malta never made it to the World Cup, so his father supported England and Joe did the same. He loved cheering and yelling with his father, though there were certain words he'd learned to be careful not to repeat.

"Well, you can play with us," Janson said. He turned to a red-haired, freckled kid named Edgar. If Janson was the captain, Edgar was the lieutenant. "Get the ball," Janson ordered.

Edgar ran off excitedly.

Joe wasn't sure what they were up to. They teased him for the mortadella sandwiches his mother made (calling him "Stinky") and they mocked his accent, and now this? Was it an opportunity to prove himself? Maybe they were testing him?

It was a test he desperately wanted to pass.

Year Seven had not started well. He had arrived in Australia three months earlier and his world had quite literally been turned upside down. He struggled to come to grips with how enormous Australia was. Malta only had small grocery stores; here they had big shopping centres. Malta only had one library; here there were libraries everywhere, with books he couldn't find back in Malta like fantasy novels, role-playing games and comics. He had seen high-rise buildings for the first time, and trains and vast arcades, the scale of which filled him with a sense of epic opportunity.

"You know," Janson said, "for a wog you're not bad. You can be in my team if you like."

It was a test.

He nodded keenly. The other kids laughed, but Janson gave them the hard stare. The laughter stopped abruptly. Edgar returned with the ball. The circle of kids split into two groups, gathering at either side of the field, with Edgar, Janson and Joe remaining at the centre.

Joe stared at the ball in Edgar's hands: It was oval in shape, not round like the ones he had played with in Malta. That troubled him.

"You know how to play footy, don't you?" Janson said.

"Yes," Joe stammered, wary of how intently he was being watched.

"Let's play," Janson said

Edgar raised the ball with both hands and slammed it to the ground between them. It bounced up and over Joe's head.

"Quick, pass it to me," Janson screamed.

Joe ran after the ball. It was like trying to catch a chicken, the ball bouncing this way and that until, eventually, it settled and he pressed his foot onto it. Breathless from the effort, he looked up to see where Janson was, ready to kick the ball.

They were all laughing hysterically.

"No, you idiot," Janson screamed. "It's Aussie Rules. Pick it up. Pick it up!"

And Joe did.

They all jumped him, slamming him down to the ground, pressing his face hard against the concrete. They beat him and kicked him and the beatings kept coming, even once he let go of the ball.

They jeered.

"Stupid wog," they said.

And that's when, in between the blows, he first caught a glimpse of the dog, watching from the opposite end of the playground, while he struggled to crawl away from the hailstorm of punches and kicks, until the teacher appeared and broke up the fight.

The kids ran off laughing, leaving him a huddled mess on the ground, lips bleeding, cheeks red and raw. His shirt and pants were torn and bloody at the ankles and elbows. His knees and palms stung to a pulse.

"Oh dear, are you okay?" the teacher asked, as she helped him to his feet.

"Yes," he said, hobbling.

"Come, let's look after those cuts. Then I want you to tell me exactly what happened."

As they got closer to the main building, Joe got a good look at the dog. It was tall and lean, all muscle, with a long, angular face and pointy ears which stood high. It wore no collar and its coat was the colour of golden desert sand.

No matter how hard he tried, he could not make out the dog's eyes.

"Where's my money?"

Joe held the cigarette between his lips and inhaled like his life depended on it. He held his breath for a long moment before allowing the wisps of smoke to escape between his yellowed teeth. His hands trembled uncontrollably. The mobile phone felt hot against his ear. A flurry of ash sprinkled onto his lap.

"Are you there? Are you listening to me?"

"I got a painting being sold as we speak," Joe said, "and two big commissions."

"I don't think you understand the situation you're in."

"You'll have it next week, Latch. I swear."

"You got twenty-four hours."

The line went dead.

"Shit."

A tidal wave of anxiety rose up from the pit of his stomach. He crushed the tip of the cigarette against the ashtray and slipped what was left into his jacket pocket for later. He reached into the glove compartment, scrabbled around for the small plastic bag, poured some of the white powder contents onto the palm of his hand, spilling the stuff everywhere in his haste.

He snorted.

"Okay, let's do this," he said. "Let's do it."

He took a deep breath.

...ah yes...

There it was. The small and precious rush of euphoria.

He sighed. It wasn't enough, but it would have to do. He wiped his nostrils. Checked himself in the mirror. Pushed back his dark hair. Grinned.

That's the spirit!

All good. Easy-peasy.

"Let's do this."

He got out of the car.

Danielle's polite smile was welcoming enough when she answered the door. "Well, look at what the cat dragged in."

She'd called him twice to make sure he was coming, for his daughter's sake of course, otherwise Isobelle would never forgive him. *Could he live with that?* she had asked.

"I just happened to be in the neighbourhood," he said and put on a cheeky smile.

Her face was expressionless. "Yeah, well, she'll be blowing out the candles any minute now."

Danielle wore a cream dress and high heels, no makeup, and no hair dye to disguise the grey in her short, expensively cut hair. Joe wore blue cargo pants and a purple t-shirt, with a leather jacket and bright orange runners. It was hard to believe that there was ever a time when he and Danielle had tried to make a go of it. He blamed that misstep on the folly of youth and the fact that she had got pregnant.

"Everyone's out the back."

He followed her.

She'd done so much better without him. She'd finished her law degree and married Stan, one of those investment-manager types. Together, they had renovated this house on the beach in

Williamstown. It wasn't a mansion, but would have cost a lot more than Joe could ever afford.

"How have you been?" she asked.

"Good."

The vast hallway made him feel small. He scanned the paintings, mostly garish landscapes and portraits. He had given her a few of his own and was disappointed, but not surprised, that they weren't on display. The laughter from the back of the house grew louder.

The cocaine helped dull the anxiety.

Her kitchen was all sterile white laminate cabinets, hardwood countertops and chrome hardware, like he'd just walked into a showroom. People wandered in and out, taking fruit salad, ice cream and soft drinks from a large dining table. A series of glass sliding doors opened to the deck and a crowd of party-goers.

"There's still food left if you like," Danielle said.

"I'm fine."

A voice yelled, "Everyone! Everyone, can I have your attention please!"

"Cake time," she said and rushed off.

He was left with a crowd of casually dressed professionals talking about money, sports and kids. Thankfully, no one made an effort to approach, though he did catch a few glances of disdain, like he was some mangy mutt that had wandered in from the streets. He grabbed two glasses of wine from a table and found somewhere inconspicuous to hide.

"Can I have everyone's attention, please!"

Stan stood next to the barbecue, pompous like a politician ready to begin his victory speech, beaming confidently, a beer in one hand, wearing a black apron pronouncing him the "BBQ King". He would have been a school bully in his time. Joe was sure of that.

"Two big things happened this year. Bulldogs won the premiership—"

"Doggies!" someone cheered.

"Boooo!" someone else yelled.

"Shut up, Dan!" Stan joked. "Let me finish."

Everyone laughed.

"And of course, it's Isobelle's eighteenth birthday."

Joe's daughter emerged from the crowd. How long since he had last seen her? A year? No, it couldn't be. More like eight months. It wasn't like he didn't *want* to see her. Life just always seemed to get in the way for both of them. For her, mostly.

She was all smiles as she stood next to Stan. Her flowery dress had more colour than her mother's. Joe liked to think that was his influence. Her glasses were different to when he last saw her: tortoise shell. They looked good on her round face. Hard to believe that eighteen years ago he had held her tiny, fragile form in his arms. It was a memory Stan would never have, he thought smugly.

Danielle came up with the birthday cake and everyone sang "Happy Birthday", followed by a lot of cheering. Isobelle made an eloquent speech, with lots of "thank yous" to lots of people Joe didn't know. There was a mention of presents. He panicked. Shit, he hadn't brought anything. But then again, what could he offer her that she didn't already have?

Isobelle reserved a special mention about her mother, and kissed Stan lightly on the cheek for putting on such a magnificent barbecue. Just when Joe thought it was all over, Danielle whispered something in Isobelle's ear. She searched the crowd.

Her eyes met his.

She waved. "Hey Dad! Thank you for coming today."

He suddenly felt the scrutiny of all those eyes, circling him like sharks, waiting for him to make an arse of himself. He raised his glass and shouted "Hey!" and people laughed. At him or with him, he couldn't tell.

Duties done, Joe saw no reason to stick around any longer. He was making his way to the front door when Danielle caught up to him.

"Beating a hasty exit from all the banality," she said.

He shrugged, already feeling the high of the cocaine wearing off.

"You okay?" she said.

"Yes," he said, avoiding her gaze.

"You don't look it." She waited for his reply that didn't come.

"Please shut the door behind you," she said, leaving him to make his own exit.

On the way back home, he passed through the suburb of Albion. He hadn't been to the neighbourhood since he was a child. He'd been thinking a lot about his old school lately and it would only take a slight detour to visit.

The heavy grey sky felt like the perfect backdrop for a trip down memory lane.

Joe parked across from the school and got out. It was Sunday evening and the streets were quiet. The rattle of a train echoed in the distance.

The school was next to a church, a Gothic revival building with steepled gables and a square belltower. A wire fence enclosed the school with signs reading "No Smoking", "All Visitors to Enter via the Front Gate" and "This is a Child Safe Zone". These fences were never around when he was a kid. He lit a cigarette and walked the perimeter of the school complex, remembering the library, where he'd spent his time exploring books about art and painting, and the classroom where the teacher read *Charlotte's Web*, a story that had made him cry.

He lingered at the playground.

At one corner was the small canteen building, where he saw himself throwing away the mortadella sandwiches to buy the pies and dim sims, just so he could be like the other kids.

Go back to where you came from, wog.

Tears welled in his eyes. For God's sake, he should have got over it by now. He blamed it on the cocaine. He reached into the pocket of his leather jacket for his handkerchief.

The dog startled him.

It sat upright on its haunches, a metre or so away to his side, watching, sandy coat shimmering, ears pointed up. It was a dingo; he knew that now, because after seeing it the first time, he had spent hours in the library looking for images to identify the mysterious beast.

"Hello," he said. "What do you want?"

It walked away.

"Hey!"

Joe followed.

On the way home from school, Janson and Edgar leapt out from behind the trees, blocking Joe's path across the park.

Janson's fist was clenched. "Did you dob on us?"

Joe's knees and elbows still stung from the beating two days earlier. His right eye was black and his lips so bruised that it hurt when he ate and spoke.

"You dobbed us in. That's what wogs do," Janson said.

"Wuss," Edgar hissed.

They advanced.

A warmth spread across his crotch, dripping down his pants. If he ran, they would only catch up to him and, if he screamed, he doubted there was anyone around to help.

It seemed he was done for, when a guttural growl came from behind him. Janson and Edgar froze mid-step, eyes opening in terror. The growl had been very real, but then again, maybe they were playing some trick to make him look away and then jump him. He didn't know which way to turn.

Only when they ran away did he turn.

A tall, lean man stood silhouetted against the sun. He wore a tan woollen coat that hung on his shoulders like a shroud. He looked haggard and misshapen, hunched forward like he was carrying something heavy on his back, his arms hanging grotesquely long at his side.

In the glare of the sun Joe couldn't make out the face.

Was it a trick of the light, or just the way the man crouched forward? His shadow resembled that of a dog.

"You're not ready yet," the man said.

Joe ran.

He finished the cigarette and lit another. Ahead, the dingo kept up a leisurely pace.

What was a dingo doing here? he wondered. Dumped and abandoned? Could it even be the same dog he had seen as a child? It didn't seem that old. How long do they live?

The rattle of the train sounded closer as they made their way through a series of streets he no longer recognised. Old rundown houses were now renovated, modernised or had been torn down and replaced with townhouses. Every residence had a neatly trimmed garden with a Range Rover, BMW or Audi parked out the front. Joe was a remnant of a forgotten past.

Eventually, with the school far behind, they came to a walking track along the edge of a park. A wire fence separated the park from a vast stretch of government-owned property, a nowhere land overrun by shrubs and rocky earth. On the property, beyond the railway tracks in the distance, loomed the old flour mill factory, a four-storey brick building backed with a series of silos. It was a derelict, heritage-protected site that had been abandoned even when he was a child.

The dingo made its way through a small, mangled gap in the wire fence, through the long dry grass, towards the railway track and the flour mill beyond. The gap was too narrow for Joe. He looked around. Kids ran circles in a nearby playground, chased by their parents. An elderly couple walked hand in hand along the path behind him.

Not a good time to be jumping fences, he decided, but tonight he'd pay the factory a visit and see if he could befriend an old acquaintance.

Joe parked his car across the street from the flour mill. Beyond a steel fence and the abandoned car park, the brick building loomed high with the towering grey concrete silos blocking out the stars from behind it. Joe took a paper bag from the passenger seat and exited. The full moon cast long shadows at his feet, as he made his way to the gate.

A sign read 'Private Property—Trespassers will be Prosecuted'. He threw the bag over the fence, then looked around. An icy breeze made the trees shake a little, but that was all he heard and saw. He clambered up the fence, struggling to hold his balance. The wire rattled beneath his weight, making a *clink-clank* sound when he raised one leg clumsily onto the top. He swung over, slipped, landing on the concrete with a jarring stab of pain up his right foot.

He picked up the bag and hobbled across the car park.

He was sweating and breathing heavily by the time he reached the first door. The throbbing pain in his foot persisted. Hopefully, it was just a mild sprain.

The door handle turned freely in his hand. When he pushed against the solid wood, it didn't even budge. He would have to find another way in. He reached into his pocket for a cigarette, but he'd left them in the car.

"Shit."

Shattered glass crunched beneath his feet as he moved along the side of the building. Rusty steel bars crisscrossed the large windows. Inside, a series of square concrete beams reached up to a ceiling shrouded in darkness. A gridwork of copper pipes spread out across the walls like roots of a tree. He could barely make out the cogs, steel casings and other bits of machinery spilled out across the broken concrete floor.

It smelt of moist earth, urine and something else.

Wet fur?

He kept moving. Strange that he could see no graffiti, no sign of vandalism, just the damage nature had inflicted: weeds reaching like fingers through the cracks spreading across the external brickwork. He reached the base of an external steel staircase. It zigzagged up the side of the building, connecting a series of doors at each level.

He ascended, relieved that the pain in his foot had dulled.

The first door was locked. He struck gold with the second.

The door opened into a long, dark hallway. As he stepped inside, the air pressed heavily against his eardrums. He pulled out his phone and turned on the dim light. The smell of wet fur grew stronger. Somewhere he heard the sound of dripping water. He made his way down the hallway surrounded by the echo of his footsteps. Eventually, he came to an open doorway to his left.

He peered inside.

The vast concrete space, lined with shattered windows and dimly lit with moonlight, had been eviscerated. The gutted junction boxes, warped steel panels, rusted chains, cogs and torn plumbing hinted at the enormous scale of machinery that had once occupied this place. Wind whistled through the window panes. Amongst the rubble, torn remains of trousers, jackets, skirts, pants, shirts and shoes were strewn everywhere.

A dumping ground for thieves?

Joe would have to be careful.

He knelt down to pick up a wallet. He took the fifty-dollar note that was inside it.

Not very good thieves, he decided, if they left all this behind.

He was reaching down for another wallet when a scrabbling sound made him spin around. The dingo watched from the threshold.

"Hello," Joe said. "I brought something for you." He took the bag from his jacket and opened it, the crinkle of brown paper shattering the sanctity of silence. "What do you reckon, ay? Looks tasty, huh?" It was the nicest bone he could afford from the butcher. A peace offering. "Come on," he said. "I'm not gonna hurt you."

The dingo didn't move.

He dropped the bone a few feet ahead of it.

It retreated.

"Hey, where are you going?"

He rushed out to the hallway. It waited; eyes gleaming in the light of his phone.

"You got something to show me, huh?"

It turned into the darkness and he followed. He came to a set of stairs going up. The stench of wet fur was stronger now, but he had grown used to its sweetness just like he'd gotten used to the dark. When he reached the top of the stairs, he stood in the middle of a hallway that branched to his right and left.

"Where to now?" he muttered.

To his right, beyond the dim outline of a door, he could hear a scrabbling and the faint sound of muffled breathing. As he approached the doorway, he realised the sound was the panting of dogs.

A lot of dogs.

So many dogs that the beam of light from his phone could not possibly illuminate all of them in that room. His eyes could not keep up with the myriad of misshapen forms crawling about in the darkest corners, hovering at the periphery of his vision; shapes that at times seemed dog or human or something in between. A small group of dogs stepped into the light. It was not just dingoes in their midst, but other breeds of all shapes and sizes, all moving towards him.

Joe panicked, dropping his phone. As he turned to run, the dingo leapt up. Joe instinctively reached out, a defensive manoeuvre. The dog's jaws clamped down on his palm and he was pushed back. For a horrible moment he thought it would bite his whole hand off, but it released him the moment it had bitten, landing gracefully on its feet as Joe stumbled backwards in to the hallway, landing painfully on his arse.

He lay on the floor, crying pitifully and grasping his bleeding hand. The dingo watched from the threshold with its ears pointed forward. He felt those black eyes sizing him up, and envied the purity of strength in the animal's poise. Dark shapes of more dogs gathered behind.

"Just wanted to be friends," Joe whimpered.

It growled, stepping forward, lips curled back, teeth glistening. Joe scuttled backwards and slowly rose to his feet. When another dog approached, the dingo growled, and the dog retreated back into the darkness.

Joe gave in to his terror.

He bolted down the stairs and out into the night. The fact he'd forgotten his phone didn't matter. He sat in the driver's seat of his car, trembling as he wrapped the bleeding hand with a handkerchief, then held it tightly to his chest. It took a moment to catch his breath. With the adrenaline rush subsiding, he could start thinking a bit more clearly.

They could have easily hunted him down, he reasoned, but they hadn't.

Maybe they were testing him? What did they want him to prove? Had he succumbed to fear too quickly? Was his offering not good enough?

By the time he reached home, his hand had healed completely, like magic. He just couldn't wipe the image of the dingo's dangerous vitality from his mind.

This test was one he desperately needed to pass.

He was asleep on the floor when they broke into his studio. He was wrenched off the ground and hurled against the wall, dropped and kicked, then left coughing and gasping for breath. He watched helplessly as the two men destroyed all of his paintings, his easels, his brushes, and splattered his paints everywhere. When he tried to speak, they beat him until he was too broken to move, his face bruised, blood and spit bubbling down his chin.

"Okay, that's enough," Latch called, and the two men let him drop to the floor like a sack of potatoes. "That's for ignoring my calls."

Joe looked up at Latch. The tall, thin man loomed above him, his lips a thin, pink slit across his face. He wore tailored pants and a hoodie with the sleeves rolled up, tattoos of red snakes coiling around both of his hairless arms. He rubbed the scar across his chin, ran a hand over his shaved head.

"Now where's my money?" Latch said.

Bullies, the lot of them, Joe thought. "I don't have it."

"What are you playing at, Joe? I mean, do you actually want to die?"

Joe spat blood. "I have something better. A stash."

Perhaps the dogs would take care of them. Maybe Latch and his lackeys were more to their taste. It was a gamble, but what did Joe have to lose? Latch might not take the bait...

"A stash?" Latch said dubiously.

"It's worth three times as much. You can just take it."

Latch thought about that for a moment. "Where is it?"

"I'll take you there right now," Joe said, struggling not to reveal his excitement. "I'll show you exactly where it is."

Latch picked Joe up by the scruff of his shirt collar, pressed him against the wall. Holding him up with one hand, Latch pulled out a flick knife. The blade sprung open. He pressed the sharp edge of the blade against Joe's neck.

"Lead the way."

One of the men retrieved the wire cutters and torches from the back of the car. "Do you want me to get the hammer?" he said.

"No," Latch said, grinning at Joe. "I've got the knife."

The three of them laughed.

They followed Joe to the wire gate and cut their way through. With the moon lighting a path, Joe led them to the steel stairway at the side of the building. It was probably midnight by now; Joe couldn't be sure. He started to make his way up the stairs when Latch grabbed him by the shoulder.

"Better not be playing games," he warned.

Joe nodded. Latch released him. When Joe reached the door on the second floor, he half expected it to be locked. That would be just his luck.

Thankfully, it wasn't.

"Down the hallway," he said. "There's a stairway. It's up there."

They switched on their torches. The crunch of debris under their feet echoed in the silence. The beams of torchlight flickered this way and that as they followed.

"Smells like piss and shit in here," one of them said.

"Shut the fuck up and watch where you're going," Latch said.

"Up here," Joe said when they got to the stairs.

But something wasn't right; he could not smell that wet-fur stink. It should have been overpowering by now, especially once he reached the top of the stairs, where he listened keenly with bated breath. There was only the sound of the wind. The place felt empty.

"Where now?" said Latch, as they came to stand at his side.

"Over here."

They followed him inside the room, the beams of torchlight searching the desolate interior before converging on Joe.

Latch said, "Where is this stash of yours?"

Joe winced from the brightness of the torches.

"Where is it?" Latch demanded.

Joe scanned the shadows, hoping for a last-minute reprieve.

But they were right, the air smelled only of piss and shit. He had failed. This was not the offering the dingo had wanted.

Latch came to stand face to face with Joe. His breath stank of cigarettes and garlic. "I don't get it. What the fuck are you up to?" His eyes looked around at the ruins. "I guess this is a good place for you to die, is that it?"

Joe held his ground. The dogs had abandoned him but, like the dingo, he was determined to be strong. Dead or alive, this would be his last stand—this forgotten, broken place of concrete and shadows, lit only by the phantom light of the moon. "Fuck you, Latch."

He relished the look of surprise in Latch's eyes.

Latch scowled like he'd eaten something sour, and thrust the knife deep into Joe's chest, pushing it up, twisting, and then wrenching it out. Joe's feet buckled beneath him. He fell to his knees, blood spreading across his shirt, oozing down his jeans.

They ran. Joe crawled on all fours to a wall and slumped against it, heart thumping loudly in his ears as the blood poured out of him. Their footsteps receded until he was alone with the darkness. He lay there gasping for air, too weak to feel anything, growing weaker with every heartbeat. His blood was hot and sticky but he felt icy cold.

There was no pain. He remembered Latch's surprised face. He would have laughed if he'd had the energy.

He waited for death as his blood drained away, his breath growing rapid and shallow. He tried to straighten up a little, to look a bit more dignified, but he couldn't feel his legs anymore and his arms weighed a tonne.

"Of course I can play football," he moaned in his delirium. "I can play very well."

The darkness throbbed. He caught movement at the corner of his eye and turned to face the doorway where the dingo emerged.

Joe struggled to keep his eyes open. "There you are." He groaned. "You should have seen me stand up for myself... I really told them, I did."

The dogs gathered around him, the sound of their panting

filling the silence. Their earthy smell embraced him like a soiled, warm blanket.

Steadily, his breathing become one with their panting. His whole body writhed and shuddered. Bones snapped, limbs stretched, his mouth elongated and teeth extended, shirt and pants tearing under the strain.

From the bloody shreds he rose, trembling unsteadily on all fours, falling and rising, struggling for balance.

The dogs waited patiently until he found his feet.

They licked the blood from his sleek black coat as he inhaled the warmth of their presence. They nudged him with their snouts, their bodies drawing him into their midst. He was a part of the pack; he belonged to them now. They moved into the shadows, becoming one with the darkness, and Joe followed.

THE SEASIDE

ROBERT MAMMONE

It might have more serial killers than God intended, Morton thought, as he shifted his bulk into a more comfortable position. But South Australia in summer more than made up for it in the glory of its coastline.

The sun beat down out of a copper-blue sky, sending light rippling across the waters of Shellharbour Bay. A light breeze danced across those waters, waves riffling against the current. Sailboarders raced each other, the riders laughing and waving as they dodged and danced around children who splashed about while precariously perched on inflatable toys. The golden sands of the Shellharbour Beach positively heaved with the half-naked bodies of sun lovers of all ages, the smell of sunscreen and coconut oil wafting into the restaurant's open windows.

Inside that restaurant, itself sitting on a slight rise across the road from the beach, Morton looked down at the feast laid before him. Had he been so inclined, Morton might've marched straight into the bustling kitchen and kissed the head chef soundly on the lips. Morton didn't believe he was a greedy man; indeed, he would take umbrage at the very idea if it was suggested to him. But there was no way he would've shared this delightful repast.

Calamari piled amidst lemon chunks. A bowl full of steamed mussels, slightly opened, teasing at the delights within. Whole succulent prawns waiting to be dunked into a tureen of cocktail sauce. And the *pièce de résistance*, an entire lobster, halved, smothered in a creamy sauce that sent Morton into shivers of expectation—as it would, surely, with anyone on the planet. His mouth watering, spoiled for choice and unassailably greedy, Morton, after a moment's pleasurable indecision, plucked a calamari ring from the golden pile and took a bite. His eyes closed for a moment as pure rapture swelled within him. A little moan of pleasure escaped his chewing mouth.

A swelling hubbub outside drew Morton's reluctant attention from the orgy of food spread in front of him. His eyes opened in astonishment. A trawler, paintwork peeling in places, was softly grounding itself on the Shellharbour Beach's golden sands. Holding the half piece of calamari between two sweaty fingers, Morton chewed thoughtfully, trying to understand what he was seeing.

A crowd of people on the beach, diverted from their efforts to burn their skin to a lovely shaded crispness, were gathering around the boat. From his vantage point, Morton couldn't see any sign of the crew, which heaped curiosity on curiosity. The block and tackle hanging from the crane at the stern of the trawler twisted in the breeze, the shriek of rubbing metal making goosebumps ripple across the exposed skin of his arms.

An elderly woman sitting at a table next to Morton's had half-risen from her seat. "I wonder where the crew is."

He glanced at her. Somehow a peeled plump prawn, drenched in cocktail sauce, had appeared in his hand. Sauce dripped on the pristine white tablecloth. Morton popped the prawn into his mouth. "Probably having a nap," he mumbled around his mouthful of food.

The woman, testament to what decades of sun worship could do to human skin, looked down her weathered nose at him as if he was some sort of fool. "A *nap?*" Her voice dripped with sarcasm.

Morton shrugged and commenced shovelling forkfuls of wonderfully tender lobster meat into his mouth. He had food to eat—wherever the crew were, it was of no concern to him.

Until it became so.

Halfway through devouring the lobster, with creamy sauce running down his chin, he glanced up, like a whale breaching the surface of the ocean to replenish its oxygen supply. The trawler glittered. For a long moment, as his working jaws slowed to a halt, Morton couldn't fully comprehend what he was seeing.

Brilliant points of light sparkled over the trawler's hull, deck and superstructure. The lights rippled like the sunlight dancing upon the harbour waters. An excited murmur similarly rippled through the watchers crowding around the trawler. Attracted by the sight, tourists on the footpath drifted across the stretch of bitumen separating the shops from the beach, ignoring the honking horns of exasperated drivers.

Sudden cries of dismay rose. Morton's nose wrinkled. A reek, as born of the abyssal depths of the ocean, rolled into the restaurant. His stomach lurched and suddenly the food arrayed before him had all the appeal of a blocked toilet. The woman who had spoken tartly to him retched, her thin shoulders heaving as a chunky stream filled her plate. Morton closed his eyes and felt vomit fill his throat.

That was when the screaming began.

His eyes flew open. All thoughts of vomiting fled. He saw a young girl, lifted by a man who appeared to be her father, reach out to touch the scintillating mass on the trawler's tilted hull. It took seconds before Morton fully processed what he saw and by that time, the child was already dead.

Like worker ants marching along a branch, the twinkling jewels moved from the hull and up her arm. Her laughter suddenly turned to chilling screams as her flesh was scythed away, blood flying as the flayed skin vanished, exposing bone. While the disintegration continued up the length of her arm, the people watching turned in abject horror and began fighting their way through the press behind.

Morton, all thought of food gone, rose from his chair, his bulging stomach lifting his plate until it fell back onto the table with a clatter of cutlery. The child's head was a mass of jewelled creatures and when they left, leaving only shreds of skin over a gore-streaked skull, Morton at last vomited.

"**P**retty," Samantha said, squirming in her father's hands as she reached out to touch the seething mass of jewelled crabs on the beached trawler. It would be the last, coherent sound that would issue from her mouth.

Derek and Jill and their seven-year-old daughter Samantha were having the time of their lives. A week away from the city and all its stresses and strains had put a smile on their faces and relieved some of the tension that many young families experience. Not even yesterday's earthquake—which had led to the beach being evacuated while lifeguards nervously monitored the tsunami alert for an hour or two before announcing the beach safe—could dampen their enthusiasm. So, when Samantha had wanted to come down to the beach to build sandcastles, both Derek, who had begun entertaining fantasies of resigning from work and relocating to the coast, and Jill, who had caught the eye of a blond, insanely buff lifeguard earlier in the week and fervently wished to see him again, had wholeheartedly agreed.

By noon the beach was heaving. Amidst all the towels and lawn chairs and umbrellas, the little family found themselves a spot near the water. Derek wrestled with the umbrella, while Samantha pottered about with a plastic bucket and spade. Jill said airily she was going for a walk to stretch her legs and followed a path that took her past the lifeguard tower and a certain lifeguard. And while this happy little family enjoyed their time on the beach, unbeknownst to them and the others nearby, a trawler with peeling paint along her sides drifted towards the shore.

It was Samantha who saw it first. She had wandered up to the water's edge, intent on filling her bucket so she could pour the contents into the moat dug around the elaborate sandcastle she had constructed, when a shadow stretched out for her. The momentary chill brought her up short. Standing in its shadow, she watched the black shape come closer. Normally a happy child who had never had a nightmare, a sudden freezing cold gripped Samantha to her very marrow. As fright oozed its way through her, the shocking experience left her mouth dry and heart thudding. Overcome, she stumbled back a pace or two before crying out, her voice a strange, fluting shriek.

Derek was by her side in an instant, sweat prickling his skin.

He was a good father; at least, that's what he thought of himself. His daughter was the apple of his eye, proof that a dissolute youth could be redeemed. A moment of anger at his wife's absence suffused him, vanishing almost as quickly when he gathered Samantha into his arms. He felt the goosebumps stippling her arms and legs as she clung to him, her face buried in his shoulder.

"Hey, hey," he murmured, breathing into her ear. "Everything's okay, Sammy."

She lifted her head and stared at him with tear-filled eyes. Now her father was here, the icy fear that had gripped her began to melt. She wiped at her face with a sand-crusted hand, then looked hesitantly over her shoulder. "Why's the boat here?"

"Good question." Derek watched the trawler heel over slightly. The vessel looked old; paint peeling over warped wooden timbers, metal fittings touched red with rust, barnacles clustering tightly across the exposed hull. "A better question might be: *where's the crew?*"

Derek glanced to his right. An old man, his skin speckled and flecked by decades in the sun, stood to one side, wearing nothing but a pair of Speedos. His forehead, already wrinkled, was further creased by puzzlement. Derek looked back at the boat. He felt a sudden sense of unease. What had been the name of the boat that had so enraptured him as a boy when he'd read about it?

"*Mary* something," he said to himself.

"*Marie Celeste*, I think you mean." His new companion regarded him from beneath bushy white eyebrows. "You'd reckon the crew would be on deck by now. I wonder where they've got to."

Despite his better instincts, Derek moved forward. Samantha had calmed down. No longer did she cling to him; she now sat in his arms, curiosity making her face come alive. The hubbub from the crowd had only grown louder, and Derek saw several of the lifeguards picking their way through, their orange caps vivid in the noon sun. He saw Jill's blonde hair blazing as she followed closely behind the last of the lifeguards, some young gun with a disarming smile that made Derek immediately suspicious.

A sudden startled shout from someone close to the trawler

caught Derek's attention. The watchers clustered behind Derek stepped away, forcing a ripple effect which packed tight the people gathered on the sand.

A mingled stench, of the ocean's briny depths and the rot of dead fish, washed over the beach. People gagged, and more than one heaved their lunch onto the sand. Derek felt the bile rise, burning into his throat. As soon as it came, the stench vanished, replaced by a faint noise, like the rustling sound cellophane makes when it is crushed. The noise grew louder, transforming into a crunching and crackling. Derek was about to turn and start pushing his way through the crowd when he saw a shine of scintillating lights sweep up and over the edge of the canted deck and begin creeping down the hull. Attracted by the lights, the crowd pressed closer towards the trawler. Muttered comments turned into gasps of surprise as the moving lights resolved into thousands of crabs.

"Pretty." Giggling, Samantha reached out to touch the nearest tiny, exquisitely jewelled crab.

Dead eyes on tiny stalks quivered. Derek felt a deepening unease as the crab lifted its claws above its head, pincers clacking. All around him, Derek heard the murmuring of the crowd begin to spike.

And then Samantha screamed.

Uncomprehending, Derek blinked as the blood spattered his face. Somewhere close, Jill too was screaming. In his suddenly slippery arms, Samantha writhed and convulsed as a winking tide of crabs swept over her. Derek saw what was happening to his baby girl, and his mind broke. Desperate shrieking filled the air around him. His feet sank deeper into the blood-drenched sand. The day darkened and his mind teetered and finally snapped as the remains of his daughter—blood-slick bones and shredded flesh and a yawning skull—collapsed into his arms. He opened his mouth to scream and something small and wriggling fell in.

"Did you hear that?" Simon said.

Elizabeth, one of several oceanographers on board, turned

away from the monitors in front of her, a question in her eyes. A bell clanged as the boat rocked from side to side. The motors thumped while the skipper held course just outside the harbour's mouth.

"Hear what?" she said.

"Noise. From the beach."

She shook her head and returned her gaze to the screen. "We're a kilometre from shore, Simon. I doubt you heard anything of the sort. Come have a look at this, will you?"

Standing on deck at the top of the stairs, Simon stared at the beach for a few seconds longer. There were gulls hovering over a craft that had seemed to have grounded on the sand. Masses of people had converged nearby, though there seemed to be movement now…

"Simon? The data coming back from the MROV is really strange."

Reluctantly, Simon glanced to the cabin below. As chief marine biochemist, by rights he should be sitting with Elizabeth, monitoring the information coming through. But the stifling atmosphere, despite the air conditioning straining to keep the servers from overheating, had driven him up top. Around him, a half-dozen men and women were focused on their tasks, monitoring the instruments controlling the Miniature Remotely Operated Vehicle, or unreeling a number of hydrophones into the water. The head of mission, Professor Henry Dirkin, stood at the stern, contemplating the placid ocean. The letters CSIRO were painted on the superstructure, with the seal of the Commonwealth positioned beside it.

Simon went below deck into the dim cabin, the largest space in the boat, with its monitors mounted on every wall. Multiple sensor arrays aboard the MROV fed images to the six monitors that Elizabeth raptly observed. Sonar, even infrared images, were all displayed in high resolution.

"What you got?" Simon said, sliding into a chair next to Elizabeth. Sweat had turned his hair lank.

"'Got'? You sure you earned that degree?"

"Don't be a snob," Simon said. He looked at the monitor

directly in front of Elizabeth. "That...can't be right."

"No," Elizabeth said, suddenly serious. "It can't. And yet..."

Simon checked the readout cascading down the side of the monitor. "Temperature has fallen. Salinity levels too. Wait. Is it saying that's fresh water?" He glanced at his colleague, brow furrowed. "How? That's—"

"Not right. But it is. I've been over these numbers for the last fifteen minutes. The salinity levels in the immediate vicinity off the continental shelf has reduced by ten per cent. The water is coming from beneath the Earth's crust. And it's spreading."

Simon whistled. "Gigalitres of fresh water?"

"I know. Extraordinary."

The boat heaved and rolled. Loose paperwork went flying. Distant shouts from the deck echoed down the stairwell. The engines coughed and went silent. The lighting dimmed further.

"That had better not be the tsunami the models predicted but didn't arrive," Simon said, picking himself up off the floor.

Wild-eyed, Elizabeth stared at the screens. Several had gone offline, and only the screen displaying the infrared imaging remained live, bathing her face bloody.

"We'd be two kilometres inland by now if it was," Elizabeth said. She swallowed. "Professor Dirkin never came up with a good reason why an earthquake measuring eight-point-two at a depth of thirty-five kilometres never generated any wave motion."

"There *is* no good reason," Simon said quietly. The monitors that had gone offline flickered. He thought he saw something on one of them, but a final burst of static obliterated it. "Anything from the MROV?"

Tapping at a keyboard, Elizabeth shook her head. "All the sensors other than the infrared are down. It's like they were shorted out. Which doesn't make any..."

"Sense," Simon offered, smiling briefly. "None of this does."

A sudden, querulous voice from the top of the steps. "Simon? Get up here with those bloody binoculars. Something is happening onshore. Tell me what it is."

"Sure thing, Professor," Simon called out. He looked at

Elizabeth. "Just a rogue wave, that's all." She refused to look him in the eye.

Tentatively, as if he expected the floor to pitch and yaw again, Simon left the control room and walked the short distance to his cabin. Inside, amidst the tumult of upended belongings, he grabbed the binocular case and hurried back along the corridor, almost falling up the steps in his haste to reach the deck. Anxiety tightened his stomach. All around the boat, the ocean was glassily smooth, the peace after the roiling waves eerie. Members of the team stood by the railing, some anxiously looking towards the horizon, while others faced the shore.

"Get over here," Dirkin called, hat askew, the sun shining off his sweaty, balding head.

Simon had never seen the professor in this state of heightened anxiety—usually the academic was the pillar of sobriety and slightly aloof disinterest. Leaning against the railing beside the older man, Simon hastily discarded the binocular case and trained the glasses on the shore. He fiddled with the focus for a few seconds, then he went still.

"Holy Jesus Christ." Simon felt his face go cold as the blood drained from it. His sister was a big fan of the Dutch painter, Hieronymus Bosch. She had put up posters of some of his most famous works on the wall of the bedroom they shared when they were younger. What Simon saw on the beach made Bosch's visions of Hell positively quaint.

Simon could only process the horror on the beach as a series of blood-stained, static images. A hundred thousand points of light failed to hide the white bone shockingly exposed against the deep, deep red that stained everything. Confused heaps of flesh. Figures clutching each other. Figures buried beneath a frozen mound of chitinous bodies. Vehicles entangled, the starred glass splashed with gore. A woman running on the stumps of her legs, tattered flesh trailing behind. A baby carriage carpeted with thousands of tiny, murderous crabs.

The binoculars dropped from his nerveless fingers. Simon gasped for breath, having held it unheedingly for a minute. His vision blurred and starbursts exploded across it. He felt a hand grabbing and shaking his shoulder.

"Simon? Simon!"

He turned, aware his face was slack with shock.

Elizabeth stepped back, fear sparking in her eyes. "What's going on?"

Simon stared at her, uncomprehending. Then a sound like a horn blowing to ring in the Apocalypse exploded around them. Looking over Elizabeth's shoulder, Simon felt a visceral thrill of terror race through him. He saw the vitality drain from Elizabeth's eyes. The muscles in her face loosened and paled, leaving grey flesh sagging from the bones. Dirkin vented an inarticulate cry, then collapsed shuddering on the deck. As the rest of the crew began screaming, an unholy reek washed over the boat. With it came a shadow, turning day into night. In that grim twilight, Simon tried to understand the mountain of cascading water that had appeared off the boat's starboard bow, several kilometres away, even as his mind began to shatter.

An immense, glistening carapace heaved itself out of the ocean. Thick chunks of primordial ooze slid from it, sending up vast plumes of water as they struck the ocean surface. Twisted knots of barnacles gave the carapace a hunchbacked appearance that only deepened its sinister aspect. A pair of bulbous and dead black eyes, resting atop twitching stalks, watched the world. There was a groan, and huge pincers on either side of the carapace emerged from the water, rising higher and higher until they towered above the creature's body.

Dimly, Simon heard Elizabeth screaming. Thousands of points of light moved across the creature's carapace, an endlessly writhing carpet of life that fell into the sea. A sound, like static, reached the stunned observers on the boat—the endless clacking of millions and millions of claws seeking to satisfy tiny, hungry mouths. And then the creature's many jointed legs lurched into life and the creature began to sweep towards the shore, its fringed mouth opening in readiness to feed.

HELL GULLY

PAULINE YATES

I just booked a ticket back to America in a body bag. The Australian team of soldiers I'm tracking turns out to be shadows cast from a clump of stunted wattle trees, and what I thought was their combat uniform camouflage pattern is the colour of the foliage. Even the branches look like rifles slung over shoulders. How the hell I stuffed this up, I don't know, but now I have the fun job of telling my team we'll be sleeping on the dirt beneath a blanket of stars instead of peeling off our sweaty socks and downing beers at base camp.

"As sure as shit, the sun'll go down," Pollock says, rolling the stalk of grass he's chewing to the other side of his mouth.

His war-hungry eyes lock on the shadows too, but his snarky comment suggests he knows I've screwed up, and he's waiting for the fallout. I peer through my riflescope and scan the area for movement. The surrounding landscape is as still as the aerial map we studied before setting out at sunup. Gritting my teeth, I lower my rifle and face Jarvis, Benson and Lenny, who crouch in the scrub behind me. If I approach this like ripping off a plaster bandage, the pain will be sharp but short.

"I lost them, boys. I don't know which way they went."

Weary heads jerk up. If dirty looks were bullets, I'd be dead.

Jarvis spits at the ground. "If we've been tailing another fucking kangaroo, I'll kill you."

I flinch. The kangaroo was my first error. The noise it had made while jumping through the undergrowth sounded like radio crackle. I'd led my team through the scrub for *three hours* thinking it was the Australian team. I'll never live this day down —

"Fuck!" Pain, equivalent to an electric shock, travels through my finger and races up my arm. Dropping my rifle, I clutch my hand. An ant the length of my knuckle has its mandibles hooked into my flesh. I flick it off, revealing a puncture wound from its stinger.

Pollock sucks the grass into his mouth, then spits it out with a glob of saliva. "Congratulations, newbie. You just gave away our position."

"Who gives a fuck?"

"Who gives a fuck, *Sarge*," Pollock warns, eyeballing me for insolence.

Biting back a retort about what he can do with his sergeant badge, I clench my hand and try to squeeze the pain away. It doesn't help. A violent, venom-fuelled throb pumps through my arm and makes my heart pound for mercy, for all the fucking good that does.

Pollock stands and shoulders his rifle. "Suck it up, newbie. Worse things out here than jack jumper ants. The rest of you, take note."

Jarvis stands and scuffs his boot against the sun-baked ground. "You'd bleed to death in this place before that little fucker killed you." To ram home his point, he wipes blood off his neck from multiple lantana scratches.

"Jack jumper venom has a recorded history of anaphylaxis-related deaths," Pollock says. "You want to question the stats? Be my guest and stick your head in a nest."

Benson sneers. "Stick Billy's head in, too, while you're at it. Might improve his eyesight."

"Shut it, Benson." Spitting on my finger, I rub the itchy, throbbing bite. If I was allergic to the venom, my throat would have constricted by now. I'm still breathing, but geez, this bite packed a punch. My heart's still pounding from the shock.

"Alright, newbie," Pollock says. "When you've finished sucking your thumb, what say you get us back on track before we lose light? I don't fancy spending the night out here with you miserable sons-of-bitches."

Picking up my rifle, I push through the lantana and hurry ahead of my team. I hate how Sarge calls me *newbie*. Sure, I've only been with the U.S. Army for six weeks, but except for Sarge, none of us has been to Australia before or taken part in the annual friendly "war games" held between our countries. After we jetted into the Townsville RAAF base, they sent half of our platoon to Rowes Bay for water warfare exercises. The other half, which includes my team, took a two-hour bus ride southwest to a rural region near Granite Vale to undertake "environment observation" exercises.

When we divvied up our sectors, our team drew the short straw and we're trekking through a zone our Aussie comrades jokingly call "Hell Gully". It's living up to its nickname. Running between two heavily-timbered steep escarpments, it's clogged with wattle, lantana, and a tangle of spiky vines I can't identify, although that's what we're supposed to do—identify. We're all covered in scratches from being whipped by thorny branches. And the heat is stifling, even with the sun going down. The predicted thirty-five degrees feels like fifty, and with no breeze, it's like walking in an oven.

A lone gum tree casts a scant patch of shade. Seeking respite from the burning sun, I stop and search for the Australian team. The last I saw them, they were heading toward the northern escarpment, but after my mistake with the shadows, they could be anywhere. Our objective is simple: track them to a mock hidden bunker and radio the coordinates back to base camp. That's it. No shooting. No fake casualties.

The objective is only a prop for the observation skill-builder exercise we're undertaking—to learn how to cope with unfamiliar climatic conditions, and label potentially hazardous plants and wildlife native to the foreign enemy's territory. I'm fast learning why Australia was the chosen venue for this exercise, but as designated team leader, thanks to an even shorter straw, I'm failing all aspects of this challenge. But I'm not quitting. I'll find the Australian team, and their bunker. I'll show Sarge I'm no newbie.

Tipping back my hat, I scowl at the trees on the northern escarpment. "Aussie bastards are probably sitting up there laughing at us."

"Better than shooting at us," Lenny says, sounding like he's got a sheet of sandpaper stuck to his tongue.

He's scrawny and bespectacled, with a crop of red hair and fair, freckled skin, so I'm surprised we're not aborting the exercise and carrying him back to base camp. Unlike Benson. His dark skin is perfect for the harsh Australian climate. He could stand in the sun all day without dropping sweat. Jarvis has a decent enough tan to protect him from sunburn, so he's coping okay. And Pollock is Pollock. Ten years our senior and seasoned with gunpowder, nothing fazes him. Or maybe his bored expression and snarky comments mask a secret desire to be anywhere but stuck in this gully with another bunch of greenhorns.

Jarvis pulls a canteen from his pack and shakes it. "I'm out. Who has water?"

"Piss in your bottle and drink that," Benson says.

"Fuck you." Jarvis rounds on Lenny. "Your canteen full?"

Lenny looks at the ground and shuffles his feet. "I got some left."

"Give it here."

If any of us needs water, it's Lenny. His face is so red you could fry an egg on it. Pulling out my canteen, I thrust it at Jarvis. "Here. Don't guzzle it."

Jarvis snatches the canteen but takes too long a drink. He hands it back near empty.

Seething, I shove the canteen into the side pouch of my backpack. "We'll top up at a creek. There'll be one around here somewhere."

Pollock laughs. "Fat chance of that, newbie."

Ignoring him, I look through my riflescope and search for greener vegetation that might lead us to water. Nothing. Just brown leaves wilting in the heat haze. Another jack jumper lands on my wrist. It looks at me. I mean, really *looks* at me. It tilts its black head, its enlarged eyes sizing me up as it gnashes orange, serrated-edged mandibles.

"Bite this, you motherfucker," I say. Flicking it into the dirt, I squash it with the butt of the rifle. The ant curls into a ball, its orange legs all a-tangle. Then it uncurls and jumps into the grass. "Bastard. Can't even kill 'em." I flex my fingers. The first sting still throbs and my whole arm aches. Sucking up the pain, I grip my rifle and—

Whack.

An electric zap shoots through my other hand.

"Fuck, fuck!" I slam my hand against my leg, knocking off another ant.

Jarvis sniggers. "Got a taste for you now, newbie. They gotta eat something out here."

Seething, I clench my hand. "They'll be feasting on your rotting flesh if you don't shut your mouth."

"Must be a nest nearby," Lenny says, looking all around us. "Yeah, look. There."

He points to a mound of orange dirt half a foot high with a hole the size of my fist in the top. Jack jumpers twice the size as the one that bit me guard the entrance to the nest.

Lenny leans down for a closer look. "Jesus. Look at the size of these things. They'd strip a carcass clean down to the bone."

He pulls out a pocket notebook and pen, and scribbles a description. He's recorded details about everything we've seen today, but I don't know why he bothers. None of us will forget anything we've encountered, especially the lantana and that damn kangaroo. But I make a mental note to tell him how easy it is to mistake shadows cast from wattle trees for the enemy.

"Let's make sure it's not our carcasses they're chewing on," Pollock says. "Newbie, get us out of here before I shove your butt down that hole."

Swearing beneath my breath, I shoulder my rifle and continue through the gully. Now that I know what the nest looks like, I see orange mounds everywhere. All have a large entrance hole. All are guarded by jack jumpers.

"Worse than walking through a minefield," I say, stepping around a nest swarming with ants. "Can you imagine getting bit by...holy shit!"

I jerk to a standstill. On the ground in front of me is a brown snake with its head up like a periscope. Three meters long, its burnished scales shimmer on a body as thick as my arm.

"Everyone, keep real still now," Pollock says. "Snakes have a short memory span. You don't move, they'll forget you're here and move on."

Bullshit. Like that jack jumper, this snake has its eyes locked on me. He's not going anywhere.

"What snake is it?" Lenny whispers.

I hope he doesn't pull out his damn notebook. One move from anyone and I'm dead.

"Eastern Brown." Pollock's low, tight response highlights the gravity of this situation. "Second deadliest snake in the world."

"Bugger that," Benson says, raising his rifle.

Detecting movement, the snake strikes. Its fangs hit my boot. Then a bullet rips through the snake's body. Flung backward, the snake writhes on the ground, twisting its body around its shredded flesh until it lies still.

"Goddammit, Benson," Pollock says. "Newbie, you bit?"

"I don't think so." Puncture marks on the top of my boot glisten with venom, but the thick leather must have prevented the snake's fangs from penetrating my foot because I felt nothing. Or maybe I felt nothing because I'm running high on adrenaline and anything other than a jack jumper bite would feel like a pinprick.

"Don't think so?" Pollock says. "Know so. Sit your butt down and pull that boot off."

I drop faster than if he'd said to give him fifty. And land on top of the jack jumper nest.

Ants jump onto my hands and wrists, latch onto my skin with their vicious mandibles, and plunge their stingers into my flesh—

It's like being stabbed with hot knitting needles. Violent throbs travel up my arms, turning my muscles to jelly. The skin around each bite prickles with itchy heat. Another ant jumps onto my neck and stings my throat. Then another stings my ear.

Frazzled from the excruciating pain, I roll off the nest and flap my hands at the ants to brush them off. Another zap to my neck makes my lips tingle. Fearing my throat will constrict, I suck in what I hope isn't my last breath, while inside my chest, my heart bashes against my ribcage in protest at the amount of venom leaching into its chambers.

"Drag him clear," Pollock yells. "Get those ants off him. Benson, what the fuck are you doing? Get your sorry ass over here and help."

Benson's kicking in the entrance to the nest, but ants jump onto his boots. Panicking, he stamps his feet and leaps back, crashing into a white-faced Lenny, who stands frozen in shock, mouth agape. Jarvis swears and strips off his belt, then lunges for my leg and wraps the belt around my calf. Confused, I kick him away, but Pollock throws himself across my waist and pins me to the ground.

"Hold still, newbie," he says. "The more you thrash, the faster the snake venom will reach your heart." He glares at Jarvis, who hovers over us, the belt dangling from his hand. "What the hell are you doing? Get that belt lashed around his leg."

Holy hell. I feel it, the snake venom. It's like dry ice slithering through my veins, leaving my limb numb. What will happen when it hits the jumper jack venom in my blood? Whatever the stats are for that deadly concoction, I don't want to find out.

I take a deep breath and force myself to remain calm. My heart refuses to cooperate. It pounds like it's chased by a sniper with their rifle locked and loaded, and that pumps the snake venom. Jarvis tightens the belt around my calf, but he applied the tourniquet too late. The snake venom mixes with the jumper jack venom and I'm flattened by a ripping pain through my chest. Eyes wide, I watch my heart burst through my ribs and drift toward the blazing sun, blood dripping from a torn aorta.

Pollock punches the hole in my chest, causing starbursts of images to flash across my vision—a kangaroo hopping through the undergrowth, crushing leaves; radio crackle. The sun sinks toward the horizon. The temperature drops, freezing the hot breeze blowing into my mouth.

"Radio for an evac, requesting air evac from coordinates 37W... cardiac arrest...snake bite...multiple jack jumper stings..."

Shadows loom over me, not wattle trees, not branches.

"...E.T.A. Twenty minutes..."

Rifles slung over shoulders, camouflage pattern uniforms.

"…he doesn't have twenty minutes…"

The shadows beckon me to follow.

"Got no pulse, sir, no pulse…"

They head toward the trees on the northern escarpment.

"Goddammit, newbie, don't you quit on me."

I see them, Sarge. I know which way to go. I won't lose them again.

MYIASIS

J.M. MERRYT

Leanne Djikstra had never liked being told what to do, and being ordered to isolate herself from others had not changed that. She never let obstacles like rules get between her and what she craved. She was prepared to lie, smuggle, and steal if the result was the fulfillment of her desires. Right now, she wanted wild mushrooms.

Venturing out early one morning, Leanne snuck from the back door of her little townhouse and into the woods. Her street was banded with a thicket of gum trees nearly crowded out by feral growth, all thornbushes and blackberries. Beyond the nature strip, a paddock stretched up a steep hill. In truth, Leanne had been ordered to stay home, but she wasn't expecting a visit from the police for a few hours and the freedom to go wherever she liked was her birthright. Leanne stifled a cough and carried on, navigating a drainage ditch partially hidden by long grass.

A tall woman, her stride was long, so soon the trees were far behind her. It was still dark, but Leanne could see enough by the torch of her phone. Minutes passed. As if reluctant, the sun slowly dragged itself into the sky, offering only a sickly half-light that sketched out a rough outline of the terrain. After a while, Leanne could put her phone away.

Three weeks of down-time had left her desperate for company, but only if it was company that would not disagree with her. Leanne had no patience for dissent. Leanne loved being the centre of attention, particularly when she was lavished with gifts and complimentary wine. Lately, she had resorted to the internet, seeking out a suitable echo chamber. Trawling through website after website, Leanne had stumbled upon a group obsessed with wild foraging. Equal parts competitive and cooperative, they traded tips on where the best truffles could be found, and which laneways concealed the best wild fennel.

How perfect.

Usually, Leanne travelled the world as a food critic, cooking whenever she had the chance. A gourmet, she delighted in trying new things. Her life, so recently curtailed, had revolved around wine tasting at local vineyards, sampling delicacies at degustation feasts, and reviewing the trendiest microbrews. Now, she ate whatever the government sent her in their food parcels; bland pap that she would usually wrinkle her nose at. How she missed her black *densuke* watermelons and her *kopi luwak* coffee—Leanne craved novelty and luxury.

After reading a blog post by an avid wild forager, Leanne had realised that the paddock next door was a prime location for mushroom picking. Dimly, she recalled seeing mushrooms on top of the hill when she'd snuck up there to get drunk a few weeks earlier. Leanne had kept silent about her hunch, determined to keep the best mushrooms to herself. No illness or police orders would stop her from getting there first.

Now, feeling smug, Leanne peered at the top of the hill and rolled up her sleeves.

It had always been difficult—deciding whether to publish a review when she found a gem of a restaurant, caught between wanting to share it with the world and the urge to keep it all to herself, hoarding knowledge like a dragon on a bed of gemstones. She had decided against sharing her plans to go foraging, fearing that someone might report her to the authorities, or worse— pick the mushrooms first. Leanne was unwilling to risk losing something she felt was rightfully hers.

A high chain-link fence encircled the hill beyond the trees. It was dark with old rust and topped with barbed wire. Big signs with high-contrast, red-on-white lettering proclaimed the paddock as private property and warned of consequences for trespassing. Her chest tight, Leanne paused for breath. A pair of wire snips hung loosely from one hand. Letting out a derisive snort, she cut a gap in the fence and slipped into the grassland beyond. A frisson of pleasure travelled up her spine and Leanne shivered, grinning.

There was something so endlessly appealing about breaking taboos.

The paddock encompassed the entire top of the hill. The barricades of bright silver on her left and right turned out to be water troughs lining the inside of the fence. A patch of gum trees perched on the top of the hill sat like hair pasted on the crown of an otherwise bald head. Cows lounged nearby, lazily chewing or else ambling about. They regarded Leanne with soft, curious eyes as she made her way up the slope. A few cows followed at a distance and Leanne hoped the farmer didn't own any bulls.

She stepped around the occasional cow pat, wrinkling her nose in distaste. Flies already buzzed around every fresh meal, voracious. At least she couldn't smell the reek of fresh shit, Leanne reflected, illness having so recently stripped her of her sense of smell.

A narrow dirt track crawled up the hill, gouged into being by the passage of tyres, and Leanne huffed and swore her way up the path. Once, she had to stop as the road twisted slightly around a cluster of rocks, and it was at that point that the cows lost interest, wandering off to do whatever it was that cows usually did.

Eventually, Leanne reached the knot of trees at the top and found what she'd snuck out of quarantine for: clusters of precious, fat, white mushrooms. They sat in rings under the trees. Someone had cleared away the undergrowth and the mushrooms had flourished. Small, slightly squarish and perfectly formed. Beautiful. The sight of the mushrooms made her mouth water. Leanne dragged a cloth bag out of her coat pocket. So plentiful were the mushrooms, it was easy for her to pick her fill.

Using a knife, Leanne cut each mushroom free of its stalk, taking no notice of how the fungal flesh stained her fingertips canary-yellow with each cut. She couldn't perceive the gasoline odour rising off the fairy ring. Settling against a tree, Leanne sighed, content, and popped a whole mushroom into her mouth, and then another. She reflected how she'd had ample time to learn about how mushrooms picked straight from the field could be so much healthier than the ones she saw wrapped in cellophane in supermarket fridges. Leanne peered into the cloth bag, thinking how delicious the rest of her harvest would be, sautéed with garlic and parsley. Satisfied, she drifted off to sleep.

Nausea roused her an hour later. Leanne doubled over and retched, her stomach cramping. Sweat beaded on her face, and she stumbled to her feet. Dizziness, sharp and disorientating, contorted the landscape and Leanne panicked. She hurried down the hill. When she reached the rocks that she had nimbly stepped around on her way up, Leanne tripped. Her bag slipped out of her grasp and tumbled down the hill, mushrooms spilling out and rolling along the path. Leanne scrambled to gather up her harvest, stuffing the mushrooms back into the bag. All care was forgotten in her haste.

Swaying, Leanne fell flat on her face. The pressure on her stomach was enough to make her sick. Drowsiness overtook her and she passed out. She lay there, braced on her elbows, with her mouth hanging open. This time, so close to the cows' waste, and stinking of vomit and foul-smelling mushrooms, Leanne attracted the attention of the flies. One after another, they crawled into her mouth. Reflexive, Leanne coughed but the flies were unbothered, greedy for such a tempting feast and a home for their young.

Hours later, when Leanne awoke once more, it was because of a sharp pain in her throat. The feel of something hatching, of a newborn *something* burrowing into her flesh. Leanne flinched into a sitting position, swore, and half-crawled the rest of the way down the hill. With massive effort, she hauled herself through the gap in the fence, skulking through the thicket that bordered her house. She glanced about for passing cars, leery of dog walkers or cyclists who might snitch on her.

Leanne sidled in through the back door, kicking off her shoes, and dumped the bag of mushrooms on the kitchen bench. A little cloth bundle on a slab of marble, the bag looked out of place in the kitchen, all razor-sharp modern lines and bright lights. Monochromatic and sterile, the kitchen often put visitors in mind of a morgue. Steadily, the mushrooms bled yellow blooms of bright poison, staining the plain beige cotton of the bag.

She hurried into the bathroom. Combing dirt out of her hair, Leanne regarded herself in the mirror. There were scratches across her forehead, fresh bruises blossoming along her jaw. Blood on her lower lip. She spat out a mouthful of gore and probed her gums with her tongue, in search of loose teeth. Leanne finally glanced down and gagged at the sight of her ruined coat—a technicolour splash of regurgitated food, cow shit, and fresh blood. She binned it, stripping off for a shower.

It was only when she was scrubbing her hair with a towel that Leanne started to feel more human, and it was at that point that the peace was broken by a knock on the door. Leanne wove her way through the house and opened the front door just enough to spy a masked police officer.

"Yes, I'm still here," Leanne sighed, exasperated.

"You didn't leave?" the cop asked, an eyebrow raised high. He shifted his weight onto one foot. He was taller than her, a copper-red beard half poking out from behind his face-mask.

Really, what could Leanne say? *Oh yes, officer. I left quarantine to go trespassing for the sake of what were probably poisonous mushrooms.* Yeah, right. Instead, she said, "Fell asleep." A practised liar, she had no trouble meeting his eyes.

The cop stared at her a moment longer, disbelieving but deciding not to press further. "Your quarantine ends in a week. I'll be back to check on you then."

"I'll count the hours," Leanne drawled, more sincere than she let on.

The cop snorted a laugh. He left.

Annoyed, Leanne sighed and locked the door.

The rest of the day passed in a blur of bad TV and trying to arrange food delivery. She spent much of her time on the toilet, her guts clenching and grumbling.

As night neared, Leanne found herself coughing more than earlier but she shrugged it off. She was ill; coughing was to be expected. Shivering under three blankets, she fell asleep on the couch, bathed in the blue glow of infomercials.

It wasn't until dawn when a pain in her throat roused her, sending her off the couch and into the bathroom. Leanne's throat hurt something awful. Sharp pinpricks of pain jabbed her oesophagus, like an embroidery needle ruthlessly pushed through tapestry. Her throat burned and she clawed at the sink as a coughing fit overtook her. Leanne gasped for air, tears blurring her vision, and she wondered if she'd have to go on one of those damned ventilators.

No, she decided. This was nothing vitamins couldn't fix. Hands shaking, she threw open the bathroom cabinet and chewed her way through a handful of multivitamins, a probiotic, and something with krill oil. Gasping, Leanne sat on the floor. She pressed her face to the edge of the bath, the cool porcelain soothing against her burning face.

The landline phone rang not long after 7am and Leanne mumbled her way through an obligatory meeting with Health Services. Yes, she was fine for food, no she didn't need financial aid—

"How are you feeling?" the nurse asked. "How are your symptoms?"

Leanne hesitated. The time she hadn't spent passed out and shivering had been full of coughing fits so bad her vision briefly went dark. Leanne convinced herself she could handle it. "I'm fine," she rasped, ignoring the feeling of a foreign object pressing against the inside of her throat. "I don't need help. Thanks, though." She coughed around gnawing pain, the sensation of internal writhing, and wondered if she needed a square meal.

Food was medicine, after all.

"Okay, that's great," the nurse chirped. "If your symptoms clear up by Friday, you'll be okay to leave isolation. I'll ring you back then. If you need help beforehand, please let us know."

Again, Leanne hesitated. "Yeah, sure. Bye," she said and hung up.

Breathing became difficult. The next day was spent gagging over the sink, and Leanne lost all interest in food. The contraband mushrooms rotted on the kitchen bench, forgotten.

Leanne clutched the wall for support as she stumbled between lounge room and bedroom, the world rolling back and forth like an endless tilt-a-whirl. Gasping for breath, Leanne turned the air conditioning on full blast and stripped to shorts and a tank top, feeling like her skin would somehow ignite the air around her.

The burning of her throat ever-present, Leanne tried to wash away the pain with glass after glass of water. But today...Leanne paused. Today, something was very definitely wriggling inside her throat. Earlier, she'd put it down to a muscle twitch, a nerve misfiring, but there was undeniably something squirming inside her. Panicking, Leanne grabbed a torch and ran to her bathroom. She opened her mouth wide and angled the light past her teeth.

She saw nothing but the rise and fall of her uvula as she breathed.

A wave of coughing struck her, and Leanne happened to shine the torch into her mouth as something small and white came up the back of her tongue. *When did I eat rice?* she wondered and spat into the sink.

A maggot, small and very much alive, wriggled across the porcelain bowl.

"What the fuck?" Leanne shrieked, recoiling. "It was on those mushrooms," she told herself. She dragged a hand through her hair, combing it away from her face. "I ate a maggot and that's why I was coughing, but I spat it out and I'm okay now. It was only one maggot." Well acquainted with the mental gymnastics of denial, Leanne wandered back to the lounge room and resisted the urge to call Health Services.

She. Did. Not. Need. Help.

She ran to the kitchen, tipping sideways and grabbing the

doorframe for support. Her eyes fell upon the bag, now sodden with rot. Gagging, Leanne dumped the whole thing in the bin, and set about scrubbing the benchtop clean. She worked for hours, thinking if she somehow removed all traces of the mushrooms from the house, everything would right itself.

Leanne spent the next few hours bent over a blue plastic bucket, spitting out maggots and gobbets of blood. Mesmerised, she watched the grubs wriggle towards her as if homesick. Too dizzy to move, Leanne began to hallucinate, convinced that the maggots grew to monstrous size. They crawled under her skin, visibly writhing inside the meat of her arms and legs, as they hollowed her out like borers attacking a plum tree. Ravenous, the maggots devoured her whole.

She woke up gasping, a flailing hand knocking the bucket which skittered across the room. She could feel something wriggling in her nostrils, mobile and starving. She cupped her hands under her nose and great clumps of maggots fell into her hands. Maggots had crawled into her sinuses, into her ears, up her nose, behind her eyes. Starving, they had gnawed their way into her brain. Leanne's vision went dark and thousands of wriggling off-white bodies filled her throat. Unable to muster a scream, she soon fell still.

The landline phone rang over and over, unanswered. The only other sound in the townhouse was the incessant buzzing of flies. Dozens of *Calliphora stygia* pupated, emerged as adults, and alighted on what remained of Leanne. A paradise of their own making, the flies set up a colony on the woman who had taken them home.

Her body was found a week later, after Leanne failed to answer the regulated number of phone calls from Health Services. Suspecting that Leanne had fled quarantine, the police turned up on her doorstep. Knocks turned into shouts, until a battering ram splintered the wood of her front door.

A cloud of flies poured out into the street, swiftly followed by a foul miasma of rotting flesh. The police gagged, overwhelmed by the roadkill stench of cadaverine. Chancing upon her corpse, one officer fled to the bathroom. Tripping over his own feet in his haste, he got as far as the hallway, where he was heartily sick.

Sprawled on the lounge room floor lay Leanne, her arms spread wide and her unseeing eyes staring at the ceiling, her mouth and throat solid with blowfly larvae, a halo of writhing maggots encircling her head.

No Frills Holiday

Geraldine Borella

Wednesday, 20th of January, 1999
Suvarnabhumi International Airport, Bangkok

Marc Rademaker jams his hands into his pockets and follows the slow line through Customs. His jacket hides lumps and bumps beneath a chambray button-up shirt, and he pulls the sides around. Thank Christ for the steady blast of air-conditioning. It's only a short layover in Bangkok, but any contact with Thai Customs is fraught with danger, and sweat equates to nervous tension which in turn tallies to guilt.

"Act natural, yeah?" Warren had said, helping him into the custom-made body vest back in Sydney. "Cool and calm. That way you won't draw attention to yourself." He filled the pockets, handling the goods with a tenderness contrary to character. "You'll be right once ya hit Amsterdam. I got a contact pickin' you up."

Marc had nodded, trying to look okay with it all, but now he wonders if he should've had the guts to back out there and then. But the money! Who could afford to refuse it? Sixteen little treasures worth twenty thousand each with a five percent cut. A few trips like this and he'd have enough to set up a bar in Bali, spend his days surfing. Fuck the suit and tie, and that accounting degree waiting like the Sword of Damocles at the end of his gap year. He'd have the resources to make his own way. Be his own man. Get out of cold, grey Brussels and find the *sun*.

He shuffles forward, the blonde woman in front reaching the

counter and handing over her passport. *Not long now.* He'll get through Customs and kick back in the lounge, grab an ice-cold Singha lager for his troubles. Maybe a plate of fish cakes too. The rest of the trip from here on in will be a breeze. At least that's what Warren said.

A step away from the counter, he turns to see a Customs officer scurry down the line, leading a sniffer dog. *Fuck!* The dog stops and sits next to Marc's backpack, which leans against his leg. Tail wagging, the dog stares, a silent surety pooling in liquid brown eyes.

Pointing at Marc and then at the backpack, the handler yells loud in Thai. Words blast in rapid machine-gun fire, syllables strung together, unknown yet clear in intent. Marc picks up his backpack and follows the handler to a stainless-steel bench in full view of the other passengers. *Jesus, couldn't we do this somewhere else?*

He's passed over to an officer who has lost his smile in some kind of personal war, and Marc's nerve falters. He reads the name on the guy's badge; it's written in English beneath Thai script: *Somchai Anuman.*

"*Sah wah dee khrap,*" says Marc and he bows his head. It's all the Thai he knows, aside from *please* and *thank you* and *excuse me.* "Here's my passport." He hands it over, trying to be helpful.

The officer flips through the pages, then checks the photo against Marc's face. Laying the passport down, he points at the backpack and then at the bench.

"You want me to put it up here?" Marc says, and the officer nods, jabbing his finger and repeating the motion. *Backpack. Bench. Backpack. Bench.* Marc hefts it up, then steps back. The officer, Somchai, points at the zip and nods at Marc. "Oh…you want me to unzip it? Sure, no problem."

Somchai gets Marc to remove his clothing from the backpack, along with his shoes, toiletry bag, MP3 player, box of condoms, his diary, pencils and sketchpad, depositing it all on the bench.

"You think there's something in here?" he asks.

"Drugs," says Somchai. "You have?"

Marc shakes his head. "No, no drugs. No way."

"But the dog detect it."

"Well I *had* some in there, but not now."

"You have before?"

"Yes. I had some in my backpack before, but not now. I didn't carry any into the country. I wouldn't."

Somchai nods but takes the backpack away, leaving Marc to stand there.

His leg jiggles and he glances around. His fellow passengers watch with interest, people he's shared a plane with for twelve hours. The family of four who sat in front stare, the youngest boy pointing. His mother pushes his arm down and shuffles him forward in the line, shushing him up. There's the chick who sat next to him, Sammy, a babe travelling to Paris to dance with the Moulin Rouge. He'd shown her Fastball's *The Way* and Elliot Smith's *Waltz #2* on the portable MP3 player Warren had given him—a Rio PMP300, cutting edge—and he'd even taught her some basic French. She'd dozed on his shoulder, damn it. But now she looks over, meets his gaze, frowns and turns away.

Announcements sound over the PA in Thai: something about London and Qantas Airways and a boarding time. Marc's heart races and sweat beads his upper lip. He wants to take off his jacket, but he can't. It'd be a dead giveaway. Sweat tracks down his spine and in-between his buttocks as he glances over to where Somchai took his backpack. He's talking with another officer, the two men staring back at Marc.

"Act cool, act cool," Marc whispers to himself.

Somchai returns and says, "Follow me please." He strides away, his black leather shoes clip-clopping against the tiled floor. Marc rushes to catch up. Glancing back, he sees his personal items still sitting on the bench in full view, waiting for his return. It's humiliating, dehumanising, frightening. Will he see any of his belongings again? What if someone steals his MP3 player? He turns away, facing front, not wanting to cause further trouble, and sucks in the anxiety rippling through his body.

Somchai leads him to an interview room and gestures for him to sit.

The room is small and stuffy. Marc can feel his face flush red and his temperature rise. He wipes sweat off his brow, pretending to brush his long fringe away, while Somchai picks up a phone and presses buttons. Somchai speaks while pulling out a pen and notepad. Then, resting the handset on the desk, he presses the speaker button.

"Hello, Marc?" says a female voice with an American accent. "I'm Kim, your interpreter. I need to inform you that, at this point in time, you've been detained for an interview."

"Oh, right, did they say why?"

"You've alerted the sniffer dog. They believe you may be carrying contraband."

"What, like drugs?"

"Yes."

Marc explains the reason for the smell of drugs in his backpack—he'd had a bag of pot stashed in there whilst travelling around Australia, but he doesn't have it anymore. Kim translates this to Somchai and then conveys his reply.

"They wish to investigate further, Marc. Take swabs and X-ray your bag. Somchai says you must remain in the room."

"I suppose I don't have a lot of choice, huh?"

"No, you don't, I'm afraid."

"What if I miss my connection?"

"Then they'll get you on a later flight."

Somchai takes Kim off speaker and talks to her via the handset. Hanging up, he stands and stares at Marc for quite some time. Marc holds his gaze—*only a guilty person would look away, right?*—until, with a snort, Somchai leaves.

Left alone, Marc sits, stews and swelters. He craves a drink. Water. Beer. Anything. The jacket needs to come off, the vest too. It restricts his breathing, makes him sit ramrod straight. He didn't think it'd be this difficult; Warren had sold him a different story altogether.

"It'll be easy," he'd said, in a cavalier tone. They'd been drinking schooners at a bar down at The Cross only a week ago. "No problem at all. Just remember to do what I told you on the plane and during layover." Warren had been particular about how the goods should be cared for, and Marc had done as asked. "You'll have no worries, and come away with a cool sixteen grand for your trouble. Easiest dough you'll ever make."

Right now, Marc wishes it was Warren facing the Thai Customs officials. Would he be quite so blasé sitting in the hotseat?

It's far too late to even think about, but he wished he'd asked more questions. Back then, he'd been hyper-focused on the contraband and the money, giving little thought to anything else since each individual ovoid represented a pure white parcel of gold. He sees now he was blinded—by the money, the goods and by Warren's entrepreneurial approach.

"I was just like you. Pushed by me old man into something I didn't want. Seriously, who'd choose to be an accountant?" Warren had said when they'd first met in the nightclub attached to Marc's backpacker hostel. "Fuck that, mate. There are far easier ways to make money. More fun too, and with perks along the way. Like being sent on a free holiday."

"A free holiday?"

"Yeah, though of course, you've got to have the balls for it." He'd grinned at Marc while raising his thick, black eyebrows. "Reckon you might have the balls for it?"

"Depends," Marc had said, taking a gulp of his beer and wiping away the froth-moustache. He'd grimaced at the taste while wishing for a Hoegaarden, something with bite. "Depends on what *it* is," he'd said, setting the glass down.

He can see it so clearly now, as though he'd been given new prescription lenses. Warren had told him what he wanted to hear, backing up his dislike for a suit-and-tie occupation, a lifetime chained to suburbia and the system. He'd validated every one of Marc's opinions, made him feel heard, seen. But it's too late for realisations now—detained in Bangkok International Fucking Airport, acting as Warren's dumb-arse mule, and for a measly five percent. He snorts. He's a mule alright, stubborn and slow off the mark, a complete fucking misfit. *What's wrong with me?* He should have agreed with his father, returned home to Brussels and followed in the family business. He should have just accepted the inevitable. *Why didn't I?*

Somchai enters the room with Marc's backpack. It's zipped up and full, as though his personal items have been stashed away. It gives him hope. *Am I free to go? Is it over?* The officer places the backpack by his chair and sits, then picks up the phone and presses buttons.

Kim's voice sounds through the speaker. "Marc, it's me again."

"Yes, hi Kim."

"Your backpack has been cleared. But they have reason to suspect you might be hiding something on your person."

"On my person?"

"Yes. They'd like to perform a strip search, Marc."

Fuck! "Can I refuse?"

"You'll be sent back to Australia on the next available flight if you do, and they'll alert the Federal Police there about the matter."

"Right."

Somchai passes over a form and points at the bottom.

"He wants you to sign."

"But I don't know what I'm signing. I can't read it."

"It's a consent form for the strip search."

Marc leans back in his chair and thinks: If he doesn't consent, he's on the next flight back to Sydney, facing the Feds there. Australian police are bound to be more lenient than their counterparts in Thailand. *It's probably worth returning. Warren will be pissed about it, but I'm the one in the shit, not him.*

"How do I know that?" says Marc. "The form's written in Thai."

Kim talks to Somchai, who huffs, then takes the form back and reads it out. Kim translates, word for word. It's a stall for time Marc needs, a moment more to collect his thoughts, weigh up his options.

But, as Somchai drones on, Marc feels something strange, a movement under his shirt, a wriggling sensation. *Shit! They're hatching already? They're not due for another week!* He lowers his chin and from the neck of his shirt emerges a small, brown-coloured snake. *What the fuck?* He jumps to his feet as the snake rears and strikes, hitting him on the cheek and sticking there.

"Fuck, fuck, fuck!"

That's no frill-neck lizard! He pulls it away, copping another bite on the hand. The snake lands on the desk in front of Somchai. It writhes about, then rises in an S-shape, preparing to launch and strike. The Customs officer shrieks and veers back, upending his chair and landing on the floor. Quick to his feet, he backs to the door and out, slamming it behind.

"What's going on?" Kim calls through the speaker phone. "Somchai? Marc?"

Alone, Marc rips off his jacket and shirt. Buttons scatter and bounce against the tiled floor. He checks the vest. Warren had painstakingly packed the eggs into each pocket with moist sphagnum moss, an "x" marking the right way up. Now there are small tears in the tops of the leathery eggs, all fifteen of them, the occupants pipping and finding their way out.

Marc touches his cheek where the snake had latched on. Is it venomous? Who can say? He pushes the thought away in a rush to get the vest off, before more hatch. Wriggling and stretching, he struggles to remove his arms from the loops and rip the self-fastening tabs away at the back. The tabs have gripped tight and he can barely reach around to pull them apart. More snakes are hatching, disturbed by the movement, and he feels bites to his neck and chest, his arms and shoulders, as they slither up and away. After ripping the vest off, a crushing wave of nausea hits. He vomits and his head pounds. It's a headache like no other, jackhammering his brain. Bending at the waist, he moans and clutches his aching guts.

"They were supposed to be frill-necks," he murmurs. "Not snakes." His words are slurred and he feels a strange sense of everything shutting down, immobilising, clocking off.

"Marc, what did you say?" asks Kim. "What was that about frilled necks? Marc?"

"I...I can't..." He sways and struggles to breathe. It's as though a 747 has taxied and parked on his chest. Staggering backwards, he veers towards the corner of the room. Small tawny snakes with lighter coloured diamond-shaped heads and yellow bellies continue to emerge from the clutch of eggs in the pockets of his discarded vest. They hiss and slither about, flicking tongues and staring with large, round, predatory eyes. They're longer than the ruler on Somchai's desk, and look like the coastal taipans

Marc had seen in Australian zoos. Marc blinks and tries to focus, fascinated by the baby reptiles—they're so cute, yet so vicious—but his vision blurs. He swipes at his eyes then checks the back of his hand. *Huh?* Blood.

He's crying tears of blood.

"Marc!" yells Kim. "Please tell me what's happening!"

It's the last thing he hears as he collapses to the floor, surrounded by sixteen aggressive, poised-to-strike hatchlings.

Warren slides a schooner of frothy beer across the table to Klaus. "All yours, buddy."

"Thank you," nods the young German. "My turn to shout next, huh?"

"No, no!" insists Warren. "I got this." He flicks his tongue and licks his lips, sizing up his quarry. "Now, what were we talking about before? Oh yeah, that's right." He snorts and shakes his head. "I know exactly where you're coming from, dude. My old man wanted me to follow him into the army too, but fuck that! There are far easier ways to make money. More fun too. As easy as going on holiday. If you've got the balls to carry it out, of course." He sips his beer, stares at the gap-year backpacker with a well-honed hypnotic gaze, then strikes. "Think you've got the balls for it, Klaus?"

Klaus reels back, taking a moment to think. "Well, I guess it depends on what *it* is."

MILK AND HONEY

JASON FISCHER

They came out of Tel Golah to see the diprotodons. The convoy left that gleaming city behind, left behind progress and glass spires, and slipped into an ancient landscape, the effect instantly jarring. The road curved through the steep mountain ranges and gorges like a secret snake, its makers unwilling to blast through the landscape in one rude, straight line. If a bridge was needed, it was done discreetly.

As to the road itself, there were no reflectors, no painted lines, and the smart-mac was the same hue as the ground it followed. A dozen cars rolled along in wake-sync, their bumpers centimetres apart even as they nudged 200 kilometres per hour. Above, a helicopter watched the surrounding landscape carefully, and the satellite above that dared anything to move where it shouldn't.

The second-to-last car was jammed full of talking heads from the Knesset, representatives from the Chief Rabbinate, and Chris Lynch, a reporter from the BBC. He'd slipped a Mossad agent a pack of marijuana cigarettes for a seat next to Eloise Hitler.

She did not look at the scenery as they barrelled through the rugged Kimberley. Whenever one of her superiors spoke to her, she would nod in agreement, lips drawn up in an approximation of a smile, and then she would return to her own thoughts. As the convoy approached the domes of Purnululu, the lead car slowed — Australia's Prime Minister no doubt wanting to admire the scenery. Everybody slowed to a crawl, and a radio up front squelched, the Mossad agents confirming that all was well.

The talking heads mocked the politician from Canberra, themselves long familiar with the beauty of the domed mountain range. Lynch leaned in close and smiled at Eloise.

"I've heard of you," Lynch said quietly. "Of your family."

"Of course you have," she said, face drawing into a wry grin. "Let me save you some time. Yes, I am a descendant of Adolf Hitler. No, I don't own any of his paintings. I'm not on the board of the Gallery, and I don't have any influence at the Foundation. I'm from the branch of the family that actually has to work for a living."

"You must get a lot of jerks asking you questions," Lynch said, and she feigned a wince until the reporter laughed out loud.

"Hey, I can't even draw," Eloise said. "I've been tempted to change back to Schicklgruber, and more than once."

"Still, the name must be useful. Look at you, big wig at the Ministry for Agriculture. You can't tell me you didn't drop the Hitler name in your job interview."

"Guilty," Eloise chuckled.

"So, what are they like? The diprotodons?"

"Magnificent."

It was a great photo opportunity: the Australian Prime Minister riding on a diprotodon. He'd brought a cowboy hat for effect, and posed on the creature's back, whooping and waving for the cameras.

It was huge, like a wombat enlarged to hippopotamus-size and then some. One of the handlers kept feeding it sweet fruits, and when the creature lost interest and lurched over to the food barrow, everybody laughed. It smashed through a watermelon as if it was a grape, huge incisors gnashing, and the cameras flashed away.

Hundreds of other diprotodons roamed around on the plain, tearing up the scrubby undergrowth. They lazed in the sun, fought playfully, and rolled around in the dust when the flies got too bothersome.

The politician spoke for a while, and then his hosts shared the same platitudes, words about friendship between the Australians and the Israelis, about free trade. The Kimberley was finally opening up for business. The cameras rolled, and no one mentioned the war.

Eloise Hitler had her own turn at the makeshift podium, long after the politicians and clerics had worn themselves out with words and beer.

"We've brought back the ultimate livestock from extinction," she told the handful of reporters still paying attention. "Six times the meat of a cow, and it will eat just about anything. It releases less methane than other animals, and its paws don't damage our fragile landscape. We even let the local Pilbara people hunt them."

"Are you going to sell any breeding pairs?" one of the reporters asked.

"No. Any animals given over to live export will be sterile. The diprotodon is our intellectual property. Next question?"

"What do they taste like?" Lynch called out, and Eloise laughed.

"I don't know," she admitted. "Our Chief Rabbinate decided that these animals are not kosher. We've had gentiles describe diprotodon as a gamey pork taste, but I'll have to take their word on that."

Laughter from the press. A lingering gaze from Lynch, and Eloise felt a blush wash over her cheeks.

"You mentioned Aboriginal hunters. Will these preserves be open for other game shooters?" another asked. She recognised him as a head writer for a gun magazine.

"No, because we don't see the point," Eloise said. "They're docile. They don't move fast; in fact, they don't have much in the way of natural defences. It wouldn't be very sporting."

The reporter grumbled.

"How about racing them?" Lynch called out. "You know, once a year, the Kimberley Israeli Territory gives the old Melbourne Cup a run for its money?"

Flemington Racecourse was long since underwater, along with most of the eastern seaboard. There was a rumble of polite laughter, but it was bittersweet, and most there were probably thinking of the great cities before the ocean came calling.

"You can domesticate and ride them, but it's a little like racing a Clydesdale," Eloise said. "Having said that, we are examining a humanitarian program. For the third world, the diprotodon is a tractor that you can eventually eat."

Lynch raised his hand once more, and Eloise smiled in his direction. The BBC seemed to be running a soft story, and she awaited his next humorous question.

"Can you address the rumours that there are significant numbers of mutant calves? I note that the press won't be allowed to see into the laboratories or the abattoir."

Her smile dropped like a steel gate. The bastard had been working up to this.

"The…the reason that we aren't permitting access to these sites is to protect our intellectual property!" Eloise Hitler said, voice rising, eyes aflame. She clenched a fist at the podium, and then slammed it down. "There are no mutations in this generation of diprotodon, and none in the three before. Your claims are rumour-mongering, sir, and I suggest that they border on antisemitism."

Fuming, she wound up her Ministry of Agriculture presentation, and the reporters made a beeline for the food and drink tents. The Kimberley Israeli Territory, or KIT, had set up a small town under the stars, milking the publicity for all it was worth. Australia had come calling with its energy dollars and groaning population, and it was time to woo her.

Eloise didn't feel much like talking, but she was required to mingle with the politicians and reporters, to answer all their inane questions about the animals. Midway through a spiel about the industrial uses for their fur, she felt a tap on her shoulder. Prime Minister Ephraim Cohen, flanked by a pair of Mossad agents.

"Excuse me," she told the guests, a wealthy industrialist and the leader of the Australian Opposition.

The Prime Minister led her from the tents and into the dark landscape, well away and over a hill. Looking back, there was only the glow from the tents, and the silhouettes of the intelligence agents as they kept a respectful distance.

"Do not let the BBC get under your skin," he said. "Of course, they will dig, that is what they do. I will not have you turn into some sort of orator, thumping the lectern and screaming for justice. Deflect him, and gently."

"Yes, sir," Eloise said.

"He has no hard data, only the rumours. Let them die. We will get the man drunk and give him a woman, and that will be the end of it."

She nodded, and then he left, drifting back towards the raucous gathering. Eloise Hitler stared up at the brilliant stars, and fought down the anger in her heart, the urge to take the reporter by the throat and choke the life from him. Lynch had risen like a snake from the grass, but she'd lived out in the KIT long enough to know just how to kill one.

The next morning, the entourage left the diprotodon ranches behind, and made for Halls Creek. With the thawing of relations between the KIT and Australia, Canberra had approved the extension of their high-speed maglev into the Israeli lands, and the first station had been constructed in Halls Creek. Work was going slowly through the fragile parts of the Kimberley, but soon the line would terminate in Tel Golah itself.

Here the Israelis processed the diprotodon meat, and the old gold town was booming with new construction, new housing. The meat plants dominated the landscape, and thousands of workers filed through the doors, gleaming in white coveralls and boots.

The reporters went nuts.

By the front doors, the two Prime Ministers shook hands and beamed for the cameras, and cut a ribbon with a giant pair of scissors. With that, the meat was finally moving, cheap protein for the Australians. Soon the trucks would roll the other way, bringing energy tech, smartwoods, the new textiles, and what few minerals the Israelis wanted.

Trucks constantly drove out of the abattoir doors, headed for New Perth and east to Toowoomba and the Townsville Islands. The first maglev full of butchered diprotodon meat left for Alice Springs, hundreds of refrigerated cars gliding along the track.

"When finished, this building will be our new Halāl abattoir," Eloise told the tour group she later led. "We want to branch out to the Dutch East Indies market. They prefer live exports of course, but we can process the meat here a lot cheaper."

"What is going on in that building there?" a reporter from the Western Argus asked.

On the edge of the settlement stood another factory, this one topped with a tall brick smokestack. It pumped out plumes of black smoke, which drifted downhill and away from the town.

"That is the rendering plant," Eloise said. "Nothing is wasted here."

Chris Lynch followed the press pack, but he was nervous, a Mossad agent dogging his every step. Eloise ignored all of his questions, favouring the other journalists, and soon the man was fuming. She seemed to delight in his sputtering anger, and made a point of answering the same questions phrased by his neighbours. He waved like a schoolchild in need of a toilet, and she never even looked his way.

"If there are no other questions," Eloise said with a smile and an arched eyebrow, "I suggest we all head for the train."

The Halls Creek maglev station was decked out in bunting and flags, both the starry Australian standard and the KIT flag with its own six-pointed star. A Sephardic group were performing traditional tunes on the platform, and there were laughs and polite applause when they made a passable attempt at the Australian national anthem.

The Australians had brought their official state maglev for the occasion, itself coated in pennants and bunting, and polished until it shone. Eloise joined her superiors from the Knesset and filed into the train behind Prime Minister Cohen. The Federal Police gently guided them into the guest carriages, well-appointed and luxurious, and soon Eloise found herself in a private booth, fitted out like a small apartment.

In mere minutes, the speedy maglev had crossed the border into Kingsland, and almost immediately the landscape changed.

The Australians had tamed their red centre, and here were solar plants, geothermal works, and dozens of market towns, fat and prosperous. Water pipes ran east, steel veins bringing life from the desal plants ringing the Inland Sea, and Eloise found the sight a little sad. Ancient rock formations stood above that incongruous greenery, as if someone had draped the English countryside over everything else.

Her department had done things the Israeli way—unobtrusive use of the existing landscape, development of native grasses and plants, and now the resurrection of the megafauna. She wondered if these steel fingers would cross the border, wondered if the convenience of water would change the Kimberley and the Pilbara that she knew.

There was a knock on the door, and she mumbled "Enter," before returning to the window. Expecting an attendant or one of her colleagues, Eloise was surprised and then a little angry to see Chris Lynch standing in the open door.

"You've got a nerve," Eloise said. "What makes you think I'll give you the time of day?"

"You'll want to hear this," Lynch said, face drawn. "Five minutes, that's all."

"I could call the Mossad in here," Eloise said, and she felt a thrill at the thought of them strong-arming this grub out of her sight.

Even still, the man stood his ground, waiting just inside the threshold. With a sigh, she invited him in, and pointed at the seat opposite the table from her.

"There are two stories I want to run," Lynch began. "Headline stories. Both of these stories affect you, so I want to allow you a choice."

"A choice, Mr Lynch?" Eloise Hitler said, jaw muscles tensing.

She stared down the man, and after a moment he looked away. Over the years she'd fought her way to the top of her department, and knew she had a formidable reputation. It was far from her first uncomfortable meeting.

"I have hard evidence of mutations in the diprotodon program," he finally said. "Not the sanitised data you've released, the real information. Our source has leaked the numbers, the lab reports, even a floorplan of the furnace in Halls Creek. You know, the one where your people burn the two-headed calves."

Eloise felt the blood rush out of her face, and thought she might be sick. Across the table, Lynch looked almost apologetic, but still he pressed on.

"There are rumours that this agreement between KIT and Australia is the beginning of something much bigger. Your rogue state wants to come back into the fold, and contribute taxes, your megafauna cloning technologies, the lot. You have everything to lose from this deal, so why would you sell out to the Australians?"

"You tell me, Mr Lynch. You're the one with the fanciful tale."

"The answer is Palestine. Your new masters have the chair of the League of Nations. They can put pressure on the Ottomans to finally permit a Jewish settlement, a real one."

Lynch looked out the window as the maglev roared over another new town. It was a temporary city, smartwood huts for the workers growing around the frames of a new arcology, the steel ribs jutting skyward. A few minutes later, another site, a new town next to an old one. They'd seeded the earth with dozens of glass domes, now surrounded by irrigated fields. A sign flickered as they passed the town's maglev platform, and it read "Yuendemu". Eloise remembered hearing about the Australians and their underground cities—one more way to preserve energy against that relentless heat.

Less than an hour left to their journey.

"I'm guessing that if the Australians learn of your deception, this deal will be off?" Lynch finally said.

"You should turn from journalism to creative writing, Mr Lynch."

"If I quote you as 'no comment' or some glib statement that discounts these *facts*, you've as good as admitted this in the eyes of the world. You and I both know that, Miss Hitler."

"Why are we having this conversation then?" Eloise said warily.

"Head office sent me out for your dog-and-pony show, but this isn't the story I want to run. I have something better, something

I've been working on for years."

Lynch stretched out an e-papyrus on the table, rotating the image so Eloise could see. It was the photo of Adolf Hitler, at work on his famous painting of Uluru. Next Lynch brought up a picture of the artist at Purnululu, smiling as he posed with a group of Gija people. Shots of the man at the opening of his Gallery, cutting the ribbon. Hitler at the dedication of the yeshiva at Tel Golah, mingling with the important people of the time. Hitler at the Knesset, delivering a fiery speech.

Hitler sprawled out in the street, dead from an Australian bullet.

"So, this is the short life of Adolf Hitler, one of your most celebrated citizens. Imagine my surprise when I discovered that he was not Jewish."

"No. You are lying," Eloise began, and then she found herself on her feet, shouting. "Filthy liar! You should be ashamed!"

A moment later came a knock on the door, and a Mossad agent poked his head in. By his side, a Federal Police Officer loomed, hand on his holster. Still furious, Eloise gathered herself and sent the pair away.

"What is it that you want?" Eloise finally managed. "Are you after money?"

"I have met with almost every surviving Hitler," Lynch said. "Whenever I tell them my discovery, they offer money, they threaten me, and they deny everything I've found. So no, I'm not after money, and no, I'm not scared of you."

Lynch leaned forward, manipulating the e-papyrus, and brought up another image. This of a young Hitler, in his Viennese days. He was in the midst of a group of men who gathered around a café table, where a portly man in a fine suit smiled and allowed his photograph to be taken.

"Georg Ritter von Schönerer, politician and virulent anti-semite. He ransacked a Jewish newspaper, and advocated for the mass imprisonment and deportation of Jews. So why did Adolf Hitler, adored Jewish son, admire him so?"

More photos from Vienna. Protests against the Jews and the Roman Catholics, and in each one was the young Hitler, waving placards and shouting. Von Schönerer's funeral, where a face that might have been Hitler's could just be made out in the pews.

"This is where young Adolf turns from politics and rededicates his life to his art. But he is rejected twice from the Academy of Fine Arts in Vienna. His money was running out, and he was living in homeless shelters.

"So, almost overnight, he invents a Jewish ancestry out of whole cloth. We hear of a Jewish man named Leopold Frankenberger who seduced Fraulein Schicklgruber, spawning Alois Hitler, who gave us Adolf. With a specious piece of paper in hand, he follows a stream of Jewish artists away from the violence of Europe, and out to the refugee sanctuary in Australia. Already, a famed art school is drawing people to Tel Golah, to your 'Hill of Exile'. There Hitler finds his fame, enters politics, encourages a secession from Australia, and is assassinated for his troubles."

He opened another document on the device, this one the scan of an old typewritten manuscript. Eloise blanched when she read the title, and then the opening text. Grand delusions, seductive madness, crude in places but undeniably the early words of the great Jewish orator, dead before he could realise his potential.

"*Mein Kampf Gegen Die Juden* by Adolf Hitler," Lynch read.

"Where did you get this?" she whispered.

"A source who is just as dedicated as me to revealing the truth of this man. Your ancestor was not only a false Jew, he was a raving antisemite, and he very nearly started a Great War of many nations. Imagine that, the whole world at war, and all because one liar wanted to become a famous artist! Eloise, I think you know all of this. Your entire family is trying to sit on this secret. There have been whispers at family gatherings, things your parents hinted at. You know this is all true."

"If you publish this, you will be laughed at," Eloise said. "A grand conspiracy theory, but anyone could have doctored those photos, that…that document."

"This is the story of the century. I don't care about your stupid mutant animals. Verify my story, and I'll list you as an unnamed source in the Hitler family."

Eloise sat there silently; fists clenched in her lap.

"It is your choice. What do you care about more, your work or your family name? You yourself said it was a burden."

"I'm…I'm going to need a drink."

Eloise fussed about on the side bar of her compartment, sloshing whiskey into a pair of tumblers. She returned, setting a glass in front of the reporter, and settled down with a sigh.

"We are fixing the mutation problem," she finally admitted. "Three more generations and we will have a dominant purity in the diprotodon bloodline. You have to believe me, Mr Lynch, we are doing a good thing for the world here. Environmentally sustainable protein, enough to feed the world."

"So, you are choosing your life's work. Admirable," Lynch said, lifting his drink. "Let us drink to both our lives' works."

"Indeed," Eloise said, and clinked his glass. "It is true that we are rushing our program," she continued. "We will not have this chance again. Next year Prussia helms the League of Nations, and they will not push the Ottomans as much as Australia means to. We want to end the Diaspora, Mr Lynch. We will gamble everything we have on going home, to our real home."

Lynch sipped at his drink, and Eloise noted that his eyes were aflame with triumph. He'd won one over her. He seemed content to let her speak now that he thought he had his source.

"It will hurt our cause to have Adolf Hitler exposed, but not as much as it will to lose our main export. Your exposé would make for an interesting footnote in history, no more. Of course, I will not allow you to tell *either* story."

"What?" Lynch managed.

He took one shuddering breath, then another. His face turned pale with shock, and he raised one fluttering hand towards his throat. He lost the strength halfway, and his hand dropped to the tabletop.

"I have a second job, Mr Lynch," Eloise Hitler said. "I am an operative for Mossad. I feel safe in telling you this, because you are in fact dying."

She moved her chair around the table, and cradled the journalist's face with her hands. His eyes jerked around wildly, and his breaths came in short, panicked gulps. He tried to cry out for help, only to find that his tongue wasn't working correctly.

"Nanotoxins," Eloise said softly, nudging his glass with her index finger. "You won't suffer long. My people will escort you back to your cabin, and you will look drunk. By the time the maglev arrives in Alice Springs, you will be dead in your own cabin, comfortably settled in your armchair. We know you are reading *Picnic at Hanging Rock,* and it will be resting in your hands as if you just dozed off. If there is a cursory autopsy, it will show that your own heart gave out."

She copied the contents of his e-papyrus to her own computer, and dumped all the data from his comm the same way.

"You no doubt have someone else in on this, with the instructions to release this data should something happen to you," Eloise said. "Within the hour, I will have a team working to discredit your work and to destroy you personally. Most likely we have enough to stop further leaks. Rest assured, your sources and your collaborators will be snuffed out, one by one."

A tear ran down Lynch's face, and she blotted it away with her thumb.

"Don't be sad, Mr Lynch," Eloise said. "You came close, but the wheels of nations crush men like you. Your life was always going to end this way."

Two plainclothes agents came to collect the man, and they caroused up the hallways, singing a drinking song and carrying their "drinking buddy" back to his bed. Eloise Hitler savoured her whisky to the last drop, and poured Lynch's down the sink.

They came into Alice Springs. As the maglev swung towards the station, Eloise saw the shimmer of water, as far as the horizon and then further. The Inland Sea. It fed in past Port Augusta and the soggy ruins of Adelaide, and filled the entire red centre of the country.

She'd seen the footage of the Australians as they had carved a great canal north, seeking to bisect the continent. Soon this would open a shipping route to the Dutch East Indies, Hong Kong and French Indo-China. Australia intended to feed the world, and now it had the means. Rice and corn, algae loaf and kangaroo, and their Jewish prodigal sons were gifting them endless supplies of diprotodon meat, a cheap protein for all.

Eloise filed out of the train behind the Prime Ministers and other dignitaries, smiling at the press. A brass band was in full swing, mangling some Jewish classics before saving face with a rousing performance of "God Save the King".

More speeches, and then the delegation was taken to the harbour. Giant cruise ships were at dock, some for the tourists and some for the new citizens who'd decided to stay. There were new arcologies and high-rise apartments all around Alice Springs, spreading from the historical township and along the coastline of this new sea.

The Australians had taken this environmental disaster and turned it into a strange mixture of the French Riviera and the old Gold Coast. Eloise had read that there were more cranes in this area than anywhere else in the world, and her mind boggled at the scale of the construction.

She found herself herded up a gangplank, boarding an enormous trimaran. Ensigns in full navy whites crewed the ship, and on board there was more bunting, more flags and bands and crowing diplomacy when one hundred years earlier they'd been at war.

Eloise was hemmed in with celebrities and politicians, all gab and glamour and even manoeuvring for favours and deals. Feeling faint, Eloise excused herself, and stood out on the foredeck of the ship.

She thought about Chris Lynch, remembered the quiet appearance of an ambulance at the maglev station. No doubt there would be an interview with the Australian Federal Police in her future, questioning her over the argument they'd had in her compartment. Her Mossad subordinates had mocked up most of an interview between Lynch and herself, a focus on her role in the Department of Agriculture. The argument would be blamed on a disagreement over her research, already smoothed over by the time he'd left her cabin and started drinking in earnest.

When she remembered the panic in Lynch's eyes, the realisation that his killer was sitting right across from him, Eloise smiled. She felt a great satisfaction from the murder, and was pleased that she could pass it off as a clandestine service to her nation.

That moment though, when she'd held a life in her hands and snuffed it out—it was heady stuff. Addictive. She gripped the railing and imagined herself one day holding a great office, something even old Adolf would have been proud of. Perhaps Prime Minister of Israel, or a power behind the throne, someone free to crush enemies, to make bloody examples when they were needed.

Eloise felt that secret darkness bubbling away within her, the heritage of her bloodline. When the great floating city of Eyre came into view, she imagined it in flames, bombs splintering the soaring glass spires, thousands of panicked people bobbing in the water and drowning.

There and then, Eloise Hitler decided that there was a beauty in death, and she resolved to explore this fully.

Nineteen Hours on Deep Creek Station

Tim Borella

We're changing the oil filter on the Robbie and it's bloody hot in the hangar. Bloody hot everywhere, for that matter, and humid. I've spilled oil down the engine and am trying to wipe it up before it gets into all the places you can't reach, and Jim goes off at me. He's ten years older than I am, and since Dad's accident in the yards he's been working on the assumption he'll be taking over, which is probably correct.

It wouldn't be right, though. The old man can be tough, but at least he's got a heart. Jim's a prick, even if he is my brother.

Bernadette's older than him and should be next in line. She's better on a horse or motorbike, can make hard decisions when she needs to. Everyone trusts her, and it feels good to think of her calling the shots. Jim—nah. But our father is old school, and to have the baton passed to you, well, you need a baton already, if you get my drift. When Jim takes the reins, I think I'll have to leave. Not something I thought I'd ever hear myself say.

Speaking of the devil, he's wheeled across a drum on the trolley and is pumping avgas into the machine.

"Aren't you finished yet?" he says. "Jesus Christ, Lachlan."

"Nearly, Jim. Just gotta put the panel back on."

"Well, bloody hurry up."

He brings the hose around my side and starts filling the main tank, ignoring the drops plinking down on me from the leaky fitting. I grit my teeth and keep doing up screws.

"Are you taking her out for a run?" I say, trying to be nice.

"Yep, and you're coming with me," he says.

"What are we doing?"
"You'll find out."

Jim flies the chopper like he rides a horse, no finesse. He got sent off to Brisbane for a couple of months to do his licence, and by the time you count accommodation, failed exams and the rest, the bill must've been at least a hundred grand. I've been up with a few of the seasonal mustering pilots and compared to him, what they do is pretty to watch—hardly moving their hands and feet at all while the machine just does what they want, beautiful and smooth. Jim must've missed that lesson. He wrestles it around the sky.

He still won't tell me what we're up to, but he's got me in the left seat holding the loaded .308 with a box of cartridges on the floor in front of me. Now we're up in the air I'm a bit less pissed off at him. The doors are off, as always, and the hundred-and-forty-kilometre-an-hour wind dragging at my sleeve cools me down as we race along the river.

I trace the winding line of trees ahead into the distance. We'd have to go another thirty kilometres to get to our boundary, and the same the other way. It makes me think of our great-grandparents doing it the hard way, mustering on horseback, felling timber with axes and crosscut saws. It'd take them all day to cover the ground we're crossing in minutes.

We're deep into the wet season, and serious storms have turned the dusty flats green and brought water and life flooding back to the billabongs. There are great standing pools of water under us; the flood plain is nearly full.

The spreading water gets feral pigs on the move, so I figure we must be out to cull a few. It's a losing battle—apparently there's twenty-four million of the bastards running around, close enough to one for every Australian, displacing native species and creating havoc. They're cunning and breed like you wouldn't believe; another triumph of human ignorance over common sense. Like cane toads or rabbits but worse.

Turns out Jim's not after pigs, though. There's a big riverbend up ahead, marked by a corridor of tall trees. He turns to circle around it, wind noise blasting through the intercom as he leans out for a better look.

"Get ready," he says, but I don't know what for.

Then he reverses the turn, tilting my side down, and I see what he's talking about. A big old croc is lying on the riverbank, not giving a shit about the noisy, clattering machine zooming around above it.

Jim's leaning across the cockpit, stabbing his finger down at the massive reptile. "Quick! Get a couple of rounds into the bastard!"

I look at him in surprise.

"Come on, hurry up!" he yells, but by then we've gone too far from the spot.

I can see he's angry at me.

"What're you waiting for?" he says.

My heart thumps and I feel a flush spread in my neck and back. "I'm not doing it."

Jim's had the crocodile argument with Dad before and won't let it go. Crocs used to be scared of people, rightly so, but now you can't go near a billabong to swim or flick a lure for fear of one lurking there ready to drag you in.

"But you used to shoot 'em yourself!" I remember him saying to the old man, back when Dad was whole and strong, tough as an ironbark fencepost. They were in the office, Jim pointing at the tanned croc hide on the wall like it was Exhibit A in a court case. I loved looking at that hide, the claws like knives, and strange patterns of ridges and knobs running from head to tail.

"Those were different times, son," Dad said. "It was legal for a start, and it's just what we did. It's like tree-clearing…you just did what you had to do to keep things moving forward. Now, any do-gooder gets a sniff of something like that, they'll take your farm off you. They've got satellites that can detect the steam off your piss these days, so don't fool yourself into thinking you can get away with anything stupid."

"But—"

"No buts. You leave them alone, or bloody look out."

Jim just grunted, stony-faced. I could tell what he was thinking—*you've gone fuckin' soft*. He wouldn't dare say it but Dad must have sensed it too, sitting up straighter in his chair and giving Jim the death stare. It took a bit to get Dad angry, but he was definitely on the way. For a minute I thought Jim would argue, but he dropped his gaze.

Now I'm getting the death stare. Jim swaps his left hand onto the cyclic stick and reaches over with his right to grab the rifle.

"Fuckin' give me that!"

I shrink back in my seat. He's juggling the controls and the gun and I'm afraid he's going to shoot one of us by accident.

"For fuck's sake, Jim, settle down," I mutter.

We come around again but instead of continuing forward, he brings us into a shaky high hover with the crocodile on his side, our rotor wash spreading ripples on the water. He's got the rifle in his right hand, braced on his shoulder, using his left on the cyclic to keep us roughly in position. The collective stick beside his left leg, which controls our height, is pretty much doing its own thing. Jim's like a one-armed paper hanger, hands and feet going everywhere as he squeezes off rounds, missing the croc by metres each time.

I'm shit scared. I've seen people fly and shoot at the same time on TV but they're proper pilots. Jim's just a dickhead likely to kill us both.

Big trees lean out over the water all along the river. Jim's hell bent on getting the croc, peppering the bank around it with bullets. We start to sink and he reefs up on the collective to stop the descent, but the nose kicks up at the same time and suddenly we're going backwards. He needs to get both hands on the controls to sort his shit out, but he's not letting go of the rifle.

I crane around to look out and back, afraid the tail rotor spinning there like a buzz saw is going to hit something, but it's not that that gets us. We're drifting sideways too, and by the time I look up it's too late.

"Jim!" I yell, just as the main rotor above us clips overhanging twigs and then branches with a sound like a labouring wood chipper. An almighty shake starts up, so violent I can hardly see, then we're tilting crazily, dropping towards the water. There's a bone-jarring thump.

It feels like later. I'm in my seat in the chopper, leaning to the right. It's quiet, and there's water up to my waist. I look around, trying to focus. The big printed barra on the back of Jim's colourful fishing shirt is facing me, leaping out with its mouth open. Good size fish. Jim's head is underwater, his hair drifting gently back and forth.

Jim's head is under water!

I pull myself together and release my belt buckle, only to fall on top of him. Bracing on the centre console, I pull his head up by the hair. His eyes are closed, tongue half out of his slack mouth, but he's breathing. I'm so angry at him, unsure if I'm relieved or not.

Blood from a gash on my forearm mixes with oil in the water, making scummy rainbow colours. I get hold of Jim's arm, feel for his buckle and unclip it. He's heavy, but the water helps so I can half-float him to my side, then out. I flip him over, get my arms around him from behind like a wrestler, and drag him onto the muddy bank.

His legs are dangling in the water, which reminds me of the crocodile—shit! Where's it gone? Now there's just a big slide mark on the opposite bank where it was before. I rush to pull Jim higher, feeling dizzy and weak. He groans, sits up and looks from the wrecked chopper to me, dumbly at first, then narrowing his eyes as if it's my fault. Jesus, I've just saved him! I can't deal with his crap, so I let him go, and walk up the bank to cool off and get my bearings.

At the top, my heart sinks. The picturesque billabongs we zoomed across earlier in minutes now stretch endlessly ahead, trackless swamps filled with murky brown water.

There won't be a search party turning up any time soon. Jim's always pissing off in the chopper without telling anyone where he's going. The machine's got an installed locator beacon but it's underwater in the wreckage, useless. Someone will notice later when we don't come back to the homestead, but how will they know where to look? By the time they're worried enough to get anything organised, it'll be dark.

My brain feels like it's starting to work properly again, and I see our choices are pretty limited. Either we stay here with the big croc overnight and get found tomorrow (if we're lucky), or we walk out to dry country before sundown. There's likely to be crocs on the way out, too, but there's definitely one here, and night's when they really come out to play.

"We've got to get moving, Jim," I say. While I'm used to waiting for him to call the shots, this supreme act of stupidity and pig-headedness has pushed me over some threshold. Another thought hits me. "And we need the gun."

"Well, I'm not fuckin' going in to get it," he says.

I'm not suicidal either, but I've got a plan. The wreckage of the chopper makes a decent barrier, so I clamber back in. The film of fuel and oil on the surface stinks. I take a deep breath and slip under, pulling myself down and groping in the mud through the low side doorway. It takes a few tries until my hand closes around something solid. Got it!

I lift the rifle back through the smashed cabin, stopping to feel around for the box of cartridges. It's still there. Feeling like a hero, I climb well up the bank before opening the bolt to check safety and drain the water out. I hope it still works. The ammo box is going to be a pain to carry, so I load five rounds into the magazine and stuff the rest into my pockets.

Jim finally gets to his feet, wincing.

"Everything alright?" I say.

He ignores me, reaching for the rifle. "Gimme that."

We've been pushing through water ranging from knee- to chest-deep for two hours, trying to avoid deeper billabongs, but it's hard to tell what's what. I'm getting sick of taking a step only to fall into a deep hole, panicking at the thought of a croc there waiting for a feed. Even though we haven't seen any yet, they'll be out here.

Big trees poking up give us some idea of where solid ground lies, and what were hillocks in the dry season are now tiny islands.

There's something wrong with Jim's right ankle. To his credit, he keeps slogging on. It's slowing us down though, and I'm getting more worried as the sun slips lower. It's impossible to know how far we've come; I'd be surprised if it's more than about a kilometre. As we get more fatigued, we're going even slower, and I'm wavering between stoic acceptance and tooth-grinding anger at Jim for getting us into this. Both emotions are equally useless.

Looking ahead, there's no end to the water. Soon, it'll be dark. I've been hearing splashes, some of which might be frogs or fish or waterbirds—or something else. I'm hyper-alert, scanning like an army scout on patrol.

Something catches my eye and I freeze.

"Jim!" I hiss, pointing.

On our right, about twenty metres away, there's something dark in the water, just a couple of lumps breaking the surface, lit by the low slanting rays of the sun. We both know what it is.

"Fuck," he says, raising the rifle to his shoulder and cocking it. He takes aim, breathes out and squeezes the trigger. The firing pin clicks. That's it.

He rips the bolt back to send the dud round spinning away, slams it home and pulls the trigger again. Nothing.

"Let's go," I whisper, backing away.

There's a small grassy mound with a couple of trees up on the left and I edge towards it, fighting to control my breathing and not make splashes. Jim follows. Looking back, I see ripples where the croc was and imagine it underwater, coming at us like a torpedo. A kind of prayer to nobody in particular goes through my mind—*Come on, come on, let us just make it to the trees.*

I'm expecting my legs to be smashed out from under me at any moment, but at last the ground rises under my feet and, amazingly, we're up on the mound. I feel slightly safer once we've put the trees between us and where we last saw the croc, which is stupid because it could be anywhere by now.

My sense of safety drains away fast as we look around. Our little island's barely out of the water and maybe ten metres across. The trees are big, solid river gums, with no branches we could possibly reach, so being here overnight's no better than if we'd just stayed where we were in the first place.

I know how stealthy and fast crocs are, and I'm picturing us fighting to stay awake, waiting for the sudden explosion of water as the first one of us gets taken. The croc we saw just before could come thrashing up right now, for that matter. This is their world, and we're helpless prey. We have to get to somewhere survivable before the light is totally gone.

"We can't stay here, can we?" I say. It's not really a question.

Jim shakes his head. "Nah."

We do a cautious lap of the mound, peering out while staying as far as possible from the water's edge. There are a couple of other islands a hundred or so metres away. While it's hard to tell in the fading twilight, one looks a bit bigger with more varied tree cover, and we really don't have much choice.

Jim's still got the gun, which with his bung leg will make him even slower.

"I can take that, if you like," I say.

He wouldn't give it to me if it was working, I'm sure, but he hands it over. Taking a long look around, I see no threats—not that it means much—and wade quietly in.

Soon we're up to our necks. I edge forward, holding the rifle over my head. Low down in the darkening water it's hard to keep my bearings. Every unidentified splash sparks a needle of fear. A chorus of frogs has started up, swelling and falling away in waves, robbing our awareness by blanketing other sounds. As seeing and hearing get more difficult, touch takes over. I'm fighting not to shy away every time I hit a slippery rock or get snagged on a submerged branch.

Keep going, keep going, my inner voice repeats. Jim sounds like he's struggling, groaning and splashing, and even as I'm willing him to quieten down, some primal part of me is happy he's drawing attention to himself.

Surely, we must be close. The ground feels like it's sloping upward, and I see silhouettes of trees looming in the near-darkness. Then there's a strange choking grunt, and I jump back as something big and dark leaps up in front of me, thrashing and churning. I fall over in the water, holding the rifle out like a staff to fend off whatever's there. The shape keeps rising, flapping, and I see at last it's just some waterbird I've nearly tripped over. I think I've pissed myself.

I don't care about anything except getting to the island, abandoning any attempts at stealth and just forging ahead until I stagger onto the bank and fall again, dropping my head to the grass like the pope kissing some airport tarmac.

Hearing Jim come up behind, I drag myself to my feet again. With a sliver of moon and my eyes adapting to the dark, I see trees with lower branches, and we find one we can climb.

Being wedged amongst hard branches, hungry and thirsty and eaten by mosquitoes isn't particularly conducive to sleep, but somehow, I've drifted off for a while. My belt's long enough to go around both me and the branch I'm on, and with other branches nearby to lean against, I feel secure enough. With my pocket knife I've cut one long sleeve off my work shirt, and used it to tie the rifle too, barrel angled down to drain.

I wake, groggy and confused, to the sound of splashes. Jim's shifting in his perch, peering down. It's big, whatever it is, and while feral pigs are pretty good swimmers, I doubt this is one out for a midnight dip. The moon's gone but starlight's enough to see a long black shape emerge from the water and waddle, with an unmistakable lizard-like gait, towards our tree.

Can crocs track a scent? I don't know. This one seems to know we're up here, nosing around the tree trunk and even raising its head as if it's going to try climbing. I'm holding my breath, afraid to make a sound. The beast hangs around for maybe twenty minutes, then slips away into the water.

I'm fully awake now, and with nothing else to do but wait for daybreak—whenever that may come—I pull cartridges from my pockets one by one, cup my hands and blow on them in the hope they'll dry out. At some point, I doze off again.

Sun in my eyes wakes me this time. I'm thirsty as hell and also busting for a piss. It takes me a while to figure out Jim's not up here anymore, and neither's the gun. I hear noises below and see him on the ground.

"What are you *doing*?" I hiss.

He looks up. "Ah, sleeping beauty. I've been awake all bloody night, unlike you, and there's been no trace of our mate since he left hours ago. Time to get moving."

I scan the murky water. There are no obvious signs of crocodiles—which means nothing.

"I don't think we should," I say. "There'll be search parties looking for us by now. Just come back up and wait."

"Wait for what? It could be days before they find us, and we won't be attracting attention with this fuckin' thing, will we?" He points the rifle to the sky and pulls the trigger. Nothing happens.

"Come on, Jim, the croc could be right *there*."

He takes a look around, spits into the water and starts back towards the tree. "Righto then, I'll give it a while if it makes you happy."

A while turns out to be about half an hour. The sun's out with a vengeance, and even in the leafy branches we're heating up. We hear a helicopter way off in the distance, then nothing. I'm so thirsty I have to get down, creep to the water and crouch to drink, scalp prickling with nervous tension. While I'm there, Jim climbs down again and leans the rifle against the tree.

"Fuck this, I'm outta here," he says. "You coming?"

"I don't think so," I say, moving well away from the edge. "It doesn't feel right."

He squats down and scoops up handfuls of muddy water, making a face. "Well, while you're playing koala bears, I'll be having a beer. If you're lucky, I might send someone back to get you."

As he stands up, the calm water erupts. Before I can even shout, a crocodile has launched, crunching its wicked jaws shut on his leg and dragging him backwards. He screams and paws at the ground, making claw marks in the muddy grass. I look around in a panic for some way to help. Jim's grabbed hold of a small sapling at the water's edge and, eyes wide with terror, is kicking at the crocodile. I take the rifle by the barrel and run at the beast, smashing the butt down on its head, over and over. There's no apparent effect and I'm afraid I'm hurting Jim. The croc has him half into the water now, rolling him one way and then the other. I think I hear his leg bones cracking. His screaming is horrific; the sapling's bending, but he's still holding on. I grab his forearm and pull. The croc's power is unbelievable and Jim's fingers are slipping, even with my help.

There's only one thing I can think to do, a gamble that means I have to let him go. The accusation in his eyes is like a knife in my gut.

I take one of the dry rounds from my pocket and load it, aiming at the rolling, thrashing beast's eye as best I can. The rifle might not fire. I might hit Jim by mistake. *Would that really matter so much?* I pull the trigger.

There's a kick, the bullet strikes, the crocodile jerks its head and is gone in a swirl of ripples.

I run to Jim and pull him clear of the water. Not all of him comes out. I feel like vomiting—the croc's taken his leg below the knee. Shreds of torn skin, tendons and crushed bone fragments hang from the bloody stump. I'm staring, shocked.

Jim's pitiful moaning spurs me into action. Trying to be gentle, I drag him further away from the edge and turn him so his leg's upslope. There's a lot of blood coming out, so I bundle up my shirt against the gaping wound to try and staunch it. That sort of works, but blood's still soaking through. I cinch my belt tight around what's left of Jim's lower leg as a tourniquet.

I think the croc will stay away now it's got food, but I reload the rifle anyway. We wanted to be found before; now we need to be. I aim into the sky and fire three rounds, pausing between each to make something like an SOS. The dried cartridges seem to be working. There's maybe thirteen left.

Jim's blood has soaked through the shirt-bandage and spread

into the leaf litter. I pull the torniquet tighter. His feeble whimper is worse than the scream I was expecting. A feeling of helpless inadequacy steals my strength.

Any movement in the water makes me flinch. I need to save bullets for protection, use them if we're to be found. The sight of Jim's pallid face spurs me to load three more, of which only two fire. I listen hard for an answering signal. None comes.

Jim's eyes are closed, and I want to close mine, too. I rub his shoulder. *You stupid bastard,* I think, tears of both frustration and love welling. Is it him or me I've got in mind? He's done this to us, but as usual I've let him. I could have stood up to him; *should* have stood up to him a hundred times before. Now it's too late.

Through the bird calls and stirring of leaves comes another sound, almost hidden. A vehicle? I raise the rifle and squeeze the trigger, holding my breath. As the echo of the shot dies away, I hear the blare of a car horn. I fire another shot, and there it is again.

Yes!

Hope flares in me. Soon we should see a boat, or the rescue chopper from the city.

Jim stirs. I'm still jumpy about the croc, but I cut pieces off my trouser leg and soak them, laying one on my brother's forehead and using the other to squeeze water into his mouth. His eyes are closed, his breathing shallow and irregular.

"Stay with me, mate," I say.

Whatever else needs to be said can wait until later.

Boyfriend Material

H.K. Stubbs

Libby zipped up her red daypack with the first-aid kit, water and snacks, and rolled her suitcase towards the door of the renovated Queenslander. She checked her watch, and reflexively ran her fingers and thumb along the length of her blonde ponytail. The window at the side of the door showed only parked cars in the tree-lined street. Pete should be pulling up any minute. Excitement jittered, hopping like crickets in her tummy inside her black jacket; she did a little run on the spot to shake out her nerves.

She'd packed warm clothes, boardgames and DVDs, seeing their intended hike was looking less likely every time she checked the weather app. The Bureau of Meteorology said an eighty percent chance of rain tonight and Sunday. Twenty mils wouldn't be enough to flood the crossings at Rathdowney, but with Pete being an inner-city Sydney boy, new to the Goldie, a wet mountain climb might not break him *in* but rather just…break him.

The cabin they'd booked had two bedrooms—separate beds— but she'd packed condoms, because, what wasn't to like? They were firmly entrenched in the friendzone, but during their last beery Thursday night at *The Cecil*, after she'd bought a round and Jen had bought another round, he'd shown Libby his indoor bouldering videos.

"It's climbing, without ropes. We fall on big mats. Carefully."

How *did* he hang on like that to, well—nothing? Woah—she'd grabbed his phone for a closer look. His shirt was off in this one. Oh, he was ripped. Over the noise of shouting outside *The Cecil*, and waving away cigarette smoke wafting in the windows, she'd challenged him to a *real* climb.

"Whaddaya mean?" he'd said.

"A real mountain. Nothing batshit like Barney. Mount Maroon. Big boulders, just a scramble, half a day."

After a moment's hesitation, an evaluating squint: "I'm not great with heights."

"How can you be a climber if you don't like heights?"

"Bouldering doesn't go high."

"You chicken?"

"No." He'd shrugged. "I'm game."

Pete had grabbed her phone and booked a cabin, right there and then. Word had gotten around by Friday afternoon. Her friends' eyes were expectant and wide within their fake lashes.

Libby pressed her forehead to the back of her wrist, against the puffy-jacket sleeve—filled with recycled tyre rubber, not feathers, to spare the ducks and the planet—and groaned. Dating a classmate and colleague…would be dangerous ground. Fourth-year med, they'd be in the same wards and study groups for years yet. So, if she *did* go there, it had to be worth it. The potential fallout was too toxic for a mere weekend fling.

A horn outside. Pete had arrived. Libby threw on her backpack, called "bye" to Jen, her housemate, and lugged her suitcase down the stairs.

She opened the hatch of the silver Tig, idling on the street outside her house.

"Are we going for a week?" Pete asked, turning from the driver's seat to look at her, his lean arm (dusted with fine, dark hairs) stretched across the back of the passenger seat. His black short-back-and-sides was as neat as always, combed to the right. He hadn't shaved, sporting a long-past-five o'clock shadow beneath his brown eyes.

Libby climbed in the passenger side and fastened her seatbelt. "My dressing gown takes up half the bag. And I bought some board games, because we won't be hiking if the rain keeps up."

"You don't like rain?" He indicated to pull out into traffic.

"I've packed my raincoat. But Maroon is slippery even when it's dry, and steep."

"And leeches, right?"

She waved away his concern. "They're just friendly pairs of suction cups joined by a rubber band. It's the chainsaw tongue that gives them a bad rap."

He laughed. "Interesting. I've gotta stop for fuel before we head up there. But leech bites get infected, right? You can lose an arm, a leg, your life—"

"Rubbish. They've got tonnes of medicinal uses, don't forget."

"Can't forget what I don't know."

"Seriously? Their anticoagulant, hirudin, was the template for modern blood thinners." She adjusted the heater blowers to warm her legs.

"My blood's thin enough," he said.

"They're helpful for vein diseases, epicondylitis, microsurgery—"

"If you love leeches so much, have them all. I want *no* leeches. You can have *all* of my leeches." He winked at her as the SUV zoomed up Smith Street.

"Gee." She rolled her eyes. "Thanks. You're so generous."

"I am." He pulled into a petrol station. "I'll pump, you pay. So we can get on the road quicker."

Libby pulled her wallet out of her bag and headed into the shop.

Two brown cows under a grey sky welcomed them to their Air BnB, a tiny cottage atop a small green hill in Rathdowney, with massive mountains looming either side.

"Super-cute little house," Libby said.

"Small," Pete added. "Imagine raising six kids in there."

"In two bedrooms, with an outhouse. Whose nightmare is this?"

He smiled. "A nightmare from the olden days."

Libby stepped out of the SUV and crunched up the driveway in her hot-pink hiking boots, taking a deep breath. Oh, so *nice* to be in the country.

"Where did they say the key was?" Pete asked.

She tried the handle on the white door. It opened. "Well, no locks required. I guess there's not much to steal."

Pete shook his head. "So how do we keep out..."

She glanced at him. "What? Snakes can't turn doorhandles. They slither in under the door, anyway."

"And murderers?" he asked.

She laughed. "Who's going to kill us? There's no one for miles."

Pete went wide-eyed. Fake fear, but with an undercurrent of the real thing. "No one to hear us scream," he said.

"Exactly," Libby smiled.

They carried their bags into the cottage, walked around the property, and pulled back a green plastic curtain to peer into the outhouse.

"Lift the lid," Pete dared her.

"You do it."

"I don't need to go," he said.

"Nor do I."

They started to giggle, and were backing away, laughing, when it started to rain. A quick run across the yard and they were in the kitchen. Libby flicked the light switch, but nothing happened.

"Don't we have power?" she asked.

"Looks like we don't," Pete said. "But how about gas? I saw a cylinder." He turned the dial on a cooktop in the kitchen. It hissed, so he lit it with a cigarette lighter. "I can make tea."

Libby grinned. No power hadn't phased him. Maybe he *would* cope okay outside the city. She prepared a fire in the potbelly stove in the lounge room, scrunching up newspaper and covering it with pinecones and sticks. She struck a match and the flames licked up over the wood. Pinecones burst and hissed like natural firecrackers. She sat back on the sofa beside the fire and Pete brought over a cup of tea. She put her feet up on the coffee table and he sat beside her.

Libby sipped her tea. "Nice."

Pete reached down to scratch his shin through his trousers.

"Feels funny." He frowned and pulled up the lower leg of his pants. "Oh crap, oh crap!" He put his tea down too fast and the cup tumbled onto the table, spilling.

"Pete!"

"Look!"

"You've got a leech already? It's okay." She grabbed it with her nails and prised it off his leg. It stuck to her fingers, but she rolled it around so it couldn't latch. She opened the front door and flicked it away.

A dribble of blood ran down Pete's leg from the wound. "Shouldn't you have used salt?" he asked.

"Doesn't make any difference to the bleeding. I thought you'd want it off as fast as possible. And this way, the leech survives."

"I don't want the little bastard to *live*." His mouth was down-turned and cheeks twitching in disgust. "What if it tells its friends?"

She grinned. "You'll be okay. Do I have to get the first-aid kit?"

He nodded.

Surprised, Libby tried not to groan. If it was her own wound, she would have let it be, but for his sake, she dabbed on some antiseptic and covered it with a plaster bandage.

"Better?" she asked.

"How did I even get one so quick?" he whined.

"Maybe it got on your shoe when we walked around outside."

"But I took my shoes off."

"Maybe it was on your sock by then. You're okay now, right?"

"Guess so," he pouted.

Libby looked towards the fire and rolled her eyes, regretting that the afternoon had taken a turn towards feeling like babysitting. Did she have to try to cheer him up? How sympathetic did she have to be? His overreaction to the little bloodsucker was... unattractive. A sticker, a lollypop, and she'd send him on his way.

"Scrabble?" she asked, trying to salvage the day.

"Sure," he said. He cleaned up the mess from the spilled tea, and she unpacked the game on the table. They drew for who would start first. Pete got an A, and made ILIAC as his first word.

"Ooh!" she said, and used his A and her whole seven to make

PARASITE, vertically. "Extra fifty points."

"God," he said. "What's next? Oh. Oh!" His hands shook with excitement as he fumbled one letter at a time onto the board, using her T and his seven letters to make INFECTED.

Libby laughed. "This isn't a big scorer, but for the beauty of the move, in the spirit of the game..." She made CYST, placing her T beneath his I.

"I hope this isn't, like, Ouija-board Scrabble."

She smiled. "I picked it up at a second-hand store. They said the previous owner bled to death. That explains the brown marks on some of the tiles."

"Really?" Pete's eyes fixed on her.

She laughed. "No, of course not!"

He turned to her, intense and sombre. "Libby?"

"Yes, Pete?"

"I want to go to the toilet, but I don't want to go outside."

She took a deep breath, groaning inside. "Because of the leech?"

He nodded.

"You'll be *fine*. I've hiked heaps in wet weather and not even seen one."

"What if they're especially attracted to me?"

"Who wouldn't be?" she joked. He didn't laugh. God, he was *serious*. "Mate, they're just attracted to warm blood. I'll come with you. And when we get back, we'll check your legs."

He closed his eyes, steeling his resolve. He nodded. "Okay."

Libby wiggled her feet into her boots and tucked in her laces. Pete was pale, staring at the door. She looked at the handle. Did she have to open it for him? Not that she minded, but...it was getting ridiculous.

As though he'd read her mind, Pete opened the door and stepped out onto the veranda. Low white clouds blocked the view up to the mountains. The rain had eased, but they weren't going to make it up Maroon after all. Libby's heart dropped. She wouldn't be needing the condoms, either. Disappointment was a sinking feeling in her chest.

While sex would be a great way to spend a rainy weekend, if

Pete was this scared of a single leech, she couldn't contemplate a serious relationship with him. She loved the outdoors. It had to be a part of her life, and of her love life. If Pete wasn't boyfriend material, one weekend's fling was not worth the years of awkwardness it would create. She walked down the steps towards the outhouse, hands in her pockets, and glanced at his Tig. Maybe they should just go home. This weekend was a mistake, booked on a whim, when they'd been pissed.

Libby squinted at the ground, finding something odd, a sight like she'd never seen before. A curving line of sticks or stitches, leading from the house all the way to the outhouse. She frowned, but didn't mention it. It could wait. When they reached the outhouse, she leant in and lifted the lid, holding her breath.

"There you go," she said, and turned away. Did she have to hold his hand, in case he fell in? Like she'd done for her four-year-old nephew when they'd camped at Straddie? She avoided eye contact as he went in and closed the curtain.

With Pete occupied, she crouched and studied the little sticks or stitches, quickly realising that they weren't either of those things. They were tiny leeches, head to tail, a whole line of them from the outhouse to the house. Which way were they pointing? She couldn't tell. She'd seen caterpillars do this before, but never leeches. They were solitary invertebrates. Their strange behaviour made her stomach burn with uneasiness. The sense of disquiet made her glance over her shoulder and all around, though she couldn't say what she was looking for.

She wouldn't tell Pete. If he didn't notice them, all the better.

"Why don't we head home tonight?" she called.

He pulled back the curtain and stepped out of the loo. "We only just got here. Why do you want to go?"

She waved at the sky. "The weather's crap. You're…" *scared shitless* "…bleeding."

"I'll be fine. I wanna do Maroon tomorrow. Dawn."

"There'll be no dawn. Not in the sense of sunrise."

"You never know," he said. "The weather forecast's wrong a lot."

"And what if you get another leech?"

He shrugged. "I survived the first one."

Libby's interest in him hadn't, though. She felt ripped off.

He smiled apologetically and stomped back towards the house, right over the line of leeches without noticing them. Libby winced, but didn't say anything. She checked all the leeches. None were missing from the line. In the kitchen she checked her and Pete's feet and legs. She bit her lip, uncertain. Riled. Seriously wanting to pack the car and get out of there.

"Don't give in so easily," Pete said warmly, touching her arm.

"Hmmm. Maroon tomorrow, then," she said, trying to convince herself there was a chance the climb might happen, and that the line of leeches was simply a natural phenomenon and nothing sinister. They were just leeches, after all.

Rain fell in the night. Drumming on the tin roof, hard enough to hammer the house down. Another percussive noise chimed in. A *tick tick tick*. No, it was a *drip drip drip*. Libby threw back her blankets and shuffled into the living room with her headlamp on, feet in her Ugg-boots. There was a leak above the potbelly stove, which had cooled overnight. A saucepan sat on the shelf behind the fireplace, so she placed it under the drip. Squatting, she scrunched up some paper to re-ignite the fire from the last few red embers. The sky was greying outside, but the rain was so dense she could see nothing beyond the veranda.

Pete was still asleep in his room. It had been an okay night, in the end. Another game of Scrabble, some laughs. Instant noodles, canned rice pudding and chopped fruit. They'd talked. He'd fallen asleep on the lounge and she'd gone to bed.

She boiled the kettle and made coffee. Sat on the lounge enjoying the fire.

Two things happened at once.

Pete opened the door of his bedroom so hard that it banged against the wall, and the rain stopped. Libby sat up, shocked. Pete was blank-eyed. Sleep walking? His five o'clock shadow had darkened his jaw, and his eyes and hair were black against his pale, yellowish face... It made her shiver. She looked from him to the window. The rain had stopped suddenly, as though it had been switched off. He strode across the living room.

"Morning?" she said, warily.

He stood at the window and shook his head slowly. "Just like in my dream," he said.

"What?" Libby put down her coffee and scrambled to the window, expecting knee-deep water, or to see the car sunk in mud, but instead… "Holy fuck."

She rubbed her eyes. Leeches, out there.

Leeches as far as the eye could see, in concentric circles, all around the house, all around the car.

"They're coming," Pete said.

She squinted. Was he right? They were so small; it was hard to tell. So many leeches. Thousands. Millions.

"We have to go," she said.

"We can't leave," he said, eyes wide as he grabbed her arm.

"They'll be in here soon."

"Why are they doing this?" he said.

"It…must be…they're starving. They can smell our blood. We're the only hot-blooded animals for miles. Grab your gear and run to the car. Unlock it from here."

Pete didn't respond, continuing to stare at the leeches. Libby's heart raced in her chest, panic burning down her arms, her hands shaking as she packed up her things, and his. There wasn't much stuff, so it didn't take long. She threw his backpack at him.

"Here. Ready to run?"

"No."

"Do you want to wait them out? Wait and see how they squeeze through the gaps around the doors and windows? Between the fucking floorboards?"

He still stared out the window, and his mouth opened a little. Following his gaze, she saw another wave of leeches inching towards them.

"The sooner we go, the better," she said.

She yanked open the door and dragged Pete by the wrist out of the house. When they reached the car, she threw their bags onto the backseat.

"I'll drive," she said, and climbed into the driver's seat, kicking off her boots as she did so, leaving them behind with a heap of hungry leeches stuck to the soles and sides. The car started, thank God, and she reversed, turned, and set off down the track.

She glanced down at Pete's feet. He was still wearing his shoes. "Get your shoes off!" she cried. "Throw them out the window."

He kicked off his shoes and leant down to grab them, as she redirected her attention to driving. They were heading off the road, towards a large tree. She wrenched the wheel to the right, overcorrecting. The back of the car swung out, but she wrestled the steering the other way, regaining control.

Pete fumbled his shoes out the window. A second later, his socks followed.

Libby took several deep breaths. Her heart rate began to settle. She was okay. They were safe. In the rear vision mirror, the cottage appeared normal, the leeches down low, hard to see.

Pete hunched forward, face in his hands.

"Better put on our seatbelts," she said.

He ignored her and inspected each foot.

"All good?" she asked.

Face lowered; he shot a doleful glare in her direction. Libby ground her teeth, annoyed. Was he blaming her for this? She'd never seen anything like it. Angry, she put the radio on. Hoping for…what? A weather report saying it had rained parasites? The mood eased as pop music played. She turned right onto the sealed road, and the clouds cleared above.

"What a nightmare," Pete said. His belly growled. "Screw Maroon."

"Maroon's behind us."

"I'm hungry. Starring in this little horror movie has given me an appetite."

Libby glanced over at him and saw humour in his eyes. It made her smile. A moment later, they both laughed.

"That was pretty insane," she said. "I've never seen anything like it. Let's get some food. They do great sausage rolls at the Outpost Café at Canungra. It's on the way home."

Libby parked and they walked into the Outpost Café. She ordered a coffee and scrambled eggs to have now, and two sausage rolls to share later at home with her flatmate, Jen. Pete was still *umming* and *ahhing* over his order, so she chose a table and sat down to check her emails. That way, for once, she wouldn't have to pay for him. Eventually, he sat beside her and a waitress brought the order. Her breakfast and Pete's...something.

"What's that?" she asked, frowning.

He shrugged. "I just felt like a big bowl of gravy. I had to get chips too. They wouldn't just give me the gravy."

"Do you always drink a bowl of gravy for breakfast?"

He looked at her and shook his head, dead serious.

"Oh. Geeze. Pete. Pete. There's something—"

"What?"

"Something in the corner of your eye. Your eyes."

"What is it?"

"I think—"

"What?"

Black spots in the inner corner of each eye. "I think they're leeches."

"WHAT?" He jumped up, feeling at the corners of his eyes.

"It's okay," she said. "Sit down. Lean back over the table, I'll mix up some salt water and put it in your eyes."

"What will that do?"

"Make them come out."

"Are you sure?"

"No. Sometimes it works."

"Sometimes? I have to get to a hospital."

"The nearest one is forty minutes away. So let me try this first."

She took a cup of water from the counter and stirred in a packet of salt. He lay his head over the table and she tipped the solution into his eyes. Customers were watching, and a waitress approached. "What's going on?"

"He's got leeches in his eyes. Do you have tweezers?"

"Oh, gross. I'll go see." She ran away.

"They're not coming out," Libby said. She tried to pinch them with her fingers. No luck. The waitress returned with tweezers.

"This is hurting my back," Pete groaned.

"Lie in my lap," Libby said, and he leaned along the seat. As she brought the tweezers towards his eyes, he closed them. "Keep them open," she said. She held his eye open with one hand and took a grip on the leech with the tweezers. But the leech's skin stretched, twanged and slipped out of the tweezer's hold.

Oh fuck. Oh, holy fuck...

"I can't get them out," she said. "I'll take you to hospital."

Pete was pale and silent as he stood up. Libby shovelled a mouthful of scrambled eggs into her mouth. The waitress put her coffee into a takeaway cup and, hands shaking, Libby drove Pete towards the hospital, pushing the speed limit the whole way.

The emergency doctor examined Pete's eyes. "I can't see anything there."

Libby looked. "Holy crap. You're right. They're gone."

"Gone?" Pete frowned. "Where did they go?"

"I guess the salt solution brought them out," she said.

"But where are they now?"

"I don't know. I guess they fell off somewhere."

Libby drove to her place in silence. She got out of the driver's seat, and Pete climbed in.

"Sorry," she said, dragging her suitcase out of the back seat.

He stared through the windscreen. "All good," he said, and drove away.

Late that night, Libby received a text from Pete's flatmate: *Pete had a seizure. He's in Gold Coast University Hospital. He hasn't woken up.*

Libby visited Pete every day. Sat and talked to him. Held his hand and stroked his arm. Described every step of the climb up Maroon. Promised him one day they'd do it together. The following week she got a 4am call from the radiologist, Dr Howard, whom she knew from her last rotation.

"I have to show you something," Dr Howard said, her voice full of concern.

"What is it?"

"The latest scan."

"Geeze. What is it? A tumour?"

"Meet me at GCUH."

Libby drove to the hospital, took the lift to the third floor, and made her way to Pete's room, where the doctor was going to meet her. She opened the door expecting to see Pete asleep in his bed, but it was empty. She went into the room, unease creeping over her shoulders.

"Pete?" she asked.

"Surprithe," he said, behind her.

Libby spun around. There was something weird about him. Dark shadows around his eyes. And the way he'd spoken. As he grinned, she glimpsed his tongue. It was silver...and serrated.

"Come here," he said, reaching for her.

She backed towards the bed, but stumbled.

Dr Howard came in the door, grinning. "You're here. Look." She switched on the screen fixed to the wall. Images writhed within a sac. "It's a recording. A scan of Pete's brain."

Libby flinched. There was something moving in there, within the scan. Many things moving in there. Like worms, but cylindrical. Stretching and reaching. Leeches.

Pete's brain was full of leeches.

"You love leeches, right?" Pete said. "I always liked you a lot." He grabbed her and pulled her close, sliding an arm around her shoulders. Before Libby could scream, he pressed his lips to her mouth, sawed his sharp tongue across her tongue and began to suck.

As Libby's mouth filled with blood, she tried to scream, to fight, to push him off. Desperate for help, she moaned and glared at Dr Howard, but all hope died when she saw the doctor grinning. Dr Howard's tongue protruded past her teeth, swishing from left to right. It was just like Pete's: sharp and serrated, more leech than human. She moved closer, reaching out, hungry to feed on Libby too.

Libby managed to reach the nurse call button on the bed, and pressed it, but what good would it do? The nurse would be the next victim. Libby knew it was already too late. The latest pandemic had been unleashed, and the rise of the Leech Zombies would make Covid look like a fucking picnic.

THERE ARE THINGS ON ME

MATT TIGHE

grit my teeth as I bump down the driveway, wincing as the underside of my car scrapes across rocks and dirt. The scene in front of me is all wrong. The place should be neat as a pin. Gran should be standing out on the trim green lawn, eager to usher me to the kitchen table, where she will fuss and click her tongue while Pop grumbles and spoons an absurd amount of sugar into his tea. Instead, the house slumps in on itself, a lumpy shadow under trees surrounded by unmanaged, weedy space. I can't see Gran or Pop anywhere.

I stop short of the turnaround, wary of the washed-out ruts that are likely hiding in the yellowing grass. I turn the car off and the frigid air I have been blasting dies a muggy, warm death. Even this late in the afternoon, the eucalypts leaning close to the house are exhausted, their leaves hanging limply in the last remnant of the day's heat. One has fallen against a wall, drunken and rotten. The grass in the yard is long and ragged and dying. The veranda is just a suggestion of wooden boards in the deep shadows and the flyscreen door is hanging open, the doorway a black, gaping hole.

Something shifts beyond the threshold, and when I squint, I see someone. I think. I get out of my car, and the heat first runs its hot breath up and down my skin and then swallows me whole.

"Gran? Pop?" I call, as sweat beads on my neck and runs down the inside of my shirt. "Gran, is that you?"

Maybe I see more movement beyond the door, but I'm not sure. I pick my way through the tall grass, searching in vain for the path.

"Pop?"

As I put one foot on the grey, splintered veranda it gives slightly. The smell of rot and dark earth rises, hot and humid.

"Shit," I grunt, as I lose my balance and go down on one knee.

My hands slap the wood and the boards feel unpleasantly spongy. A thin grey figure appears in the doorway, framed in darkness.

"Come on, then," Pop says, his voice soft, and then he disappears into the dimness.

I stand in the doorway, peering into shadows. "God, Pop, open some curtains."

"Leave them," he says, his voice low and wet. He moves with the exaggerated care of someone who distrusts their own bones, and settles carefully into the tired recliner in front of the boxy old television.

It is marginally cooler inside, but it smells like that puff of air from under the veranda, thick and festering. I move slowly as my eyes adjust.

"Is everything okay?" I ask, even though everything is obviously not.

Pop isn't okay either. He was never a big man, but he used to have the wiry, knotted appearance that takes some small men as they age. Now, his face is too thin, his cheeks empty and sagging, and his skin is too grey, even in the shadows of the room. He is shrinking, collapsing in on himself as if in sympathy with the failing house that surrounds him. My guilt rises up, as cloying as the air in the room. I live far away, but I should have come sooner. More often.

He doesn't answer, but I can hear him breathing. He pulls at the air with a faint gurgling effort.

"Pop," I say gently as I kneel by him. "You don't sound well."

"Fine," he says. "We are...I am fine."

His breath on my face is too warm, and I try not to pull away from the wet earthiness of it.

"Where's Gran?"

His eyes, too dark and too large, roll towards me and then away. "Sick," he says, and then coughs. "In bed." He shifts and moves absently, rubbing at his arms.

The voice is high and querulous, but bubbly as well. "Is someone here?"

Gran is standing in the bedroom doorway. I am too shocked to speak. Her nightgown hangs off her, and her skull looks both bulbous and too heavy on her thin neck. She takes a step forward, and turns her head this way and that, the shadows covering her features.

"I can hear them again," she mutters.

"It's me, Gran," I say, standing up.

She keeps swivelling her head back and forth. Then she takes another step forward and I can see her more clearly. Her hands move incessantly, feverishly, and when I look down I almost gag. She is scratching at her own arms with her long, bony fingers, and both of her stick-thin forearms are split and torn, weeping blood.

"There are things on me," she whispers, and she rolls her yellowed eyes around the dark room. "Things in me."

"I'm taking you both into town," I say as I wipe Gran's arms with the cleanest cloth I can find. I've also found an old tube of antiseptic and some oversized plaster dressings, and the scratches look like almost nothing by the time I'm done. When I finish, she is staring at me, eyes glazed. Her breath on my face is as hot as the sullen air outside.

"Into town? No," Pop says from the recliner, his voice so liquid it almost gurgles as he stares at the dead television screen.

"Pop," I say. "Look at this place." I gesture around the room pointedly, at the drawn curtains, the blank TV. "Look at you. Look at Gran. What does she mean? What does she think is on her?" *In her,* I don't say. I can't bring myself to say that.

Gran moans.

"Neither of you are well," I say. "And the house—"

"Shh!" Gran interrupts. "Can you hear them?" She cocks her head, and her eyes are suddenly bright.

"Hear what?" I ask. There is nothing beyond the quiet ticking of the corrugated iron roof cooling slightly, and my grandparents' wet breathing.

"Look—" I begin.

"Hush!" Pop says without looking around. He also seems to be listening to something that is not there.

"I'm going to call the doctor," I say. "Tell him I'm bringing you both in."

Neither of them replies straight away. For just a moment, a slight rustling rises all around, the sound of things moving in the dimness, there and then gone. The air itself seems to press close, to rub against my skin in feather-light touches, and I shudder and glance around. I see shadows and neglect and my own guilt staring at me from every dark corner. Gran is listening intently. I strain, but now there is nothing.

"There are things in me," Gran whispers. "Can you hear them?"

I gawk at her, unsure of what to say. The silence stretches out, full and heavy. Finally, Pop speaks.

"Too late to leave now," he says, so softly I almost don't catch it. "It's almost dark."

"Tomorrow then?" I ask.

He nods, and Gran nods faintly as well.

I hesitate. There is something very wrong with Gran. Pop doesn't seem much better. But I don't know how I would get them into the car if they refused, short of dragging them both. I nod. Tomorrow will be soon enough.

The setting sun bleeds orange through the kitchen window. I've tried the lights but they don't work, and the shadows are growing towards me from the corners of the room. For just a moment I think there is a faint rustling sound again, and then I hear a shuffling step behind me.

Pop is standing just beyond the kitchen door, back in the dark.

"You should not have come," he says, and then draws another struggling breath.

"Are you kidding?" I say, and my anger at myself sharpens my words. "Why didn't you tell me things were like this? What happened to the electricity?"

I step towards him, my anger growing. Pop is sick. Gran is sicker. He should have done something. I should have.

He shifts back as if he doesn't want me too close. The last of the sunlight briefly washes his arms in dark orange. He is rubbing at them again. As he does, I think I glimpse, just for a moment, small movements under the skin. Tiny lumps, shifting this way and that.

"What...?"

I take another step forward, but there is nothing to see.

Pop breathes wetly for a second before speaking. "Too late now. Dark soon."

I swallow my anger with some difficulty. Tomorrow, I will get them into town and away from here.

I flick on the light in the spare room and nothing happens, of course.

"No light," Pop mutters from behind me.

The room is hot and smells thick with dust. The bed is barely a grey outline now the sun has set. I fumble my phone out and turn on the flashlight.

Pop grunts and shifts back into the hallway. I barely notice, given what I am looking at in the bright white illuminated circle.

"What the..."

The corner of the room is a huge, misshapen brown pillar. It spreads across the floor and rises up to the ceiling, across the ceiling, tendrils of brown material wending outwards and plunging behind the panelling, as if burrowing into the struts and supports that make up the bones of the place. In the middle it bulges out, like it has paused in the act of bubbling across the room. Half of the bedside table has been consumed, and what is left is split and rotten.

"Is...is that a termite nest?" I ask, but there is no answer.

Pop is gone. I don't need an answer anyway. That first stab of light from my phone has shown more than the dark spreading trunk and tendrils. The brown surface is dotted with hundreds, maybe thousands, of small, moving white bodies. They scurry frantically away from the light, and a sound rises from in front of me, from behind, from all around. A rustling—no, more like whispers.

"Gran?" I call. "Pop?"

There's no answer. The rustling sound stops when I speak, and silence falls, heavy and full. The termites stop as well, all of them, all at once. They should be rushing away from the light, but they are just…still. I think of Gran and Pop, going still, listening.

Gran and Pop in this house, sitting in the dark with this *thing*.

I turn towards the hallway, to get to them, to get out of here, and the floor that seemed solid enough a minute ago now sags underneath me, like on the veranda. Momentum keeps me moving, and my next step sends my foot straight through the boards. I throw my hands out in front of me as I fall and my phone goes flying, the light flashing across the walls as the thing clatters into the hallway. The space underneath the floor is deep, and I drop in up to my thigh. My other leg twists out painfully behind me. The broken edges of the wooden boards dig through my pants and into the muscle underneath.

"Fuck!"

I pull myself forward and the floor sags further but holds. I roll onto my back and put my hand to my leg. It comes away wet—I'm bleeding. Bleeding and laying on the rotten floor in the dark.

"Gran! Pop!" I call, but there is no answer.

It's too dark. I put my hand back to my leg. There is blood, but it doesn't feel like much. A scratch, really. But then something runs across my hand. Some*things*. Lots of them, light touches as whatever they are run up my wrist and forearm. The scent of wet rot fills my nose and my mind. I can't see all those eerily still termites in the dark, but I can guess they are not still anymore.

I haul myself up, trying not to gag, and focus on the circle of light from my phone in the hallway. I limp out to it, shaking my hands and brushing them up and down my arms, trying to get the damn crawling things off me. Trying to stop those insistent touches. Trying to brush away the sweet, sickly smell of decay. There must be hundreds of them. They creep over my shoulders, under my shirt, across my stomach.

I snatch up my phone. The light jitters and jumps across my front, my legs. I am covered in the tiny white creatures. My arms are smeared with wet, pasty remains where I have squashed them in my frantic brushing, but there are so many more, crawling all over me. I yell and brush at them with one hand as I stumble down the hall and towards the front room, holding my phone out in front of me. There are feathery touches up my neck, and that rustling sound comes back, rising and falling like whispers.

"Gran!" I scream as I hold my phone up in front of me. "Pop!"

Pop is sitting in his recliner. He is scratching frantically at both of his arms, the skin of his forearms torn and bloody. He rolls his eyes in the flickering white light.

"There are things," he moans. "Things on me. In me."

I shriek and turn, even as the tickling sensation reaches my ears. The rustling rises again. My phone light washes across the walls, pushing feebly at the shadows.

Gran is standing in her bedroom doorway. She takes a step forward, and it looks as if her head is more bulbous than before, swollen and misshapen. Her arms hang in bloody tatters by her sides.

Something tickles at my ears, and inside my ears, and the rustling becomes louder.

Gran falls forward. She makes no effort to catch herself, and her head hits the floor with a soft, ripe sound. She lays still, the pale light from my phone reflected in her staring eyes as I shout her name. Termites are streaming from her ears, her nose, her mouth, and I realise dimly that I am brushing frantically at my neck and my ears with my free hand even as I stand there. Those light, feathery touches move into my ears, into my head, caressing, feeling, *burrowing*. The whispering builds until it is everything. I think I might be screaming now, but I can't hear it. There is just darkness, and that whispering.

The curtains are drawn against the heat of the day, against the terrible light of the sun, and the room is dark. Pop is in his chair but he is so very still now, as still as Gran. My breath bubbles, as if my throat is full of something. The rustling, the whispering is all around and inside my head. I sit on the floor and scratch at my arms. Things run across my skin, even though I cannot see them.

There are things on me. There are things in me.

CONTRIBUTOR BIOGRAPHIES

EDITOR

DEBORAH SHELDON is an award-winning author from Melbourne, Australia. She writes across the darker spectrum of horror, crime and noir. Her latest titles are *Man-Beast, Liminal Spaces: Horror Stories,* and *The Again-Walkers.* Her award-nominated titles include the novels *Body Farm Z, Contrition* and *Devil Dragon;* the novella *Thylacines;* and collection *Figments and Fragments: Dark Stories.* Her collection *Perfect Little Stitches and Other Stories* won the Australian Shadows Best Collected Work Award, was shortlisted for an Aurealis Award, and long-listed for a Bram Stoker. She has won the Australian Shadows Best Edited Work Award twice: for *Midnight Echo 14,* and *Spawn: Weird Horror Tales About Pregnancy, Birth and Babies.* Deb's short fiction has appeared in many well-respected magazines, been nominated for various awards, and included in *Best of* anthologies. Other credits include feature articles for magazines, non-fiction books (Reed Books, Random House), TV scripts such as *NEIGHBOURS,* stage plays, and award-winning medical writing.

Visit Deb at http://deborahsheldon.wordpress.com

AUTHORS

GERALDINE BORELLA is a writer, poet, songwriter and podcast narrator. She writes fiction for children, young adults and adults. Her stories and poems have been published by Deadset Press, IFWG Publishing, Busybird Publishing, Celapene Press, Wombat

Books/Rhiza Edge, AHWA/*Midnight Echo*, Antipodean SF, Black Ink Fiction, Shacklebound Books and Raven and Drake Books. She has a story published in *Spawn: Weird Horror Tales About Pregnancy, Birth and Babies* (IFWG Publishing Australia), a horror anthology that won the 2021 AHWA Shadows Awards for Best Edited Work. She lives in Far North Queensland, Australia, on Ngadjon-Jii land with her writer husband Tim, and enjoys plotting the rise and demise of her main characters while hiking around the local volcanic crater lakes. She is currently honing her craft, working on several longer projects in between writing for short story call outs. You can find more about her at https://geraldineborella.com/about/https://www.facebook.com/geraldineb4/ and at https://mobile.twitter.com/geraldineborel2

TIM BORELLA is an Australian author of speculative and other fiction published in print, online and in podcasts. He's also a songwriter, and has been lucky enough to spend most of his working life doing something else he loves: flying. He lives in beautiful Far North Queensland. For more information and details of Tim's recent work, please visit his website https://tim-borella-author.mailchimpsites.com/ or see Tim Borella—Author on Facebook.

RENEE DE VISSER currently lives in Brisbane, Queensland, Australia with her partner and daughter, and her dog and cat. When not working and writing, she enjoys reading, cooking, gardening and entertaining, and she has a modest collection of horror memorabilia. Her dream is to someday move out of suburbia to a mountain retreat where she can write stories surrounded by free-ranging chickens. Her first published story, "Keep Them Close", won the AHWA Short Fiction category in 2018 and was published in the 2019 Italian anthology *Leucosya e altri racconti dal Trofeo Rill e dintorni*. Her story, "The Surrogate", can be found in the multi-award-winning anthology *Spawn: Weird Horror Tales about Pregnancy, Birth and Babies*.

ANTHONY FERGUSON is an Australian-based writer and the secretary of the Australasian Horror Writers Association (AHWA). Anthony has published numerous short stories, flash fiction pieces and non-fiction articles in Britain, the United States and Australia, in a range of magazines, zines and anthologies. He wrote the novel, *Protégé*, the non-fiction books, *The Sex Doll: A History* and *Murder Down Under*. He edited the short story collection *Devil Dolls and Duplicates in Australian Horror* and co-edited the Australian Shadows Award-nominated *Midnight Echo 12*. Shortlisted on four occasions, he won the Australian Shadows Award for short fiction in 2020. He is a submissions editor for *Andromeda Spaceways Magazine (ASM)*. Visit his website at anthonypferguson.wixsite. com/mysite

JASON FISCHER is a professional writer who lives near Adelaide, South Australia. He has won the Colin Thiele Literature Scholarship, an Aurealis Award and the Writers of the Future Contest. Jason facilitates writing workshops, is an enthusiastic mentor, and loves anything to do with the written or spoken word. He is also the founder and CEO of Spectrum Writing, a service that teaches professional writing skills to people on the Autism Spectrum. He plays a LOT of Dungeons and Dragons, has a passion for godawful puns, and is known to sing karaoke until the small hours. Visit him online at jasonfischer.com.au

FOX CLARET HILL is a transgender fiction writer who has been writing horror stories since he was old enough to spell. However, despite his adoration for the genre, writing was nothing more than a shadow-shrouded hobby until submitting his first story to DarkLit Press in 2021. That same story saw the light of day, and he has been confined to his office ever since. Born in Mothman's home state and raised in the hills of Malvern, Fox now resides by the beach in Australia with his husband and two dogs, Herbie and Gizmo. You can find information about his published and upcoming works by following him on Twitter @foxclarethill or going to foxclarethill.com

ROBERT MAMMONE has been writing since 1989, but it was only in 2009 that he decided to try and be professional about it. In between navigating suburban life in Melbourne, he has been published in *Doctor Who Magazine*, *Pseudopod*, *Midnight Echo* magazine, the *British Fantasy Society*, *Sword and Sorcery Magazine* and in a number of Doctor Who spin off novels with

Candy Jar Press in the UK. You can find him haunting Twitter @DreadSinister or if you can stand to listen to his witterings, as co-host on the *42 to Doomsday Doctor Who Podcast*.

BEN MATTHEWS is a physiotherapist who graduated from Curtin University in 2013, and who now works with people living with terminal and life-limiting neurological conditions. Having always had a passion for writing, he completed a Master of Writing through Swinburne University in 2021 with a focus on short fiction and horror. Ben spends his time writing, drawing, and exploring the human experience within weird and supernatural horror stories. He is a finalist in *Dark Regions: Survive the Night* horror competition. Ben lives in Perth, Western Australia, with his amazing wife who thinks horror stories are silly. You can find him on Twitter: @benmatt322 or Medium.com: @bjcmatthews

Contributor to the critically acclaimed competitive-entry anthology *Spawn: Weird Horror Tales About Pregnancy, Birth and Babies*, **J.M. MERRYT** mixes folktales with cosmic horror. Her latest stories feature creatures that feed on the corpse of a murdered god ("The Bargain") and a dead language that should have stayed that way ("Necroglossia"). Obsessed with ghost photography and failed arctic expeditions, she hopes to visit haunted places and see what she can dig up. See more of J.M.'s work at https://jmerryt.wixsite.com/website-1

HELENA O'CONNOR is an Australian writer of speculative fiction who lives near the coast and writes with an assortment of flavoured coffees and a nice view of the sea. Her work tends towards bittersweet themes and dark vibes with a dash of hope. Previously an academic in neuroscience research, her writing explores identity, relationships, philosophy, and ethics, particularly with regard to advancing technologies. Her short fiction has been published in several anthologies and highly regarded literary magazines such as *Aurealis, Andromeda Spaceways Inflight Magazine,* and *Nature: Futures*. She also likes video games and cake. Her favourite marsupials are quokkas and quolls. She can be found occasionally on Twitter: @HelenaFiction

STEVEN PAULSEN is an award-winning speculative fiction writer. His bestselling spooky children's book, *The Stray Cat* (Lothian/ Hachette), illustrated by Hugo and Oscar Award-winning artist Shaun Tan, has seen publication in several English and foreign language editions. His horror, science fiction and dark fantasy short stories, which Jack Dann describes as "rocket-fuelled with narrative drive", have appeared in books and magazines around the world. The best of his weird tales (including new fiction written expressly for the book) can be found in his short story collection, *Shadows on the Wall* (IFWG Publishing Australia, 2018), which won the Australian Horror Writers Association Shadows Award for Best Collected Work. His exciting new historical fantasy novel, *Dream Weaver*, set in 15th century Ottoman Turkey, will be released by IFWG Publishing in 2023. Readers can find out more about Steven's work at: www.stevenpaulsen.com

ANTOINETTE RYDYR is an artist/writer working in the genres of science fiction, fantasy and horror usually bent into a surrealist and satirical angle. She works with fellow creator, Steve Carter, and together they have produced graphic novels, award-winning screenplays and esoteric electronic music. Antoinette's story "Mother Dandelion", published in *Spawn: Weird Horror Tales About Pregnancy, Birth and Babies* (IFWG Publishing Australia), was a Finalist for the 2021 Aurealis "Best Horror Short Story" Award. In 2018, Antoinette's and Steve's collaborative steampunk western novels, *Weird Wild West*, were published by Bizarro Pulp Press, USA. They have also published graphic novels including *Savage Bitch, Weird Worlds, Bestiary of Monstruum, Femonsters, New World Disorder, Kill of the Spyderwoman* (Canada), *Mundo Monstruoso* (Spain) and the celebratory resurrection of the infamous *Phantastique*, ingloriously presented in full bloody colour! More grotesque delights can be viewed on their website: https://www.weirdwildart.com/

CHARLES SPITERI is a writer, film director, producer and editor. He has written two (unproduced) screenplays, taught filmmaking and written academic articles on film culture. His short films have been shown at international film festivals. He has also written several short stories and articles, including the

2006 Australian Horror Writers Association Flash & Short Story Competition winner, "Vara". He loves watching movies and playing board games and whilst his wife loves board games and movies too, they're yet to convince the cat to join them. Follow Charles on Twitter @strangemachina

H.K. STUBBS is an Australian writer, journalist and creative producer who loves following stories and paths—both her own, and others'—for the discoveries along the way and the surprise at the end of the journey. Stubbs's stories have been published in *Apex Magazine*, *Kaleidotrope*, *Midnight Echo*, and anthologies by IFWG Publishing, GSFG, Knightwatch, Black Beacon Books and more. Her non-fiction appears in *We Are Gold Coast* and *Nevertheless*. She's happiest rock climbing and exploring the mountains of South East Queensland...snakes, ticks, leeches and all. Follow her adventures on Twitter @superleni, Instagram @ helenstubbs, and her blog https://helenstubbs.wordpress.com

MATT TIGHE lives in northern NSW with his amazingly patient wife, not-so-patient children, Sherlock the dog and Mycroft the cat. He is an academic in his other life. His work has appeared in *Nature Futures*, *The NoSleep Podcast*, *Daily Science Fiction*, and other places. He received the 2021 Australian Shadows Best Short Fiction Award for his short story "A Good Big Brother", published in the award-winning anthology *Spawn: Weird Horror Tales About Pregnancy, Birth and Babies*. You can find his sporadic attempts at humour on Twitter @MKTighewrites and other info at https://matttighe.weebly.com/ (including a cool picture his son drew of his father's brain).

KEITH WILLIAMS was born in a galaxy far, far away... Okay, Scotland actually, but it was a bloody long time ago. He has worked as a production designer, kitchen designer, gaming manager, carer, yada, yada. Long retired now, Keith has written 10 novels (only four published...BASTARDS!), numerous short stories and won the AHWA short story competition in 2014 with the brilliantly haunting (his words) "Sundown". Despite his literary genius the judges have steadfastly refused to award him another win since...BASTARDS! Keith spends his time writing insane stories to stay sane…HAH! Some of Keith's works are available at Kobo.com

PAULINE YATES lives in Queensland, Australia, and writes horror and dark speculative fiction. She's an Australian Shadows Awards short fiction finalist, and her AHWA contest-winning short story, "The Best Medicine", was translated for the *Mondi Incantati* series produced by Riflessi di Luce Lunare (RiLL), Italy. Her short stories appear or are forthcoming in numerous national and international anthologies and magazines, and her debut YA sci-fi novel is due for release in 2023. When not writing, which rarely happens because thinking about her stories is the same thing, she enjoys reconnecting with nature and taking photos of the sunrise. Links to her website and publications can be found here: https://linktr.ee/paulineyates